FAME

A LOVE STORY

R.J. ROME

ISBN: 978-0-578-59374-6

To those who say you can't, you can.
For my family & my true friends

1

"Oh my God, Jenna. He's coming over here, and he's even hotter in person!"

I turn to look in the same direction as Max. My crush Mark McGinley was indeed walking my way. I hear Max whispering to me, but I can't look away, my gaze is riveted on Mark's stride as he walks over. My hand shakes slightly, and I hold onto Max's shoulder, squeezing it gently for support.

"I still can't believe your parents let you do this."

"Oh, God," I whisper, ignoring Max completely. Up close, Mark has impeccably perfect white teeth and a smile that renders you speechless, and here he is standing mere inches from me.

His band Tainted Innocence, an alternative rock band from Anaheim, is on fire right now, topping billboard charts and currently in the middle of an epic nationwide tour.

Mark, the lead singer and guitar extraordinaire, who totally fits the bad boy rocker persona, complete with ripped abs, spiked blond tips in his hair, and tattoos that cover a good percentage of his body, he's a work of art.

Then there's Jamie, also on guitar, Dave on bass, and Steve on drums. They're all hot, but Mark is the fan-favorite.

Tonight happens to be my first night as the band's newest backup singer. I nailed the audition earlier in the day and got an immediate callback from the band's manager to sing in tonight's performance. Depending on how tonight went, I'll occupy the spot for the rest of the tour. At least, that's what I'm hoping for.

"You were flat out there." Mark's words snap me out of appreciating all of the things a sixteen-year-old girl shouldn't.

"Excuse me?" Of all of the things I expected him to say, that was not one of them. How about, 'great job on your first night' or 'thanks for coming on such short notice.'

And fuck him, because if I had a nickel for every request to sing the national anthem, I wouldn't be standing in front of Mark McGinley, hearing the word "flat" come out of his mouth.

My silence and confusion have no effect on him as he continues his verbal assault.

"Yeah, your tone, it was off. In fact, you were way off-key, and it was very distracting."

After the callback, I had only a short rehearsal with the other backup singers, nearly an hour before the band took the stage.

Everyone else I've seen since the end of the show has praised my performance.

I steal a glance at Max. His mouth is gaping wide open. I'm not sure if he's in shock at seeing Mark up-close or from the insults he's slinging at me, because Max knows my vocal range and my accolades back home.

Not to mention, Max is probably more infatuated with Mark than me or anyone else I know.

I square my shoulders and open my mouth to speak, but before I can manage the words swirling in my head, I'm left staring at Mark as he walks out the stage door, his arm around some girl.

2

JENNA - JANUARY 2015

The steam billows in the air. Circling the bath like a dense fog and the thick air makes it difficult to catch my breath. I sip from a bottle of sparkling water, desperately wishing it was the sting of a whiskey or even a cheap glass of wine.

Recalling the events of my first encounter with Mark today at Dr. Wild's office was incredibly difficult, and the singular reason for me currently wanting to relapse on my newfound sobriety, along with my resolution to finally seek professional help.

I sink deeper into the soaking tub, still trying to catch my breath.

I think back again to meeting Mark that day. I don't know what it was about that moment.

Maybe it was meeting a celebrity for the first time.

Or, the fact that Mark didn't kiss my ass after a lackluster performance when everyone else did.

Or, the more likely scenario is that nothing could have prepared me for the shit-storm that would become my life.

After all, I was a singing sensation back in New Jersey. The lead vocalist in both my high school and church choirs, both of which won several competitions and many trophies, lined my bookshelf in the modest three-bedroom ranch I grew up in.

No.

No one could have predicted that the sweet girl from New Jersey, would rise and then fall. Hard. Not once or twice but *every* single time. As soon as I stood up, something would have me landing on my ass again.

I know I got tired of it, so I know it wore down those around me. I just couldn't crawl out of the addiction. It was easier to forget everything with a bottle in my hand. I could handle anything with a little liquid courage.

This explains why I'm totally and completely screwed up and grasping at anything that will keep me from hitting rock bottom, yet again.

I lift myself out of the water that has grown cold and wrap myself in a fluffy white towel before stepping out onto the cold tile floor, resolving once again, that no matter how painful talking about the past is, I *will* return to Dr. Wild's the day after tomorrow.

3

JENNA - MAY 1996

"I'll meet you back here after the show, I'm going to find your parents." Max kisses me quickly on the cheek before heading out of my makeshift dressing room. The dressing room I'm currently sharing with two other backup singers.

I don't mind them, though. Generally, we get along, and besides the fact the other singers are older than me, we have a lot in common.

They also happen to be the only people I've spent considerable time with besides Max, who trails along with me from show to show.

I've barely seen my parents over the last few months while on tour, but they are here tonight, and I'm excited for them to see the show.

I'm in the middle of fixing my lipstick when the band's manager, Jerry, walks in.

He's a short, stocky, middle-aged man. My guess, in his early fifties, and up the ass of the band members riding the pinnacle of their success train.

"Jenna, Mark wants to talk to you." He shouts as if we all couldn't hear him come in.

"Now? The openers are closing their set."

Jerry shrugs his shoulders as he heads toward the curtain. "Yes, he said now."

Debbie grabs my arm before I follow obediently behind Jerry. "Jenna... I just thought you should know. Mark fired the last girl the same way."

She has that worried mother hen look on, but I simply nod and walk through the curtain and down the hall to the door where I know behind it, Mark is waiting for me.

I contemplate saving face and just leaving. Saving us both the exchange that will take place in mere minutes if I knock on the door.

I lift my hand to knock, but the soft rapping that I manage can't possibly be heard over the blaring stereo on the other side of the door.

I knock again louder this time, before turning the knob and stepping inside the room.

Mark is the lone occupant, drumming a beat on the table. He turns briefly to acknowledge my presence before casually lowering the volume.

"Led Zeppelin?" I ask, and he nods before standing and walking toward me.

"You a fan?" He asks.

I shiver ever so slightly, folding my arms in front of me, hoping he doesn't notice how uncomfortable I am. "I listen to a little bit of everything."

He nods as if he expected my answer. He stands there silently, his hands in his pockets for what feels like an eternity before he finally speaks.

"How old are you?" I'm momentarily distracted by his thick muscular arms that are decorated in ink.

I'm not sure where he's going with this, so I answer carefully.

"I'll be seventeen, in September."

Another nod. "And your parents? Do they want you to be here?"

"Listen, you don't have to fire me." I shift from foot to foot, surely my nerves are about to get the best of me.

"I don't? And why is that?" He smirks, obviously pleased with himself for making me squirm during what is sure to be an unpleasant experience.

"I'll just go." I say simply, hoping this won't ruin other opportunities for me when word gets out that I was fired by Tainted Innocence.

Dread builds inside of me, knowing that I'll have to return to Jersey, a failure looming over me.

He just stands there smiling, his smug face fills my vision until I can no longer see the periphery of the room.

He takes a step closer, one more, then another, lifting my chin so my eyes meet his. The bright blue hue of his eyes burn into mine and it's hard to keep focus but I cannot look away.

"Where's your boyfriend?" His eyes interrogate me.

"Boyfriend?" I asked confused. I haven't dated anyone since I left home.

He raises his eyebrow. "The one always following you around like a puppy."

"He's not my boyfriend." I say baffled that Mark could confuse Max for my boyfriend.

"Let me guess, you want to be a star. Because you're so great. You're just here so someone can notice you. You want a record deal. Am I right?"

I shake my head. "I don't understand what's happening here."

"I want you to sing a solo. Tonight."

I'm frozen in place, torn between wanting him to remove his finger from my chin and him keeping me like this forever. "A solo? Like on the stage? In front of the crowd?"

"Show me what you got. You go on in fifteen minutes." He drops his hand quickly before backing away and taking a shot of some amber liquid.

"No. I can't do that. Are you serious?" A few months prior I would have been confident to sing, even welcomed the opportunity, but that was before Mark told me I was flat and off-key.

"Very." His presence fills the room and I feel stifled.

"You haven't said a word to me in months, besides that I'm terrible, and now you want me to sing a solo? What do you propose I sing?"

He shrugs. "Sing Zeppelin, Aretha, Old MacDonald, I don't care."

"You think this is funny? I haven't rehearsed. I have no music." I stand firm with my hands on my hips, my fingers toying with the cheap sequins on my thrift store jean skirt.

I suddenly realize what's going on, he's going to make me look like a fool or a chicken and I'll never get anywhere in Hollywood.

Not because I don't fit in, but because this will surely be career suicide. I feel lost as he stands and stares at me, amusement glittering in his icy blue eyes.

"If you can really sing. Like, truly madly sing, you don't need a rehearsal. Rehearsals are for people like me who just get by. I mean, shit, we're lucky people actually show up." He turns and walks to the door, holding it open as he swigs another shot straight from the bottle, then lets the door close behind him. He's gone, and I stand alone, deciding my fate.

4

"How do you feel today?" Dr. Wild asks me from behind her desk, while I laze on a chaise lounge with a pillow over my stomach.

How do I feel today? I've asked myself that question every day for the past nineteen years.

I often thought of it as keeping track of my mental health.

Some days, my answer scared the hell out of me, but I always had the answer. Today when Dr. Wild asks this question, it feels like a trap because I don't know the answer.

I just know that I don't feel like myself. *Whoever that is.*

So, I don't answer. Instead, I focus on the fact that I'm here, in therapy, and it feels like I'm about to bear my soul to the enemy.

"It's ok, Jenna. You don't trust me." She lifts gracefully out of her chair, walking around to the front of her desk and taking a seat on top of it. "You don't trust me, even to ask you a simple question, but you will. You told me that you need to be here, but you're not sure you do. You don't believe deep down that I can help you."

I shake my head to disagree but clutch the pillow to my chest. "I didn't say that."

She nods, but I know she's already noticed my defense mechanism. "Ok, then. I think it's best if we pick up where we left off last time." She takes my silence as acquiescence and continues. "When was the last time you had any contact with Mark?"

I squeeze my eyes closed.

Just hearing his name. Picturing his face, no matter how long it's been, still kills me inside. "Five years," I whisper, knowing the answer right away. I could never forget that day.

I feel her staring at me. "Can you tell me more? Was it a friendly exchange?"

My eyes sting, the tears that I've held at bay now threaten to unleash themselves. I sit up, suddenly feeling very vulnerable. "Not today, I just can't." I've spent the better part of my life keeping people out of it, unable to divulge the private details to anyone. Asking me to talk about the last time I saw Mark is too personal, it's opening an old wound. "It was the beginning of the end," I confess sullenly, knowing full well that was the day my addiction swallowed me whole.

I'M LYING wide awake in my modest four thousand square foot house in the hills. It's a culmination of everything I thought I wanted and everything I don't need, but it's mine.

It's almost five A.M., but I've been wide awake for hours. I sit up quickly, pushing the covers off me. Everything feels too heavy on my skin like I'm drowning.

I had nailed the performance that night when Mark made me go on stage with only fifteen minutes to prepare.

It was the scariest thing I had ever done, but when the crowd actually cheered at the end, I was amazed. It was incredible, and I was hooked.

Performing became my first addiction. *Or maybe it was Mark?*

I was obsessed with him, though he never knew it. I would follow him after the show just to see where he was going. Some nights he met up with a woman, and I went back to my room to sulk.

He would often go to a club or bar close to where the show was, obviously, I was too young to get in so I would wait outside. Max was constantly scolding me, but back then, Mark didn't even know I was alive.

I strip off my nightgown and pad across the room to the bathroom. I step lightly, but there's no need to, there's no one that I'll wake even if I stomp across the floor. I turn the faucet on and blink blindly into the water. This is why I can't think about Mark, this is what he does to me. I'll have to address some boundaries with Dr. Wild.

I wrap my arms around myself as I step under the cold water. I let out a shrill cry because I've been here before, many times.

It's a mixture of frustration and temptation.

And I've tried many times to stifle this feeling of want and need.

Just one sip, and I'll be back where I started. I'll feel better temporarily, though, and it's that temporary feeling that I crave.

A month ago, everything was different.

A month ago, I was a drunk.

A month ago, I stood in front of a cemetery plot, burying the one person I trusted with all of me.

A month ago, I was a drunk, but I had Max.

Max knew everything about me. He knew who I was and who I wasn't in front of the camera, that I was an addict, but he cared for me anyway.

And that night, a month ago, I came home and poured every bottle down the drain.

Deciding for the first time in my life, I couldn't make up an excuse to keep being an addict.

5

JENNA - SEPTEMBER 1996

"Happy birthday!" My parents yell to me as I run through the airport to them.

I haven't seen them in weeks, and between being on tour with the band and flying back and forth for school, I'm exhausted. I feel around in my pocket, making sure that the caffeine pills Debbie gave me are still there. I've been taking them for weeks now. They give me a little boost and make the exhaustion of touring a little more tolerable.

This break couldn't come at a better time, and luckily enough, this time, I get to be home for a whole week.

"Hey, Max! Is she getting into trouble?" My Dad says in his dry sense of humor tone.

"You mean Miss. Goody-two-shoes?" Max rolls his eyes, and my Dad laughs as he puts his arm around him like the son he never had.

I honestly don't know what my parents think about Max's sexuality, especially since they are so religious. Being gay in our community isn't socially acceptable, and I've heard my parents say 'he's confused,' or that 'he might come around.' Thankfully though, my parents took him in when Max's family kicked him out. They couldn't handle their only son betraying them.

When we get to the baggage claim, Max and my Dad collect the bags, and my Mom wraps her arm around my shoulders and pulls me in close for an awkward mother-daughter moment. "So... Tell me what's going on? Have you met anyone special?" My mom is joking around, but I know deep down she is curious as to what her teenage daughter has been up to. She hates me being on the road.

"No, Mom, we don't have time for that. If I'm not on stage or doing homework, then I'm trying to write songs."

She drops her arm and steps away from me. "Alright, alright. God, Jenna, you don't have to have such an attitude with me."

"I'm sorry. I'm just tired." *Traveling days on end isn't easy, maybe she should try it.*

Even though I'm not the main act, and no one cares if I show up, I promised myself I wouldn't quit. This is my dream, and I figure soon enough, I will meet the right people.

Being back home, though, I can't help but think about just going back to my normal life, be a normal teenager, doing normal teenage things. I know my Dad would be disappointed, though.

As if on cue, Dad senses my rotten mood. "Don't worry, Jenna. Someone will notice you. We all saw that solo. You blew the crowd away. All your hard work will be worth it." He says while loading our luggage into the trunk.

I smile, remembering the solo. I was damn lucky that the band knew *Pat Benatar's 'Hit me with your best shot'* and that I had practiced it a million times in my room. *Nice try, Mark. Shame on you for trying to make me look like a fool.*

"I hope you're right, Dad."

6

I t's too early to call my Dad, but I want to talk to him, so I shoot him a text asking him to call me when he gets up.

He had seen something in me when I was a kid, that had convinced him that I could be a star. I played the part and did everything I could to make him proud.

So, when my Mom said no way is her only child going off to L.A. at sixteen, we pushed her to say yes. Yet, I always wonder what my life would've been like if my Mom had stood her ground and said, 'no.'

Would I have been able to avoid becoming an addict?

Would I have become a recording artist anyway?

Would I be happily married?

I sigh, I guess at the end of the day it doesn't matter, this is the hand I was dealt.

I dress quickly and head down the hallway to the recording studio, which occupies a large portion of my square footage but totally worth it. Before Max died, we wrote and recorded most of the songs for the album here, but there were a few songs I struggled with, and we never got around to fixing them.

Since the funeral, I haven't had the heart to come in here and try again, but something is drawing me to the studio this morning.

Maybe I need a distraction from therapy? Lord knows Dr. Wild is by no means taking it easy on me, but music has always been my therapy, and I know I can battle pretty much anything that ails me through the power of a song.

I let myself into the studio and shut my phone off, so I don't get distracted, then I sit down the old-fashioned way with a pencil and paper and try to work it out. Scribbling down the words flowing around in my mind, hoping it translates to something good in its tangible form on paper.

I spend several hours on one track, writing and rewriting and still try after try it's awful.

I'm about to scrap the song when I decide to try something. Something I haven't done in such a long time. I stand, pushing buttons on the computer until the melody I'm looking for comes through the speakers. I slide the headphones over my head and lean into the microphone as I close my eyes and sing the song that started it all, my first single.

The song that catapulted me to stardom, to the top of the billboard charts. The catchy pop single that everyone loved, but after a while, I secretly hated.

Before long, it made me sick to sing it, but here I am, years later resorting back to it. I've sung it a million different ways over the years, but it always leaves me emotionally drained. I fall to the floor in a heap of tears as the last chords of the song ebb through the room, and the last ounce of my sanity has evaporated along with the melody.

7

"You shouldn't have that."

I'm standing on the beach, a few feet from where the waves meet the shoreline with a glass of champagne in my hand. No one has noticed that I'm down here, nor has anyone here tonight thought that I needed a babysitter. When you travel with the band, no one really cares what you do, so long as you show up and perform.

I don't turn around to see who is admonishing me because I know his voice even though he doesn't usually talk to me.

The other guys in the band are always friendly and include me in conversation, but I get the impression from Mark he thinks I'm just a silly kid because he's six years older.

"It's only champagne," I say, defiantly turning just in time to see the icy blue eyes glittering and the reflection of the moon in them.

"Your point?" He takes the glass from my hand, puts the glass to his lips and gulps it down. "You're underage."

"What the hell Mark?" I stand with my hands on my hips, my buzz is starting to kick in, and I try and play it cool.

"Why aren't you back home with your family? It's New Year's Eve."

I shrug my shoulders. I could've stayed home after Christmas, but

I felt lost and out of place, and I couldn't wait to get back to writing my own music. Being home just wasn't the place to do that.

I shrug again, I don't have the answers he is looking for. I saunter the few steps toward him, closing the distance between us.

Mark may be older, but that doesn't matter right now, because what Mark doesn't know, is I've already consumed several glasses of champagne, and I'm feeling extremely promiscuous.

I stare up at him expectantly, hoping, waiting, even daring him to show me something other than the cold, asshole attitude he usually shows me.

His eyes meet mine and then quickly avert my stare. I reach out to touch his arm.

"Jenna..." His voice trembles ever so slightly, but I pick up on it. Then without a second thought, he grabs my shoulders, pulling me to him.

I gasp suddenly, unsure of my intentions. Mark's chest is firm, and I feel his erection against my stomach.

Our faces are so close our noses are almost touching.

I'm breathing heavy, and my pulse is racing, and I'm sure he must smell the alcohol on my breath.

Despite what impression I've just given him, I'm very much a virgin and very inexperienced, even at seventeen.

He rubs his thumb over my bottom lip then sucks in a breath.

Something behind me catches his attention, breaking this magnetic feeling that has me frozen in place.

"Max is looking for you." With that, he pulls away and trails up the beach, toward the Santa Monica beach house that the record label rented for tonight's soirée.

I stare after him as Max walks toward me.

"What was that all about? He told me to take you home."

I shrug my shoulders because honestly, I don't understand. *Maybe he does know I'm alive.* "Come on, let's go."

8

Three months later...

I smile back at the host of a very popular east coast morning show not because I have anything to be happy about, but because that's what we do in the 'biz.'

No matter what smile.

I'm advocating for a new animal charity, and the special segment is supposed to bring in beaucoup donations for the non-profit and put me back in the limelight ahead of my new album.

After she asks me the last of her prepared list of questions, most of which have nothing to do with the charity but more to do with my personal life, the show goes to commercial, and I walk off set tossing the mic on the floor.

I don't know why I agreed to be interviewed, I have no business being around people right now. I'm barely clinging to sobriety, and honestly, I've always hated doing interviews as it is. I take out my phone fully intending to fire this new manager that my record label set me up with.

"Jenna, I'm so sorry, did I say something wrong? Your manager approved the questions before..." The talk show host says behind me.

I've obviously given her the impression I'm offended or bothered by her questions. I put my hand up to interrupt her. "No, it's fine. It's just been a while." I lie because this is the first interview without Max as my manager, it's the first time walking off of a set and not seeing his face, and it's probably the first time I've been completely sober during an interview.

My nerves are shot, and I don't know how the hell I'm supposed to promote a new album without Max by my side. *Where the hell is my manager, anyway? Shouldn't he be here?*

I blow air kisses to the host and promise her once again that it's not her, it's me, before I grab my coat, clutch my purse to my side, put on my big sunglasses and head into the blustery cold of February in Manhattan.

I stand close to the building. Stopping to take a deep breath, but the air is cold, and it burns my lungs. I take a quick step forward, which enfolds me into the stream of people on the overcrowded street in Times Square. Luckily, I blend in here, which is why I opted for no bodyguard today.

I used to wish for this, to be able to walk down the street unnoticed but I couldn't, I was too recognizable, and someone always had to be with me. I'm either lucky today, or I've been out of the limelight too long, and I lost relevance.

That's the problem with fame, you want it until you have it, and when every ounce of privacy you have is stripped away, you're supposed to just take it because that's what you wanted. Maybe I'm certifiably insane for wanting to release a new album.

I text Dr. Wild my thoughts on this so we can discuss in our next session before I step into the first Starbucks I find. Coffee has become my new addiction, but I guess it's better than alcohol.

I leave my glasses on for good measure because once I take them off, I'm not just the weirdo wearing sunglasses in the coffee shop. I'm Jenna, six-time Grammy award-winning artist with multi-platinum albums, and anyone who takes a photo or video gets rich from it.

The barista clears his throat as he looks me over and hands me my cup calling out the fake name I ordered under. I generously grace the tip jar because if he realizes who I really am he doesn't call me out. I pull my phone out text my driver and wait just outside the Starbucks. That's when I hear him.

"J?" I know it's *him* because only he would call me that, not a fan, not a family member. *Him.* I must be losing my mind because it's not possible we're in the same place at the same time.

But I turn and it *is* Mark, and he's had a head start, obviously seeing me first that now he's only steps away.

I panic and walk briskly toward the curb, ready to cross in front of midtown traffic just to get to the other side of the street and away from him.

"J!" He calls again, but I'm able to run across, narrowly missing a cab. "J, stop!" He follows behind me obviously determined to make this as uncomfortable and awkward as possible.

"What?" I say sharply as he successfully crosses the street and catches up with me. "How are you even here?"

He pulls me out of the middle of the sidewalk and looks me over from head to toe.

I'm wearing a pea coat over a simple pantsuit with stilettos and suddenly, I'm very self-conscious of how I look.

Suddenly I'm sixteen again, intimidated by his presence and I tuck my hands inside my coat pockets and look down at my shoes.

"I was going to ask you the same question. Work," he clarifies. "I'm here for work."

"I see. Well, it was good to see you." I turn to walk back to the other side of the road where my driver is sitting when he grabs my elbow. I wince, the contact, even though it's through my coat is too much to bear.

"I sent flowers." He says a little above a whisper.

I nod in acknowledgment. "You did." I'm lacking crass, I need to be better than this, but I just can't, not today. Not when everything in my world is fucked up.

"Jenna, I'm sorry. I know how much he meant to you."

He's right, he did send flowers, I stared at them for an hour debating what to do with them. Eventually, I decided they had to go, and I threw them in a dumpster behind the funeral home.

"Yes, you reminded me quite often." I remark snidely.

"That's not fair, Jenna. He was always between us."

"No, he wasn't, you put him between us."

He sighs and throws his head back because this is what we do, we fight. Our relationship was always a tumultuous one. "Ok, fine." He puts his hands up in mock surrender.

"Are we done here?" I ask as I clutch the vibrating phone in my pocket and say a quick prayer that my driver doesn't leave me while I'm in fight or flight mode.

"Yeah, just... are you sure you're ok?" He looks at me with so much concern.

I could lie and move on or I could tell the truth, it wouldn't make any difference and we both know it.

"No, I'm not ok. But I will be."

9

JENNA - JANUARY 1997

"Jenna, look," Max calls me from the bedroom of the posh hotel we are staying in just outside of Portland. I run over to the bed, jumping on it as he holds out a tabloid magazine for me to see.

"Oh..." I don't know what else to say. It's pictures of me at the New Year's Eve beach party. The captions are less than flattering and accompany a picture of Mark and me on the beach. Someone must have captured the last few minutes of us on the beach. Right before he pulled away.

Obviously, they didn't capture him walking away. The captions are distasteful accounts and assumptions of what is happening between us.

"Why didn't you tell me?" Max pouts.

"Oh my God, shut up. Nothing is going on. Mark took my champagne away, and I was snarky to him." I defend myself.

"Jenna, a picture is worth a thousand words. And this picture clearly says he's fucking you with his eyes."

"Oh, no. My parents." I rush off the bed and over to the corded phone on the nightstand. I dial the number and wait, one, two, three rings later, my mom finally picks up. "Hey, Mom."

"Jenna! Hi sweetie. Where are you now?"

"I'm in Portland, you have the schedule, Mom. Why don't you keep track?" I say frustrated that she never seems to take interest or care where the tour is now.

"Jenna, is everything ok?"

"Yes, Mom, fine. Listen, I just wanted to tell you something." I hear my Dad pick up the other line.

"Jenna." He says his voice high pitched.

I expect the worst now. He's probably already seen the photo. "Dad..."

"I have great news, sweetheart."

Huh? This is not what I was expecting. "What is it?"

"I got a call from a Randy Reed. He's a talent manager, he wants to meet you. Said he saw you a few weeks ago at one of the shows. He said he can make you a star! Jenna, this is it! What we've been waiting for."

There's a loud bang on the door.

I look from Max to the phone. "That's great, Dad."

"I'll make the arrangements to meet with Randy, see if he's legit, and we'll catch up with you on tour."

Another loud bang.

"Sounds good Dad, I have to go." I hang up quickly, and Max and I sprint to the door. As soon as I open it, Jerry bursts through the door, yelling and cursing. Mark comes in quickly behind him, shutting the door. All eyes are on Max and me.

Jerry speaks first. "You know this is a big problem, right?" He's holding the magazine in his hand. "Did you have someone take these pictures?" His anger terrifies me, and I listen as Mark tells him to calm down repeatedly before he takes a seat on the chair next to the bed.

"Jenna," Mark begins. "Just tell Jerry what happened."

I shake my head. "What happened?"

"Yes, the night on the beach."

"Jesus Christ Mark, you're twenty-three, and she's seventeen. Why are you alone on a beach with her?"

I look to Mark, whose brow is furrowed, and he also seems to think this is a problem. "I was drinking," I say truthfully. "Mark stopped me."

Mark stands relived and claps his hands. "See, I told you, no big deal. Come on, let's go." He pulls Jerry toward the door, but Jerry pulls his arm out of Mark's grasp.

"It is a big deal because someone took a picture of it." Jerry yells.

"Ok, well, she didn't do it."

"Mark, if something else is going on, you better tell me now. We're gonna have to run damage control once they find out how old she is."

They're both talking like I'm not even in the room, and I'm about ten seconds away from bawling my eyes out. "I came on to Mark," I yell, "I was drunk, and it won't happen again." They both turn to look at me. "I didn't know anyone else was on the beach." I look over at Max, who's smirking at me.

"One more problem, and you're gone. We don't need bad publicity or statutory rape charges!" Jerry swings the door open and storms out of my room while Mark stands on the threshold. We share an intense moment without words, neither of us looks away, our eyes are lock until he breaks and turns to leave. The sound of the door closing reverberates around the room and speaks volumes.

"You slut." Max laughs and feigns a shocked expression.

I roll my eyes and fall onto the bed. I stare up at the ceiling, this talent manager couldn't come at a better time. I have to get off of this tour. I have to get away from Mark.

10

MARK - APRIL 2015

"Wow, I can't believe you were both there, same place, same time." Jerry is shaking his head as he repeats that same line over and over.

"Yeah, it was surreal." I shake my head like a swarm of bees are circling as I recount what happened. It's been two days since I saw Jenna and she shook me to my core.

The last time I talked to Jenna was five years ago in her lawyer's office, dissolving our joint assets, signing divorce papers, and me promising not to contact her again.

She wanted a clean break, and I gave it to her. I gave her more financially than she was entitled to, not that she asked for that, but I felt that it would get her on the right foot again.

I kept my word for the last five years, no contact. Sure, I had seen Jenna plenty of times, but I upheld her wishes, that is, until two days ago.

"That little girl always did go straight to your head," Jerry says matter-of-factly as he takes a bite of his burger.

"What are you talking about?" I ask, tossing him a napkin, grease from the burger is dripping down his chin. He's such a slob.

"You got that puppy dog look. Always did when it came to her."

He's right, I always had a weak spot for her. Which is why those first couple years she hung out with the band, I tried like hell to avoid her at all costs.

"Nah, it's not like that. I'm over her, it's been five years." I say casually. Like I'm over her.

I'll never be over her. Sure, there's been others after her, I'm only human, but no one ever came close to her. Jerry doesn't need to know that, though.

"Over her? Huh? That's funny." He wipes his chin and crumples the napkin, tossing it onto his plate. Thank god, I was about to lean over and wipe his face myself.

"What? You don't think so?"

He leans forward, folding his hands on the table. "Why you still wearing the ring around your neck then? Some badge of honor or something? Or, is it a reminder to never get tied down again?" He erupts into a fit of laughter like he's just said the funniest thing ever.

"You're a real asshole, you know that." I stand and toss some cash down on the table. It doesn't matter how much money Jerry has, he never lets you forget how much you owe him, even for an eight-dollar burger.

"Oh, come on, Mark, don't go. I was just messing with you."

"I gotta run anyway, there's somewhere I gotta be. I have an appointment."

"Oh yeah? With who?" He asks with curiosity.

Jenna's new manager happens to be someone I've known for a long time, and luckily, he put me in touch with her assistant. I made an appointment with her under an alias. "Jenna."

He raises his eyebrows either in surprise or satisfaction that he was right because while Jenna's addiction is alcohol, mine was always her.

"I thought you weren't allowed to see her." He questions.

"I'm not an ax murderer." She's probably going to slam the door in my face anyway, but I have to see her again. If only for a few seconds, I have to see her, look into her eyes, and hear her tell me one more time that she feels nothing for me. Yes, her eyes will tell me everything I need to know, which were cleverly hidden behind shades two days ago.

I walk out of the restaurant and grab the chain around my neck, rubbing the platinum ring between my fingers for good measure. I glance quickly at the inscription inside the ring.

I'm yours forever.

If only she had meant that.

11

JENNA - APRIL 2015

I'm sipping a double shot of espresso and pacing the floor of my home office. "Ugh, I don't know, Tom. Max always did these things. I don't care what the stage looks like behind me. He was the creative one." I'm whining and cranky because I don't know what set matches with the eight wardrobe changes that Max had planned for my "comeback tour," and my new *super* manager, Tom is even more clueless than me.

"Fine, I'll summon the stylist and the team that handles the set design. I'll be back shortly."

Maybe we are getting ahead of ourselves planning out this tour. The album isn't even fully recorded, I don't have a release date from the label, and the tour planning is spiraling out of control. "Great." I rub circles around my temples. Max and I always joked that he could never leave me because I knew nothing. But that was the truth, he shielded me from so many things, and he just knew what I wanted and didn't burden me with the details.

My cell chimes with a text. It's my Dad. He's called me several times in the last few days, but I haven't been in the mood to talk. Especially since I saw Mark in Manhattan. I know he will hear it in my voice, so I keep putting off actually answering his calls.

IS EVERYTHING OK? LOVE DAD

I shoot off a quick text back, telling him I will call him later, then I spend the next hour on social media. I have thousands of followers who are always making contact, and I do my best to connect with as many as possible. *Thank god social media wasn't around in the nineties.*

Lily knocks on the door. "Hey, Lily. Come on in." She has dark skin and the most gorgeous green eyes, she's exotic looking, and she keeps her long dark hair braided, pulled back off her face. She's been my assistant for almost two years now.

"What's going on, girl?" She asks.

"Not much. Living the dream." I wave my hand around the office.

She laughs. "I guess I should make it look that way on your Instagram then."

I have to admit, social media sometimes makes me want to throw a temper tantrum. Because of that, Lily usually handles the brunt of it.

"Ha-ha funny." I say and look back down at my screen.

She clicks a few times on an iPad then looks at her phone, while I continue to scroll through the Twitter universe.

She stands abruptly. "Your appointment is here."

"Who is this again?"

"A designer that wants you to be the brand ambassador for his new clothing line. I figured it was ok since Max had been looking for something like this."

I pretend to bang my head on my desk.

"Come on, girl, keep an open mind." She admonishes me.

I sigh. "Ok, send him in." That was me, brand ambassador. No one wanted Jenna, the musician anymore.

She walks out, and I take a seat behind my desk, praying that this meeting is short and sweet. I know I need to branch out and become relevant again, I'm just not sure this will be the right move.

Then again, I'm not sure of anything anymore, which rings even truer a few minutes later my appointment waltzes in.

"What the hell are you doing here?"

12

I see the shock register on her face the minute I walk through the door, pretty much the same face I got from her assistant at the front door, but thankfully, Lily still let me in.

I answer her shock with a smile. She stands in front of the window, the sun is at her back, the glow surrounds her, and she looks like an angel. It's not the first time I've seen her like this, yet every time I do, it's like the first time. Her glow is captivating.

Millions of people have always seen it too, that's how she became successful so quickly. It didn't matter if it was an arena full of people or just me, she owned every single performance.

"I want to talk." I didn't plan this out too well, I only presented the idea to the designer a few hours ago, and he was all for it. It may have been impulsive, but I had to see her again, and I don't really know where to begin. I shove my hands into my pockets and pray that this won't end badly.

"So, you lied to my assistant in order to what? Corner me into talking to you. Again."

Obviously, I knew when she crossed in front of a cab to avoid me, I shouldn't tempt fate, but I'm weak. "No, I mean, yes, partially. There is a clothing line, and we do need a face."

Her eyes are angry, she feels broadsided, and I can't say that I blame her. "We? You're designing a clothing line?" Her tone is incredulous, her posture is stiff. I've had several business ventures over the years, this shouldn't surprise her.

"Investor, actually. The designer wanted to come alone, I thought that it was best if you knew I'm involved, should you be interested."

She scoffs and folds her arms over her chest. "How considerate of you." She rolls her eyes. "I think you know that's a very slim chance. Tell me, what's in this for you, Mark?"

Seeing you, even if you're looking at me with such distaste, hearing your voice, even if its angry words aimed at me.

"Besides a successful brand?"

"I don't believe you."

I take a seat in one of her fancy chairs and stare out the window before I answer her. "Why?" I eye her skeptically.

"Don't make yourself comfortable."

I need to get in her space, make her feel that connection again, it's a fire burning inside me, I don't believe she doesn't feel it too. So, I stand and cross around her desk, till we are toe to toe. "Why don't you believe me?" I notice her visibly shiver. She feels it too.

"You haven't talked to me in five years, and now, here you are two days after we 'happen' to see each other in New York?"

I lean against her desk, crossing my arms over my chest. Her eyes are drawn to the ring that's on the chain around my neck. "Are you really suggesting that I followed you to New York?"

"I'm not suggesting anything. I just want to know what your motive is, upfront this time."

"Jenna, are you interested or not. We can go back and forth all day long, but at the end of the day, whatever you think I did back then is all in your head."

She rolls her eyes. "I don't think—I know what you did, Mark, and it was extremely hurtful and unforgivable, and five years hasn't changed that."

"Ok fine. I knew this was a bad idea." I stand and start for the door, I never should have come. I need to get over her for my sanity and hers. Gone are the days of loving her, protecting her and her running to me when she needs me.

"Yes, one of many." Her words cut like a knife.

Lily is at the door eavesdropping, a worried look on her face. I nod to her, then let myself out.

Jenna's right in the fact that nothing has changed in five years.

Five years hasn't changed her anger toward me as I had hoped, there's no going back, no way to recover what's been lost.

13

"Jenna, over here." I hear him before I see him. *A Paparazzo*.

I turn to go back inside, but the photographer steps in my path. I try sidestepping him, but he follows me.

"Come on, Jenna, let me get one shot."

It didn't take long for the media to figure out who I was from the pictures of Mark and me in that magazine. My best guess is someone back home sold me out, everything is about a payday.

They have been following Mark around trying to catch us together again, while Jerry has been trying to run damage control.

"Excuse me. I forgot something." I've never experienced anything like this before, but I know I need to get back inside, now.

"Just one shot, smile for the camera." He pleads.

I can't get by him, every step I take, he matches it. He's drawing attention to us, and other people with cameras start to surround me. I shake my head 'no', but he's still harassing me, asking me questions.

"How old are you?" "What's going on with Mark?"

I think about lying on the ground and crying, hoping they might take pity on me and leave me alone.

"Stop it! Leave her alone now!" A voice shouts over the flashing and calls of photographers. Mark. I see him as he barrels through the growing crowd, then grabs me by the wrist and pulls me through the now *very* large crowd of not only photographers but bystanders as well.

He isn't gentle or subtle, as he has to literally push people out of our way.

Finally, we make it back inside, and he clutches me to his chest, his breathing is ragged, and he's holding me tightly. I'm crying, I'm shaking, I'm a mess, but I feel safe in his arms.

I look up into his face. His emotions are a mix of anger, fear, and compassion as he stares down at me. "Thank you. I didn't think—"

He cuts me off. "Are you ok?"

I nod, tears still streaming down my face.

"You need a bodyguard, maybe two. I'll talk to Randy, he shouldn't have let you leave alone." Whatever compassion that was there a second ago is now something else entirely. I'm not sure if he's angry at me or with Randy or both.

"Ok." I grab onto his shirt.

He pulls away quickly as if he's just committed a cardinal sin by touching me. He backs away slowly, still looking at me before he turns and heads down the hall toward the recording studio I just came from, where Randy is still inside listening to the track I just cut.

"Mark!" I call out just before he enters the room. I want him to know I'm grateful, but also, I want him to know I feel it too. Whatever it is that he's trying not to feel, whatever we aren't allowed to feel. Instead, I stick with a simple "Thank you."

He doesn't respond. He turns the knob and walks inside the studio.

I slide down the wall, pulling my knees up to my chest as I listen to the yelling going on behind it. I rest my forehead against my knees and sigh. I'm not sure what's worse, Mark pulling away from me or the paparazzi following me.

14

JENNA - APRIL 2015

"He wanted you to do what?"

"I know, Dad. He's crazy! How could he think I'd be a part of anything that has to do with him?" I pull off the freeway toward my house in the Hills, yelling inadvertently at my father, who has always harbored ill will toward Mark, so he's obviously on my side.

"You sound really upset. I think I should take the next flight out."

I shake my head even though he can't see it, slowing down for a red light. "No, Dad, you don't have to do that. I'm fine, really. I'm not going to let him set me back."

He sighs, expecting me to say that. "I'm overdue for a visit anyway." He's lonely without my Mom, and he knows that I'm grieving without Max.

"Dad, you were here not that long ago."

"I know, but that wasn't a good visit." There's no arguing with him there, funerals shouldn't be the only reason you see family.

"It's not that I don't want you to come, I just have a lot going on that doesn't have to do with Mark." My Dad used to be in denial about my addictive tendencies, worse than I was. He's an enabler.

"Ok, just promise me you'll call me if things get too crazy. I'll come right out."

"Thanks, Dad." I say gratefully, and hang up as I pull into the driveway where Tom is parked and leaning against his car door. I impatiently swing open the car door.

"Uh... hi. Were we supposed to meet?" I quickly check the calendar on my phone.

"I was hoping we could talk."

"Sure. Come on in." I walk to the few steps and lead him into the living area. "Water?"

"No, I'm good." He looks around, not meeting my eyes.

I grab one out of the fridge and sit at the island. I'm trying to remain friendly despite the unannounced drop-in. Still, he *is* my new manager, so I need to get over this feeling of replacing Max and understand this is just business, not an invasion of privacy.

"Listen, J—" My skin crawls at the sound of the nickname that only Mark has ever called me.

I slam my hand down on the marble countertop, cutting him off. "Do not call me that, ever, no one calls me that." I can tell I've surprised him, but he continues.

"I'm sorry, *Jenna*. Listen, Jenna, the clothing line... the one Mark asked you about. I know you guys have history, but I think we need to discuss—"

"History?" *Is this guy for real?*

"I don't mean it like that. I just mean, hasn't it been long enough that you can work together on this?"

"No. Absolutely no. And don't pretend to know what history we have, because you have no idea. I'm sorry, I just can't do it."

He takes the seat across from me, analyzing me.

"You don't know what you're asking me to do." I say once again.

"I know with Max gone, you have reservations..."

"Don't dare bring Max into this either. You have a lot of nerve right now. You need to leave." My voice louder now.

"I'm going to be honest with you, and I need you to do the same. The record company heard about the clothing line. They want you to do it, because they are worried about your comeback. They're forecasting negative sales."

"Ok, well, they can't really believe that a lot of artists knock it out of the park after a long hiatus, especially with a Vegas residency."

"I actually agree with you." He leans on his forearms, clasping his hands in front of him.

"Then what the hell is the problem?"

"They're gonna drop the record if you don't do it Jenna."

15

JENNA - JUNE 1997

"Go straight to jail, do not pass go, do not collect two-hundred dollars." I'm sitting on the band's tour bus between Mark and Jamie. We usually separate after a show, but all the flights to D.C. were canceled due to bad weather, so Max and I tagged along with the band.

"How come I've spent more time in jail than actually playing," I whine, and everyone laughs.

Mark leans over casually, I can feel his warm breath on my ear, and it makes me shiver. "Maybe because you're a bad girl." He whispers, and I close my eyes, swallowing hard.

After months and months of touring together, it feels like Mark is always toying with me. A cat and mouse game, but I'm not sure if I want to be the cat or the mouse.

I look around. No one seems to notice or care that Mark's hand is on my thigh. I lean forward to roll the dice, rolling a four and a one, no doubles, which I need in order to get out of jail. "Dammit."

Mark grabs the dice with his free hand. The other is still resting quite comfortably on my thigh drawing circles. "Better luck next time." He squeezes gently, and I nearly orgasm just from the sexual tension of his hand so close, yet so far from where I want it.

I steal a glance at Max, who is sitting near the window writing in his journal.

"Max, can you finish the game for me? I'm beat." I stand and walk to my room without waiting for him to answer. I change quickly into a T-shirt and sweatpants and climb into bed, pulling the blanket up to my chin.

My heart is racing, and my skin is clammy, I'm beyond aroused, and I'm struggling to take deep breaths as I desperately try to calm myself. Startled, I respond without thinking when I hear a knock. "Come in." I swing my legs off the bunk and hop down, expecting it to be Max, but I swallow hard because Mark fills the small space instead of Max.

He raises an eyebrow at my Backstreet Boys t-shirt, making me self-conscious of not only the t-shirt but the lack of anything underneath it.

"It was a gift," I say, defending myself and folding my arms across my chest.

"Everything ok?" He asks.

"Yeah, fine. Just tired."

He eyes me warily and lifts my chin to meet his eyes. "Tired?" He questions all the while keeping his eyes pinned on me.

I nod, I'm not sure what else to say, and I don't know why he's followed me back here but what I want is for him to sprawl me out on this tiny bunk bed and make love to me. But that's not happening because where I lack self-control, he excels.

"I see. Listen, J... I can behave myself for the next three months. But once you're eighteen, I want you. I want you more than anyone or anything. I've never felt this way before, and God help me, I don't know if it's because you're the Goddamn forbidden fruit or my savior. So, if you don't want that, you need to tell me soon, ok?" He moves a piece of my hair off my forehead.

I nod my head. I can't formulate words. I've dreamt of this moment over and over, so much so, that now I'm not sure this is real.

"Goodnight, Jenna." He gently kisses my cheek then leaves me standing stunned.

I touch my cheek as I sit back on the bed and replay the last year. He's been so damn cold to me at times that I don't understand his sudden confession. One thing I do know, I want him, and I don't want to wait.

16

MARK - JUNE 1997

"Great show, dude!" A fan with VIP access shouts as I walk down the stairs to the backstage area. The show was great, but I'm distracted, and I can't help it. Jenna drives me crazy on stage.

"Thanks, Man!" I shout back and stop to pose for a quick picture. Then I sign a few autographs for other fans who paid an exorbitant amount of money for the VIP experience.

Another half-hour of frontman obligations and then back on the bus. Usually, that's an unbearable thought to be getting back on the bus, but since Jenna has been traveling with us, I can't wait.

The next show is only a few hours away, and that will give us most of the day tomorrow to chill with the guys or do something fun.

I'm stuck in my head, thinking about taking Jenna shopping when a middle-aged man grabs my arm and pulls me aside. "I need a word with you, Mark McGinley." My bodyguards are about to tackle him, but I call them off.

"And who the hell are you?" I ask, brushing the guy off my arm.

"Jenna's father." *Oh shit.* Well, that explains the angry look, I fucked up. Jenna didn't tell me her family was coming, and I'm guessing right about now he's very unhappy about me grinding with her on stage.

I walk toward my dressing room, waving off my bodyguards because I can feel the wrath of her father, and I'd rather not do this in front of anyone.

He follows behind. "You have a lot of nerve."

Ok, I was hoping this was going to go better in private, but now I realize he may kill me instead because we are alone.

So, I figure, I can handle this two ways. The punk asshole who doesn't give a shit or the sorry asshole who just crossed the line with his daughter on stage in front of thousands of people. I take the middle road.

"Listen, Mr. Foster. I care about Jenna. It's just part of—"

He pushes me against the wall. "You have no business being that close to my daughter. She's seventeen for Christ sakes. If I'd have known this is what was going on, I would've tagged along. I guess Max wasn't keen on keeping his word to keep her out of trouble."

"Sir, with all due respect, it was a spontaneous moment, and I swear I haven't—"

"No. You don't get to say anything till I'm finished. My daughter is a good girl, and being with someone like you will ruin her. You hear me, McGinley? If I find out you lay one finger on her. I'll make sure any future women in your life get no pleasure out of you, got it."

I stare blankly at him. "Got it." I could cower or rebuke his argument, but he's made up his mind.

He turns to leave, satisfied that he has the last word.

"Mr. Foster, one more thing." He turns, with a smug grin on his face, it makes me sick. Like I'm a monster like I'm not good enough. "She'll be eighteen soon, and there's not a damn thing you can do about it."

He looks pensive as if he had already realized this. "You may be right about that. But you know as well as I do, you won't be any good for her."

17

Hollywood is cutthroat.

Girls like me are a dime a dozen in the pop world, and ever since Mark drew attention to me on stage, I'm the flavor of the week.

Several record labels are interested in me, and this is the moment I've been waiting for, but today, I need to be in two places at once.

Starlight Records for a meeting and my parents' house Jersey for my eighteenth birthday party. There's no way I can do both, and Randy is no help in the matter.

I'm torn because I am new on the scene. I don't want to lose the opportunity by rescheduling the meeting, but I know my parents have a big thing planned for me, and I don't want to disappoint them.

So, I'm sitting on the tour bus trying to decide who to let know I'm not coming. I know my Dad will understand, so with tears streaming down my face, I decide I will have to call my parents and pray he can make my Mom understand.

The door swings open, and Mark steps on. I stand and try to hide my face, but he sees that I've been crying and immediately comes to me.

"Who do I have to kill?" He asks, grabbing me by the arms.

I cock my head, then realize the tears are more of a sobbing, and I'm borderline hyperventilating. Every word I'm trying to get out is inaudible.

He pulls me up into a tight embrace. "J, relax, tell me what happened. I can't help if you don't tell me."

I hold him back, clutching his shirt, staining it with tears. His arms feel like home like no one else could ever hold me this way. Finally, I'm able to calm enough to tell him about the problem.

"I don't think they will reschedule if I cancel. You know things don't work that way. They'll forget about me before tomorrow."

He pulls back to look at me. "Tell them you have another offer."

I pull back, meeting his eyes. "But that's not true." I say earnestly.

"They don't know that. They will want to beat out their competition. Tell them to give you their best offer, and you'll let them know tomorrow." He assures me.

"I can't do this." I wave my arms around emphatically. I want this more than anything, but suddenly the reality of it all is too much. "What if they don't take the bait?"

He smiles and reaches for a large Manila envelope. "Happy early birthday. I wanted to wait till after your meeting, so it didn't sway your decision." He explains.

Puzzled, I tear it open and find a Contract. There are tabs on several pages that say, 'sign here.' I skim it quickly and gasp when I realize what it is. "You're offering me a record deal?"

"Well, 'we' the whole band owns the label."

"I don't know what to say." I swipe at my face with the back of my hand to dry up my tears.

"Think about it. Let us make it easy for you. A big record label will eat you alive and kill your creative freedom. We just want you to have fun and of course, be successful."

I laugh, he sounds like a used car salesman. "You really think that I can do this?"

"I do. Really. We all do."

I drop down onto the couch and flip again through the pages. It looks like pretty standard wording, and I'm sure Randy will kill me for signing without him, but call it a gut feeling I know it's the right thing to do. "You got a pen?"

He smiles. "I'll drive you to the airport."

18

JENNA - APRIL 2015

I trusted Mark with everything that day, my heart, my career, and I took them from a little record label to one of the biggest still to date.

It was easy to sign with him that day, I knew he wouldn't let me fail. He was emotionally and financially invested. My parents were so happy for me until I told them who I signed with, then continued to add insult to injury by showing up to my party with Mark.

That was the first of many times that my Dad told me to stay away from Mark, but I never listened for my own good.

I pull up to Heartbeat Records and throw the car in park. I know my hunch is a gamble, but Mark has manipulated me before into doing what he wants, and my gut is telling me he's behind my label suddenly wanting to drop me.

When I walk in, I can't tell if my heart is racing because of the memories that are flooding back or because I'm about to see Mark for the third time in recent days.

"Hi, can I help you?" A bubbly, bright blonde says from behind the desk. I haven't seen this woman before, and I was hoping Olivia would still be at the desk so I wouldn't have to explain myself.

"Please let Mr. McGinley know that Jenna is here to see him."

"Jenna?"

I groan inwardly, these damn kids today. Don't they listen to nineties music? I roll my eyes because this girl is clearly in the age demographic I'm supposed to be reaching with the new album.

"Yes, is he in?" I answer politely.

She's flustered but manages to tell me. "He's by appointment only, I don't see your name..." As she scrolls on an iPad.

I pull out my phone and dial his cell number, which I still know by heart despite deleting it from my phone.

He answers on the second ring.

"I'm in the lobby, your receptionist is about to turn me away, you have two minutes." I hang up and tap my heel as I wait. It's less than two minutes when he steps off the elevator and walks toward me.

"Jenna."

He looks... amazing. My stomach lurches and then flops as I get a good look at him in dark jeans, a black t-shirt, and old school Adidas sneakers. My knees feel weak, and I lean on the counter to steady myself. Obviously, he's aging well.

"You should have let me know you were coming." His words hit me, and I snap out of the fantasy.

"Why? So, you could plan your next move?" I raise my eyebrow and start for the elevator. "It's more fun this way." The door opens and closes behind us, and in the close proximity of the elevator, his masculine scent makes me lightheaded.

"You look amazing, J." He's looking at me like he used to. Like he wants to devour me. I swallow over the lump in my throat because it is too tempting to move across the elevator.

"I really wish you would stop calling me that." I keep my voice steady, which is hard while he is looking at me like that. "Where's Olivia?" I shift nervously in the tiny space.

"VP of Marketing." He says proudly.

"Wow," I say, truly proud of her accomplishments.

The elevator stops, interrupting any further conversation. The doors open and he leads me out with his hand at the small of my back, he's done this more times than I can count, but the contact is like a head trip. The greatest high. I guess, once an addict, always an addict. Every single nerve ending is on fire.

"Does this visit mean that you've changed your mind?" He asks once we're in his office taking a seat on the couch closest to the door.

The office is pretty much the same as I remember. Laidback California style with couches and bean bag chairs and a table instead of a single desk. Totally Mark.

I don't sit because right now, I'm feeling very vulnerable. I can't ascertain what these feelings are that suddenly have me feeling... sentimental. *I can't feel like this right now.* "My label is threatening to drop me. You had something to do with that." It's a statement, not a question.

"Yesterday, you accused me of stalking and now, sabotage? Poaching?" He seems hurt by my accusations, but I know better. I know the heartless man behind the mask.

"Yes. Now, what do you want from me? Haven't I already given you everything?" I hadn't been able to give him everything, but I certainly tried.

He stands, so we are face to face, toe to toe. It's hard not to look away, but I stand tall and take a staggering breath that I hope he doesn't notice. "For the record, I was in our New York office three days ago on business. Second, the music business is volatile, I had nothing to do with your label dropping you, it's the business we're in." He says matter-of-factly and then walks toward the window.

"So, it's all just a coincidence? You want me to believe that?"

"You won't believe me no matter what I say."

"Fine, Mark. I'll do the clothing line, but I don't want to deal with you. Have the designer call me." I leave pausing just outside the door to catch my breath as I remember how we used to be.

19

"Maybe you should sing country, you sound twangy."

I give Max an if-looks-could-kill stare. "Shut up, Max." I throw a pillow at him, but he's right. It's not poppy enough. It's not even good.

Jamie and Mark are listening to the last four cuts I've recorded. I'm watching them behind the glass, their reactions are stoic. They know it sucks too.

My palms are sweating. I dry them on my ripped jeans then reach for my Evian water bottle.

Mark throws the headphones down and walks out of the control room.

It's been two months since my eighteenth birthday, and despite his promise a while back, Mark has made zero moves on me. I'm starting to think I dreamt the whole thing of him telling me how much he wants me.

Jamie puts his headphones down and comes into the studio. "Alright, Jenna, that's a wrap for today."

"I'm not tired, Jamie, I can fix it," I say nervously.

"Nah, we've been here too long already. Go home. Rest your

voice." In the music biz, that means go home because you sound like shit.

"Ok." I sound meek and frustrated.

Jamie kisses me on the cheek and waves bye on his way out.

I've gotten close to all the guys in the band, so it's not unusual for us to hang out or for them to peck me on the cheek, everyone that is except for Mark, who still avoids me like the plague.

"I have to go anyway," Max says, bringing me back from my pity party. When I don't ask why he continues. "I have a date."

"Oh? Are you going to tell me who?"

"You don't know him."

I pull him into a hug, happy that my best friend is finally living his best life after his family disowned him.

He grabs his backpack and heads for the door. "You coming?"

I shake my head. "I need a few more minutes. I'll see you tomorrow." I say solemnly and run my hands through my hair before grabbing the mic once more.

He nods and the door shuts loudly behind him.

I lean forward and close my eyes, pretending I am recording, imagining the music, the beat, and I feel it flowing through me now.

I belt the song out one more time, hitting every note the way it should sound, right on key. It's perfect, so damn perfect that I'm disappointed that everyone missed it, but then I hear a slow clap coming from the other side of the glass, and my eyes fly open.

Mark is at the control desk, he pushes a button so I can hear him. "It's about fucking time, Jenna Foster." He barrels through the door to the studio, slamming it open.

He doesn't wait, he doesn't ask permission, he takes what he wants as he strides over, grabbing both sides of my face and kisses me. Oh God, does he kiss me. Our mouths are sinful expressions of everything we want, yet everything we have been deprived of.

He reluctantly pulls away, still holding my face in his hands, he kisses the tip of my nose. I'm breathing hard and aching with need, one kiss has set me on fire.

"That was awesome." He slides his hands down my arms, still holding me close.

"I've never been kissed like that before," I say slightly embarrassed revealing that to him.

He laughs. "I meant the song, but yes, the kiss was equally amazing."

"Too bad we didn't get it on record." Once again, I'm disappointed.

"Yeah, about that. I came in right before you started, I saw you close your eyes, and I knew you were going to nail it. I guess you missed the light go on."

"You recorded it?" I say in disbelief. He takes my hand and pulls me into the control room to rewind the playback.

"Jamie might let you walk away, Jenna, but I won't let you go that easy."

20

"She still thinks I cheated on her." I say in disbelief.

Jamie sits next to me as I throw back beer after beer.

"She thinks I'm messing with her." That couldn't be further from the truth. Everything I did before, during, and after our marriage was for Jenna.

"Of course she does. You never told her the truth." He slaps me on the back.

"I couldn't. She asked me to let her go."

She asked, and I obliged. In the end, all we did was try to hurt the other more.

I know better than anyone else recording an album is risky business. The music business isn't like it once was, old fans are nostalgic, and new fans are hard to get when you're 'that old guy from that nineties band.'

Jenna might have an easier time resurrecting her old fans while acquiring new ones, but it's still a risk. No label wants to take that big of a gamble.

If my business venture cost her the Contract, they wanted out anyway. Jenna won't change her style, she wants to record what she writes. I always gave her free reign to be the artist she wanted to be, and luckily it always paid off. I believed in her when no one else did, and she carved a path for many other pop artists to merge sounds between genres.

"Well, I still think you should just tell her. I would think she would want closure after all this time."

"It's best if we just leave things like they are. Back then I tied her down because I was terrified to lose her. The worst already happened, I don't want to go there again." I admit.

"Ok, well, I'd like to see her. She didn't have to disown all of us when she left your sorry ass." He throws back his own beer.

"Fuck you, Jamie." I motion to the bartender for another round. If I can't make Jenna listen, the least I can do is drink her away.

"Hey, she changed her mind about the clothing line, right?"

I shake my head. "Her label threatened her. It's not like she wants to do it. Oh, and they want her to have a single in the ad."

"You don't care about that, right?"

"I told them no. We have artists we could be promoting in the ad. We're cutting our nose to spite our face, it's a total conflict of interest." This was a terrible fucking idea.

I reach for my phone and text Damien, the designer and tell him to find someone else, throwing my phone back down on the bar. He will be disappointed, but he'll just have to understand.

"So, you're just gonna let Jenna go, for a second time?"

I grab my phone and stand carefully. "She's not mine to let go. She's... nothing to me."

21

"Go out to dinner with me." It's been a month since that kiss with Jenna in the studio. It's all I've thought about day and night. I'm trying like hell to take things slow with her, but I can't wait much longer.

We just played our last show, the tour is over, and I want to concentrate on her, on us.

We've hung out plenty with the band and with Max, but our time alone has been limited. It's time to change that.

"Are you asking or telling me?" She walks down the stairs of the bus. I'm blocking her escape. She looks gorgeous, her light brown hair is cascading around her shoulders. Her hazel eyes are glimmering.

"If I ask, will you say yes?"

"Try it and find out." She's playing coy. Most of the women I've been with have thrown themselves at me. Jenna has been different since day one, and I don't want her to throw herself at me.

"Jenna, will you please let me take you out on an actual date, and not one that ends with you in one bed and me in another. I want you. I can't wait one more day."

"No." She says.

I look up at her stone face. She's deadpan serious. "No? You just made me go through that whole thing, and you never intended to say yes?"

She shrugs her shoulders. "I can't. I'm flying home tonight."

This is news to me, the tour is over, but I never considered she wouldn't be going back to LA. Only now do I see the duffel bag behind her. I'm desperate to keep her here with me.

"You can't leave, your album needs *a lot* of work." My words wound her, she looks disappointed.

"I know. That's one of the reasons that I'm going home. This just doesn't feel right. I'm not cut out for all of this." She looks defeated.

The tone in her voice breaks my heart. She *is* made for this, her record will be amazing. I don't know what has changed her mind, but someone is getting inside her head. Maybe Randy or her parents?

"We have a Contract," I say bluntly. "You can't record with another label."

"I know, and I'm sure you will do what you have to. Sue me." She steps off the bus and over to the cab that has pulled up, Max is already there waiting for her.

"J, wait..."

She turns. I need her to stay. She's everything to me, we need more time, so I throw it all out on the line. "Stay. Forget the music. Stay for me, stay with me." I plead one more time.

She walks back to me despite the cab driver honking and yelling for her to hurry up. I breathe a sigh of relief, she's changed her mind, but instead, she pulls something from her pocket and hands it to me.

"What's this?" I ask as I unfold it, revealing several pictures of us torn out of a tabloid magazine. Someone is following us.

"We are just one big conflict of interest. You're my... what? My label? My friend? A guy who wants to get in my pants?"

I scoff at her characterization of our relationship. "I think if I wanted to just get into your pants, I would've done that already."

She stares at me hotly. "You don't know what this is either, you're hot one minute and cold the next. I can't follow you around anymore. I'm not some groupie."

"Goddamn it Jenna, I know that." I reach for her, but she pulls away.

She points to the tabloids. "But they don't."

22

JENNA - APRIL 2015

"They're going in another direction?" I'm juggling my phone in one hand and my coffee, keys, and purse in the other while Tom throws another curveball at me.

"That's what he said."

I roll my eyes, another one of Mark's games. I finally manage the door and step into the foyer. "Ok, so now what?"

"So now we meet with the label execs about still moving forward with the album."

"Ok, let me know, make sure they know I'm not changing anything." I hang up and throw the phone down on the kitchen island. "Fuck him," I say to no one, just out loud so I can hear myself. "God, I need a drink," I scream because that's what Dr. Wild has told me to do when I'm overwhelmed. *Acknowledge it. Breathe through it.*

I storm into the living room, kicking off my shoes one at a time and grab the plush blanket off the couch and wrap myself up, cocooning myself within it, so I'm not tempted to jump in the car and drive to the nearest liquor store.

Then I sit on the couch, swaddled in my melancholy. I heard that grief would creep in at any moment, without warning.

That grief would eat you alive and spit you out. Right now,

between grief and addiction, I feel like a black tunnel is swallowing me whole.

I don't realize that I've been crying and curled up on the floor for hours until I hear the doorbell ring, and I sneak a glance at the clock.

I don't want to deal with anyone, so I ignore it, hiding my face in the blanket until it rings again and again. I roll my eyes, it could be my Dad who decided to make the trip after all and has shown up unannounced.

I answer the door with the blanket still wrapped around me and inwardly curse myself for not checking the camera when I see Mark standing there.

"Can I come in?" He asks gently, obviously seeing me in my current emotional condition.

I can't imagine what I must look like right now. I hold the door, so he can't push inside. "It's not really the best time."

"Just a few minutes, please." He looks at me with so much compassion, and somehow this man has always been able to get to me, break me down.

I step aside to let him in and take a seat on my white leather couch.

"Are you ok?"

I roll my eyes. "Don't worry, I'm not crying over you."

"Jenna... I—I never stopped caring about you, if you need to talk to someone, I'm here for you."

"I'm good, I pay someone extremely well to listen to me."

He sighs and sits down on the other end of the couch, rubbing his palms on his thighs. "I didn't want the label to force you into the ad. So, I told them we were going in a different direction. I didn't want you to think—"

"It's fine. You're right, I didn't want to do it. Now I don't have to."

He's silent for a moment. "Where did we go wrong? When did we go wrong?"

I scoff. I can't believe he's even asking that he knows as well as I do. "Does it even matter?"

He's quiet as he considers that. "No, I guess not." He says finally.

I sneak a glance at him, he's looking so intensely at me.

The truth is, when we first got together, I thought the intense chemistry and passion we shared would be enough to keep us together forever, but eventually, fame and life got to us and tore us apart. *Wishful thinking.*

"Anyway, I just came by to tell you that and to let you know if they don't move forward with the album, I know a guy who owns a label." He winks at me.

And there it is, his motive, getting me back under his label. "I'm surprised you would get behind something so dark and edgy, and namely about you without hearing it."

He sighs. "It wouldn't be the first time, but I know what you're capable of."

I'm sure he means this in more than one way, but I don't take the bait. "It's not a pop album, like I said it's dark. I knew it was a risk, but I needed to write it. Besides, they were probably just looking for an excuse. You made it easy for them."

He nods solemnly and stands to go. I follow him to the door.

"Did you know?" He asks.

"Did I know what?"

"That Max was suicidal?"

I sigh, because I had a hint of an idea a few years ago but I kept him busy thinking it would go away. Maybe I was too deep in denial or too wrapped up in my own problems, but I never thought he would leave me.

"I should have." I say as the tears fall.

He shocks me as he grabs my hands, squeezing gently, then leaning forward to kiss me on the cheek before he turns to go.

The warmth of his lips on my skin spreads a warmth through me that I haven't felt in a long time. It's that feeling of being home, of being loved.

I stare after him for a long time, then finally, I realize the only way to forgive myself, might be to forgive Mark first.

23

JENNA - JUNE 1998

"Smile!" A crowd of parents gathers around to take a picture of us in our cap and gowns.

I'm standing in the middle of a group of my friends huddled in a pose with our arms linked around each other.

Max is standing to the left of my parents. We've been back home since December, but he didn't want to return to school with me. It took me a lot of work to catch up, but I was able to, and here I am, graduating.

I've been pushing Max about getting his GED, but he says he's not ready. I, on the other hand, wanted normalcy, even though a lot of the kids at school treated me differently, it was still better than being attacked by photographers or reading into Mark's hot and cold signals.

My Dad and Randy agreed that I would finish school and then get back on the bandwagon to stardom.

I agreed because I was able to attend my senior ball and walk at graduation.

I was thankful for the normal teenager experiences except when all my friends were applying to colleges, I was writing songs or meeting with Randy about business.

While all my friends were dating, I was home pining for someone I couldn't have. Leaving Mark after the last show still haunts me, and I hadn't heard from him or the other guys except for one letter I received from the label saying that I'm legally obligated to produce a record under their label. Randy thinks with a good lawyer, I can get out of the contract with the rights to my songs still intact, but so far, Randy's word doesn't mean much.

"Good luck Jenna!" One of the girls in my class calls to me before running off the field with her boyfriend. I wave to them as my Mom puts her arms around my shoulders.

"Jenna, I'm so proud of you, honey." She gleams.

"Thanks, Mom." She's been thrilled to have me back home and has been trying to encourage me to apply to colleges instead of running back to L.A. I dreaded either option.

We're walking the long walk back to the car when Max leans into me to whisper in my ear.

I look in the direction he's quietly telling me to look and gasp.

"Go, I'll distract them." He says, and without much thought, I nod and start walking in that direction.

I turn back once to look over at my parents and Max. He has them occupied talking to a few other parents.

I take my cap off before I reach my destination because now it feels silly and childish.

"Hey," Mark says when I'm about a foot away, lifting his dark sunglasses on top of his head.

"Hey." I say shyly.

"I didn't think you would notice me."

"Max saw you. What are you doing here?" It's a lame thing to say, but I don't know what else to say. Seeing Mark leaning against a fancy car in my high school parking lot is surreal, and others looking our way surely recognize him.

"I wanted to congratulate you, in person."

"Thanks." I scuff my shoe on the ground and look back once more to my parents. They're walking in the opposite direction from us, back to where we parked.

"Here." He says, reaching behind him and handing me an envelope similar to the one he gave on my birthday, the one that held the recording Contract.

"What's this?" I reach forward, taking it from him.

"A graduation present."

I shake my head. "You and your presents." I quickly tear it open and stare at the contents inside the envelope.

I pull out a bunch of papers as well as a key from the bottom of the envelope. I quickly scan the documents. "You're absolving me from my contract?" I look up, he looks laid back, sitting against the car, his tan, toned arms holding him up.

He nods, and my stomach sinks. "You're a free agent. Keep reading."

I flip through the other pages, finding a signed lease and another recording Contract. I hold the key out to him. "Ok, you got me. I don't get it."

He lifts himself off the car and walks the few inches to me, closing the gap. "I'm letting you out of the Contract because I think you signed it impulsively, and I don't want you to feel obligated." He takes the key and puts it into my palm, closing my fingers around it. "This is the key to an apartment in Studio City for you and Max, no strings attached. And this," He grabs the blank Contract and puts it back into the envelope before handing it to me. "Is because I still want to throw my hat in the ring. I want to sign you, Jenna, but I want us more. So, if you choose to sign with another label, I'm ok with that. If you want to stay here, I'm ok with that too, I'll make it work. I want you."

"What if I say no?"

His smile is cryptic, eery. "I've heard you say no before. I've watched you walk away, get on a plane, and I've spent the last six months without you. Sure, I could find someone else, pretend she is better than you, that I have this magical connection with her, that you leaving didn't hurt me. I just don't want to." His words affect me more than I want to admit.

"Good." I say. His eyes are intense like the eye of a storm, I could fall into them. Hell, I want to fall into them.

"Good?" He looks at me perplexed.

"The guys around here are pretty lame, I think I prefer older men."

He laughs and pulls me to him. "Hey, watch it." He strokes my cheek with his thumb and leans forward, our noses are touching, his breath on my lips. I take a shuddering breath. "I'm going to kiss you."

Yes, please!

"I'm waiting." And he does he kiss me, like he's been starved, like he's baring his soul to me, and my heart feels like it might burst out of my chest.

And when we pull in front of my house hours later, and I tell Max the plan I never look back.

24

"Have a good show." Marissa smiles and winks at me. She's been hitting on me for months, making it no secret that she wants me.

Marissa is gorgeous with long straight black hair, eyes that make the ocean look dull and the body of a supermodel that would make any man weak in the knees.

She also happens to be the coordinator of this special nineties tour the band signed onto.

Of course, I find her attractive, and had I not seen Jenna again, I probably would've occupied my time with her, but now I just can't. I swallow a heavy-handed shot of Jameson to dull my emotions.

I kissed Jenna and left her standing at her door two weeks ago. Since then, I can't stop obsessing about her.

It's driving me mad not knowing what she's up to.

Max and I continued talking after Jenna, and I divorced. He would give me periodic updates on how she was doing, and I lived for those updates.

With that connection gone, I'm starving and restless and the need to take matters into my own hands in consuming me.

Even being on this ten-show tour isn't helping to distract me because when I think back to that time, all I see is Jenna.

Jenna, on stage behind me, her long, light brown hair swinging as she sings. Jenna sunbathing at the hotel pool, her long tan legs on the lounge chair. Jenna, on the tour bus, driving me crazy in every way possible. Her voice filling the room when she sings. The way her eyes gleam when she comes under me, the way our bodies melted together.

She's everywhere in my mind yet nowhere in my reality.

"Mark? You ready?" Marissa is next to me, her long manicured nails dig into my bicep.

I toss back another shot of Jameson and climb the stairs as we take our places on the stage, the crowd roars to life. We don't often perform anymore, but it's cathartic to be back on stage.

The crowd is great, the music is bringing me to life, and I've got a great buzz.

We are the final act to perform for the night, and with one song to go on the setlist and a few too many shots of Jameson, I'm feeling a little too nostalgic.

I wave my arms around to get the guys to stop playing, this is off the cuff, and no one knows what I'm doing.

I put the microphone in the stand, grab my solo cup, and close my eyes as I down the rest of its contents.

"How many of you have ever been in love?"

The crowd claps, the catcalls and whistles buzz all around me.

I look over to Jamie. He's laughing, but I know he's terrified where I'm going with this.

"How many of you are with your love tonight?"

Again, the crowd's response is loud and buzzing.

I take the mic out of the stand and walk from one side of the stage to the other as I rattle on.

"Anyone ever lose someone they love? I'm not talking death, I'm talking life on earth, without that one person you can't live without. The universe meddling in what's supposed to be?"

The response is there but milder than my first two questions. "Good, then this is for you poor bastards like me. Jenna, this one's for you."

25

MARK - JUNE 1998

"You're doing fine, just keep going." She shakes her head.

"I don't want to do fine, Mark." She yells and throws her headphones down. God, help me. This girl is going to drive me crazy. I clear the studio and step inside the booth.

"What do you want to do, Jenna? You want to take five? Take the day? What?"

She sits on the stool and folds her arms over her chest, she's angry at me, at herself, and at the song.

I stand and stare at her. I can't help but think that Dave is right, that me producing her is a conflict of interest. Maybe it's making this harder on her than it has to be.

"Why don't you show me what I'm doing wrong since you know everything." She pouts.

I go back to the soundboard, hit the button for the music, and run back into the booth. I lean forward into the microphone, wait for the first verse, and I let it rip.

It's not nearly as good as she was doing, so I stop just after the chorus.

She's laughing uncontrollably, which makes me laugh too. "Please tell me you did that on purpose to make me laugh."

I wrap my arms around her waist and pull her close, she smells like apples. "You have to lighten up. You're going to burn out just from recording. This is supposed to be the fun part. You have to find your happy place while you're in here."

She exhales a breath she had been holding. "I don't want to sound like everyone else on the radio." She's trying to sound objective, but it comes out whiny.

"You won't. You're doing something fresh. Everyone else is just pop, this is... this is something entirely different, and no one is writing their own songs, not like this."

She groans. "Fine, let's do it again."

I kiss her lips, once, twice then a longer one, she groans, and I'm instantly hard.

I love kissing her, I love that she's here with me and I love the fire she has when she's creating music, but her self-esteem and desire to be perfect are getting in her way.

Reluctantly, I let her go and call everyone back into the studio. "Ok, everyone, from the top. Jenna, you good?"

She winks and gives me the thumbs-up, and we start again.

Our eyes are locked as she starts out slow but perfect, she nails the chorus, and by the time she's at the second verse, she hits her stride, and it's magical.

She sounds like she's been recording her whole life. She found her happy place.

She closes her eyes as she sings the last of the lyrics, her voice fading out with the notes of the music.

She's breathless when she finishes, and I motion for the engineers to play it back. I pick up the headphones, listening as we play the whole thing and then look at each other.

We all nod in agreement, it doesn't need to be re-cut or stacked. The one take is perfect.

Dave pushes the button so Jenna can hear him.

"That's a wrap, Jenna. You just recorded your first single."

She jumps up and down, clapping, then bursts through the door and jumps into my arms. "Thank you." She whispers into my ear, and I kiss her cheek. "What would I do without your pep-talks."

I grin. Her excitement is contagious. "Hopefully you never have to find out."

26

JENNA - MAY 2015

"Jenna, wake up. You have to see this." I look over at my nightstand. It's six in the morning, and I actually slept the whole night, for once.

Lily is standing over my bed with her iPad in hand.

I stretch and turn over. "Lily, this better be an emergency."

"No, Jenna, but you have to see this. Your social media is blowing up."

"Why?" Thank god when I first hit it big, there was no social media. I thought things were bad back then, but today social media can destroy you.

I sit up and take the tablet from her. Thousands of people tagging me in videos. Thousands of retweets and shares.

I immediately recognize who it is in the video and cringe.

"Oh no, did you watch this already?"

"Of course, I did."

"What did he do?"

She smirks and hits play. I watch the whole thing and then hit play again and again. I hear my name on his lips over and over while the crowd claps and cheers. I watch it several more times and conclude he's drunk. Very drunk.

"What the fuck." At first, I'm angry, then I'm... I'm something, not flattered, but something in that ballpark.

The truth is I hadn't stopped thinking about him since that night two weeks ago when he kissed me on the cheek.

That innocent kiss caught me off guard and stirred something inside me. Something deep down. Something I've told myself daily for two weeks, I can't feel. *Don't do this.*

"Coffee, please," I say to Lily before swinging my legs out of bed. I pull on my robe and stare out the window before impulsively dialing his cell.

It's early here in LA, I have no idea where he is now, if he regrets what he said, or if I'm interrupting someone beside him, lying on his chest while he sleeps off his drunkenness. I wonder if he's still wearing the chain that he had on the other night—the one with his wedding band hanging around his neck.

"I know. I'm sorry." He says, answering after a few rings.

"What on earth, Mark?"

"I was hoping you didn't see it."

"See it, it's plastered all over my feeds. I don't know how I would miss it."

Lily returns with my heavily caffeinated coffee, and I wave for her to leave.

"God, Jenna, I don't know. It's like..." he trails off, but I hear the sadness in his voice. "It's like seeing you and being on this nineties tour is messing with my head."

"Nineties tour?"

"Yeah, it's nostalgia city. I just lost it for a minute, that, and I'm sure the Jameson didn't help."

I swallow over the lump in my throat at the mention of Jameson, and take another sip of coffee. Jameson on the rocks sounds great right about now.

"Are you ok?" I ask because I do genuinely care.

"Getting by. It's hard to get over something I fought so hard for."

I wince, not knowing how to respond to that. I take a deep breath before responding. "I don't hate you, Mark."

"That's good, Jenna. Because hate is the furthest emotion I could feel for you."

I sigh, I'm not going to get sucked in again. I have to shut this down. "Then let's go back to the way things were, before we saw each other in New York, no contact."

He's quiet too long. I look at my cell, thinking the call has dropped.

"Mark?"

"I'm here."

"Ok..."

"I shouldn't have let you go, Jenna. You caught me off guard that day, we had just... we had just made love. You leaving me was the furthest thing from my mind. You never let me explain."

Tears start to form in the corner of my eyes. I can't do this. I can't maintain sobriety and deal with Mark, it's too painful. "It just wouldn't make any difference." I manage to croak out.

Out of the corner of my eye I see Lily come back into the room and take a seat in the chair next to my bed. My voice is about to shatter into a million shards of glass tears. "I have to go, I think you just need to forget about me, move on. That's the best thing for both of us." I hang up and throw the phone for good measure.

Then I fall to my knees and let a violent cry escape me. One that I may have been holding in for the last five years.

Lily is holding me when I come back to reality. I'm sore and weak from occupying this spot on the floor, but I let myself feel all the feelings that rush through me like an angry ocean.

It's unbearable, but therapeutic, and when I can't shed one more tear I stand, holding onto Lily for support.

"Two things," I say between breaths. "Call Dr. Wild, I need an appointment right away."

She starts to walk away then turns back. "What's the other thing?"

"Get the schedule for the tour Mark is on."

27

JENNA - JULY 1998

"We should put it over here, near the window." Max stands with his hands out like an interior designer, imagining the space through a small square in his fingers.

I drop onto the second-hand couch and turn on the TV that's sitting on the floor.

"Honestly, I don't care how you arrange the furniture." We've been moving into the apartment for the last two weeks, and I'm sick to death of unpacking and arranging what little furniture we have. Max obviously is not.

The buzzer rings, and I run over to the intercom. "Friend or foe?" I say jokingly into the speaker.

"Let me in, beautiful."

I giggle and buzz Mark into the building, standing waiting by the closed door until he knocks, then I swing the door open and jump into his arms the minute he crosses the threshold, my legs straddle his waist, and he greets me with the same passion, kissing me senseless as he carries me into the bedroom.

"Thank God for a two-bedroom." He mutters through labored breaths as he drops me onto my bed and climbs on top of me.

This is how it's been the last two weeks, hot and heavy but not leading to where I really want him the most. I'm sorry I told him that I'm still a virgin.

He lifts my shirt and fondles my breasts, his mouth nipping and sucking and driving me totally crazy.

"Mark, please," I beg. I want to move beyond foreplay, but for some reason, he never goes all the way.

"Jenna." His tone is a warning or a slip in composure, I'm not sure.

He unbuttons my jeans, sliding them down my hips so he can slide his fingers under the waistband of my boy shorts.

I gasp at the contact and the ministrations of his fingers, and I lift my hips to push him in further. His mouth reclaims mine, and I'm all sensation and angst as he presses over that magical spot. Over and over, until the pressure builds and breaks.

He swallows my cries as I come. Once again, sated but not fulfilled. He kisses the tip of my nose and pulls me up to my feet before he fixes my pants.

"I'm really ready, I promise."

He laughs and pulls me into his embrace. "I waited too long J, I don't want to screw this up."

I groan. "Leaving me frustrated is a good start to screwing it up."

He looks down at me, with stark seriousness. "It's gonna be special. Not just some quick lay on your twin size mattress Jenna, and not with Max in the other room."

I drop onto the bed frustrated. I wouldn't care if it was in the back of a car at this point.

He sits next to me, and his voice is softer now. "I want there to be more between us than just the guy who took your virginity."

I smile and link my arms around his neck. "You know, they say you never forget your first." I wink at him, and he kisses me sweetly before pulling me out the door.

"Hey Max, when did you get here?" Mark says jokingly with a coy smile as he pulls me toward the front door.

"Ha, ha. If you two weren't always sucking face as soon as you walk through the door, maybe you would notice someone other than Jenna."

Mark smiles that breathtaking smile. "Good point. Don't wait up." He tosses a set of keys to Max as we head down the stairway.

"What was that?" Mark's good mood has me curious.

"I'll let him tell you later. Just thought he should have some fun too."

I shrug, dropping it for now and follow behind him. "Where are we going?" I ask excitedly.

"We're going shopping."

"Shopping? For what?"

"Our first date."

"Our what?" I stammer.

He laughs. "I'm taking you out to dinner." His smile is so bright, it's infectious.

"Oh." Then I realize something. "Mark, wait." I drag my heels on the sidewalk and pull him to a stop. I look around for good measure, making sure we're alone. "What about... the paparazzi?" I whisper.

"What about them?" He opens the door to his fancy Corvette so I can get in.

"What if they see us? Won't they think we've been sneaking around this whole time?"

He motions for me to get in, but I'm terrified. Terrified of what they will write.

I lower myself slowly onto the leather seat, and he closes the door before he gets in on the driver's side. "I don't care, J. You're an adult, I'm an adult, and you're not gonna be stashed away like my dirty little secret." He puts the key in the ignition, and the engine roars to life before he quickly peels away from the curb. He grabs my hand as we head out of Studio City and toward Rodeo Drive.

I must still wear the worried look on my face because he grabs my hand and kisses over my knuckles. "We know the truth J. That's all that matters."

28

I'm nursing the worst hangover since probably my early twenties. My head is pounding, and I'm feeling sorry for myself. *What was I thinking?* I had no business having any sort of hope that Jenna would start talking to me again.

She's right, it's been five years, I have to move on.

After all, how much longer can I harbor hope for someone who doesn't want me in return?

My phone buzzes next to me. It's Marissa *again...*

I lift it, shielding my eyes from its brightness until they adjust. She wants to talk to me before the show. I consider making up some excuse, but I don't.

Instead, I agree to meet her for a drink. She could serve as the perfect distraction.

Standing slowly, I make it to the bathroom, grab two Advil out of my bag, and chug with an airplane bottle of vodka from the mini-fridge. I've been here plenty of times, and when all else fails, hair of the dog is the cure.

I take a quick shower, then meet up with the guys for a sound-check and a quick bite to eat.

"So... Jenna, ream you out for that romantic proclamation?" Dave asks with a smirk.

I knew they weren't going to let me off that easy.

I shrug my shoulders. "Could have been worse."

"So, now what?" Jamie looks at me, expectantly, waiting for me to say more.

"Now nothing. She wants to go back to the way things were, no contact."

The guys look from one to the other.

Steve leans forward. "So let me get this straight. You had the chance to tell her the truth *again*, and you didn't."

I rub at my temples and take a sip of water. *Fuck this hangover.*

"Listen, guys, it's not like if she knows the truth, she'll jump back into my bed and forget that the last five years happened. We can never pick up where we left off." It's the hard truth.

"Maybe that's a good thing." Jamie says.

I look over at Jamie. "How so?"

"I don't know, maybe you both needed time apart, maybe it would be better this time around." He knows everything we went through, I don't know how he could ever think that.

I push my plate away, disgusted. "I guess we'll never know."

I'm sitting at the bar waiting for Marissa, who is fashionably late.

I ask the bartender for another seven and seven, and while I wait, I scan the bar. People are starting to arrive for the show, and the place is filling up quickly.

I look around once more, then I see Marissa. She looks beautiful. Her skin is bronze, her long hair is down around her waist, and she's wearing a low-cut leopard print shirt, skin-tight black leather pants and red heels that scream 'fuck me.'

"Hey, you." She says casually as if she's not half-an-hour late.

I kiss her on the cheek and pull out the stool next to me as she orders herself a glass of wine.

"I'm so glad you agreed to have a drink with me." She says excitedly and casually places her hand on my lap. "I thought that you might be trying to get back with Jenna after last night's show." She smirks.

I smile warmly at her and steer the conversation elsewhere, that is until I see someone out of the corner of my eye.

It's only for a second, but I swear I see Jenna. I blink a few times and scan the area again.

No way. There is no possible way she is here.

"Are you ok?"

I look back to Marissa, who's looking at me concerned.

"You just missed everything I said." She whines.

"I know I'm sorry. I thought I saw someone I know. Go ahead." She rattles on and on for the next hour, and I do my best to give her my full attention, until I finally excuse myself for a bathroom break.

Just before I reach the men's room, I see the Jenna look alike again by the table selling band T-Shirts.

"I'm losing it," I say to myself, then I take care of business and return to Marissa.

She stands as I approach. "I guess we should head backstage, we don't want to be late for your set."

I nod and walk her backstage with my hand on her lower back. I'm doing all the right things, but everything feels wrong. I stand behind her as we watch band after band, and I ignore her body pressing against mine and her fingers as they intertwine with mine.

At five minutes to nine, she gives the band and me the go-ahead to take the stage. I'm a few steps behind the guys, and she catches me off guard when she grabs my arm and kisses me roughly. "I'll be waiting, naked, in the green room after your set." She whispers, and honestly, I didn't see that one coming, so I just nod.

Up on stage, the crowd is really feeling us as we play song after song. I stick to the setlist this time, instead of making any more drunken outbursts.

Then I see her, the Jenna girl.

She's in the middle of the crowd wearing a Tainted Innocence t-shirt, jeans and big sunglasses. I squint to see her but it's hard with the lights. I can't make out her face, but I'd swear on everything that it is Jenna swaying to the music.

I think about calling her out. Making her come up on stage, but I don't. She must be here for a reason, she's trying to blend in, or maybe she's dating someone from another band. Maybe it's not her at all.

When the song finishes, I say a final few words and then scramble off the stage but I'm too late.

She's gone and the crowd isn't helping the chase as I stop to sign a few autographs.

Finally, I make it to the exit but there's no sign of her.

I'm about to turn back when I see her and with every fiber of my being, I know it's her. Not a look alike, but the real thing. *Jenna.* And she's about to get into the back of a black SUV. I run over just as she opens the door.

"You didn't come all this way just to see the show."

She turns and smiles. A real fucking smoldering smile. "What if I did?"

Is she flirting with me? I grab her hand off the door handle. "Then you should get your money back."

She casts her eyes down and then looks up at me under full eyelashes. "Oh? And why is that?"

"Because it wasn't good. You see, I was distracted." I shut the door to the SUV.

"Was it the tall leggy brunette?" She lifts her hand back to the handle.

There's no way I'm letting her leave.

"Not in the least. I thought I was hallucinating. I saw you, a few times."

She clears her throat. "I saw her kiss you."

"She's no one." Tonight has proved that. Her hazel eyes flicker in the moonlight and I'm transfixed.

"It doesn't matter if she is." She says casually.

I sigh and shake my head. A limo beeps behind her driver. We're holding up traffic. "Please talk to me. Give me one hour." I plead.

She turns her head back toward the SUV contemplating her choices. "One hour." She agrees and I don't waste a second. I open the door handle and help her inside, then climb in beside her.

I tell the driver where I'm staying, and he pulls off quickly. The SUV is dimly lit but I stare at her silhouette, she's breathtakingly beautiful and her apple-floral scent that I remember all too well, is intoxicating in the small space.

I resist the urge to take her hand during the ride, it's much too personal, and she's already conceded so much.

The ride is short, once we are finally out of the club area and when the driver pulls to the curb in front of my hotel, I grab her hand and pull her out, practically sprinting inside the lobby.

"Bar or room?" I ask breathless, stopping when I feel her falter beside me. I look over to see if I've already made a mistake.

"Room."

Jenna never turns down a drink and once again, surprises me with her answer. *Do I even know her anymore?*

On the elevator I anxiously watch as the floors count up. We've already wasted twenty minutes of the hour and I'm sure she will punctually abort all talk once the hour is up.

Once inside the room, I reach into the mini fridge and pull out two mini vodka bottles, needing some liquid courage here. *Tell her the truth.* "Are you sure you don't want a drink?"

She looks up at the ceiling and blows out a breath. "I'm sober, almost five months." I stare at her too long, beaming like an idiot.

"Jenna... that's great!" Which sounds condescending. Like I'm speaking to a toddler, but I quickly put the bottles back in the fridge and realize I'm already screwing this up.

She looks uncomfortable, tapping her foot as she glances again at her watch.

I collect myself and motion for her to sit on the bed. I don't know where to start, but I have to get it all out. I take a deep breath then sit in the chair across from her.

"I didn't cheat on you." I blurt out.

Her face remains impassive. "I've heard that before." She clasps her hands together over her thighs.

"Jenna, why would I cheat on you?"

Her head drops in disappointment and I stand and pace nervously, worried now that the truth will be worse for her. "I don't know Mark, why does anyone cheat?"

"Well, I didn't." I lock eyes with her, so she knows with every ounce of my being, that there is truth in that statement.

"Fine. The pictures were photoshopped. Go on."

I kneel down in front of her, taking her hand and by God's grace, for the second time tonight she doesn't pull away. "I wasn't sleeping with those women. I was vetting them."

"Ok, sure, vetting them." She shifts on the bed. "For what exactly?"

"As Surrogates. Well, potential surrogates. I was trying to find someone discretely, confidentially. I figured you would be more open to the idea after the process was done. You said it would be too overwhelming. They all signed non-disclosures that's why they didn't say otherwise. I didn't think you would want anyone to know." I blurt out the truth.

She eyes me skeptically. "If that's so, why not just tell me?"

"You just left. You made up your mind about me, after everything, it felt like the truth was harder to hear." It was the truth. The infertility topic was off-limits.

"Times up." She rips her hand out of mine and stands, crossing the room quickly to get to the door.

I look at my watch, time is not up. "No." I say firmly as I catch up and grab her elbow.

"That's a low blow. Using your affairs as an excuse for me being infertile."

"Jenna…"

"I need to go." She tries sidestepping me.

"Why did you come? Why did you agree to talk to me tonight?"

"I didn't know you were gonna tell me nonsense." She's got that fighting look in her eyes.

"No. I mean why did you come to the show tonight?"

She's quiet. "I thought it would help... I was trying to remember a simpler time in my life that didn't involve booze or pills or..." she trails off.

I close the gap, we're toe to toe. I lift her chin, so we're eye to eye. "Or what?"

"Being alone."

"You're not alone." I whisper between us.

"Really?" She pulls out of my grasp. "Well where the hell is everyone Mark? Where is my Dad? Where are my friends—that aren't on my payroll? Even Max was on my damn payroll. And goddamn it Mark, where were you? When I was alone laying on the fucking bathroom floor bleeding and cramping. Where were you?" She falls to the floor, shuddering sobs escape her, racking her entire body.

I fall in front of her and wrap my arms around her. I never understood back then what the miscarriages did to her. "I'm sorry, I tried fix it. I never realized..."

She looks up at me, even with her tear stained face she's beautiful and it takes everything to hold myself back from kissing her. "I never felt whole after. I started to feel incompetent as a wife, as a woman. Five miscarriages and you weren't around. I just figured you didn't want to be around me, you were disappointed in me. And then, seeing those women with you... hotels... I just added it up."

"No. No. No, to all of that. God no." I shake my head and put my head in my hands.

The last five years could've been cleared up. I let her go on thinking I was unfaithful, and I should've put an end to the rumors long ago.

Somehow, I just always thought she would come back. Max did too.

I look up at her, she's quietly analyzing the last five minutes, maybe the last hour, hell, maybe even the last five years.

"I have to go." She stands abruptly and I follow her to the door.

She turns back once before she crosses over the threshold. "Can I ask you something?" She says quietly.

"Anything."

"Why are you still wearing the ring around your neck."

I grab the ring and hold it between my fingers and shrug. It's a simple reason, one that seems kind of silly now. "I just couldn't let go."

Something in her eyes flicker but she nods and turns to go.

I hold the door open and watch her, waiting to close the door until I can no longer see her. Then I drop down onto the corner of the bed, resisting the urge to empty the mini bar while I reflect on the last hour.

I'm so deeply absorbed in my melancholy that I barely acknowledge a knock at the door. I don't move, I don't want to see anyone right now. A few minutes pass and there is a second knock, quieter this time, but obviously whoever it is, isn't going away.

"Fuck!" I yell and cross the room, swinging the door open in a rush, half expecting it to be Marissa standing there giving me shit for standing her up.

I do not expect it to be doe eyed Jenna.

She rushes into me, wrapping her arms around my neck, her lips claiming mine. The shock takes a minute to wear off. My heart is racing, and I respond feverishly, my breathing is ragged, my cock is instantly hard, and I fist my hand in her hair, angling her mouth so I can claim her deeper.

She puts her hands on my chest, pushing me back until my legs hit the bed and I'm under her.

My hands are restless. I want to touch her everywhere, all at once, but I don't know what her end game is, so instead of touching her I flip us so that I'm on top.

She stares at me with swollen lips and lust glazed eyes.

"Jenna." I break away breathless, I feel like I'm dreaming. I look at my watch. "One hour is up."

"Fuck the hour." She says adamantly and puts her arms around my neck.

I lean down tenderly kissing her lips. "Is this what you want?" I whisper, praying that she doesn't come to her senses now.

She reaches for the hem of my shirt and lifts it over my head. Her fingers trace across the tattoos on my chest and arms. She closes her eyes and swallows hard.

"Don't make me wait like last time."

29

JENNA - MAY 2015

I sobbed the whole way down to the lobby when it hit me. *I want him.* I want him more than ever before. I was scared he'd shut the door in my face, but I had to go back.

And when my lips met his... God, that spark, that flame that he always lit burned inside me again. I haven't felt that whole in so long.

If he doesn't make me wait, if he fucks me right now, I have no idea where we go from here, but right now, I'm where I want to be. Beneath him.

He stares at me, surely contemplating my request. To be fair, if I were him, I would throw me out.

He shakes his head, and I close my eyes, he's turning me down, not that I blame him. "Just so I know, what is this? What will this be to you Jenna? I just have to prepare myself mentally, because I'm in love with you. I've never stopped loving you."

I know that from the way he looks at me and the ring around his neck. I know he's been carrying a flame for me for the last five years and yet, I'm selfishly asking him to do this.

"I thought about that the whole way back here and I don't know. I can't give you an answer."

He lifts off me and pulls me to my feet. I look down regretting that I came back here.

He tips my chin back and kisses me reverently once more then lifts my arms over my head, gently tugging off my corny Tainted Innocence t-shirt that I bought at the show.

"I'm going to give you what you want." His hands glide down my breasts, rubbing my nipples over my unimpressive cotton bra and leans forward to kiss the top swell of my breasts. "I've always given you all of me."

I close my eyes and swallow hard.

He pushes down my skinny jeans, letting them fall in a pool of denim on the floor and I shiver in anticipation as his finger brushes over my stomach down to my sex and I bite my lip as he rubs me over my panties making me groan, appreciating all the ways this man already knows how to turn me on.

"Turn around." He says, his voice gruff.

I'm lost in a sensual haze at his command, and when he brushes my neck with the back of his knuckles, then down between my shoulder blades, as he quickly unhooks my bra and tosses it across the room.

With his firm hands on my shoulders he spins me back to him, bending forward to take my puckered nipple into his mouth, gently rolling it between his teeth.

"Mark." I sigh his name, unable to say anything else. I'm frozen in place as he continues, moving onto my other breast as his hands shimmy down my panties, squeezing my cheeks.

He stops abruptly and I squeal when he gracefully scoops me up and places me down onto the mattress, captivating me as he undresses and swiftly settles himself between my legs. He's still in such amazing shape and I can't help but stare, appreciating his erection as he stands before me.

When I finally look up, his eyes aren't on mine. He's focused lower, between my legs, my sex wide open for him. "Still perfect in every way." He chokes out and kneels before me closing his mouth over my pussy, making me arch and writhe from the sensation of his tongue swirling around my clit. It's fantastic and I'm climbing quickly. The sensations epically building as his tongue plunges in and out, up and down.

He's relentless and I let out an incoherent cry and my fingers grip the comforter as my body shudders, the chemicals firing in my brain as I climax into a crescendo of pleasure. My body is limp as I come back down to reality.

He settles his hands on each side of my head and moves in between my legs, spreading them with his knees and he's so close that I feel his cock right near my swollen seam.

He's hesitant when I look into his eyes. He's overthinking this, and I know that orgasm was nothing compared to how his cock will feel inside me.

I'm reckless with no regard as I bait him.

"Fuck me."

He stares at me with a pained expression, before thrusting forward.

I'm floating above myself as our bodies connect, amazed how they still fit together like a puzzle, intersecting as only it's matching piece can fit.

He captures my mouth and pushes us further up the bed. I tightly wrap my legs around him so there's no space between us and I revel as he moans with each thrust, pounding into me faster and harder each time.

"Come with me." He pants.

We're tangled slick bodies, moving together in this beautiful rhythm of ecstasy and as if on cue, my body responds to his command, and we climax together. If there is heaven on earth, this is it.

He kisses the tip of my nose softly just like he used to and leans on his elbow next to me.

As the euphoria wears off, I want to get up and leave, run out of here. *I'm a monster.*

I don't want to make this more than it is, but I'm sated and warm and before I can argue with myself a deep exhaustion takes over.

THE PROBLEM with being an alcoholic is numbing reality. Skewing the perception between right and wrong. I've considered the problem of doing that for years.

Yet, I never considered the problems of being sober. Sobriety is knowing your actions and their effect on the outcome.

Being sober means that when you wake up in someone's bed you have nothing or no one to blame but your own actions.

No, I didn't wind up in bed with Mark because I was drunk. Alcohol did not make me choose this path. Instead, I acted on emotions, nostalgia and impulse.

It feels like there are a million reasons for me not to be here, yet here I am, watching him sleep. His arm draped over my stomach as I contemplate where we go from here.

I was upfront with Mark that I don't know what this is, that I don't have the answer.

But now, seeing him peacefully sleeping next to me I realize this will be something more than a one-night tryst with my ex-husband. I took advantage of his feelings by asking him to sleep with me and now I have to deal with the downfall of my actions.

Not even alcohol would be able to fix this problem.

Gracefully, I slide out of his embrace, he stirs for a second, but doesn't wake as I pad lightly around the room, collecting my clothes. I retreat to the bathroom where I stand under the horrible halogen bulbs and stare at myself as the monster that I am.

I don't shower because the scent of him still lingers on me and selfishly I want to bask in that a little while longer, so I dress and fix my hair, throwing it up onto a messy bun.

Quietly, I grab my shoes, I don't put them on until I'm out in the hallway leaning against the wall and contemplating if I should stay and talk this out, or if leaving is the best recourse.

I decide that playing the part of a monster is easier than seeing the love in those glacier blue eyes. Those eyes that will hold so much promise if he wakes next to me.

So, I catch the next elevator and wait in the lobby for my driver, who will take me back to the airport and back to the reality that Mark and I are over.

Once I'm in the SUV I pull out my phone and stare at it, debating as the minutes tick on what I could say to him that will relieve him of any regret when he wakes.

He beats me to the punch.

I open the message and read the two words over and over.

I'm sorry

He throws me off with those two words.

What is he sorry for? Sleeping with me? Not telling me the truth? That we're too far gone?

I put my phone away in my bag and lean my head against the seat. I'm sorry too, that I can't be who he wants me to be.

30

Mark's two-story beachfront Mediterranean is set back from the road. It's somewhat lavish from the outside with a nice size pool, but inside is laid back, warm, and inviting.

I step out of the master bathroom and into the bedroom, it's the first time I've been at his house just the two of us, and Mark told me to make myself at home.

"Damn." I stand in front of the mirror spinning from side to side. I can't help but stare at myself in the little black dress and stiletto pumps. I look older, more mature. I look... sexy.

I sit on the bed, running my hands over the comforter, imagining what it will be like sleeping here with him. What it will be like to finally have sex with him, I flush at the idea.

He clears his throat, his frame fills the doorway, and I look away embarrassed as if my thoughts are written on my face. "J... you look... amazing."

I twirl around for him, and I know he appreciates it when he comes up behind me, wrapping me in his arms and pressing his erection against me.

"Ready?" He asks, and for a minute, I'm hopeful he wants to skip dinner and get right to the having sex part of the evening.

I stare at him, at his attire, he's not dressed up, not like I am. He's dressed a step up from causal in a black t-shirt and dockers. I pray that I don't call attention to us with my outfit.

To be honest, I've been dreading our date for hours now. I know we will be seen, someone will post us in some paper or magazine, and it will taint this evening for me.

He doesn't wait for me to answer, he grabs my hand and pulls me through the house. My heels clack on the floor in a loud echo that matches my heart, but with his fingers wrapped around mine, it's the safe feeling I need to keep walking. But we don't head toward the garage or the front of the house.

Instead, he releases my hand, opening the door that leads out to the balcony, which overlooks the beach.

The warm breeze rushes over my skin as I step out, and I gasp when I notice hundreds of candles along the balcony. The warm glow is mesmerizing against the dusk sky.

There's a table set up with dinner for two, and Michael Bolton is playing softly on the boom box.

I turn back to Mark. He's standing with his hands in his pockets appraising me, as I take it all in. "I'm sure that we could remember this night on our own, without being in the tabloids."

"Mark." I'm astonished and so grateful. I throw my hands around his neck and kiss him like my life depends on it.

He pulls away, resting his forehead on mine. "If you keep kissing me like that, I'm not going to feed you, and all this effort will be wasted."

"Thank you," I say, meaning those two words full-heartedly because he put so much thought into this knowing how worried I was.

He pulls my chair out and then sits across from me.

The meal is delicious, the conversation is lighthearted, and I feel like a woman instead of a silly kid.

After dinner, we move to a loveseat at the opposite end of the balcony. I slip off my shoes and pull my feet under me comfortably, and Mark pulls a blanket over us.

I rest my head on his shoulder and watch the water glisten in the distance.

We stay there quiet and content for what feels like an eternity, him absentmindedly stroking my arm as I entwine our fingers.

"Mark?" I whisper.

"Hmmm?"

I turn my head so I can see him. "Kiss me."

He politely kisses me, then sits back, and once again, I'm frustrated and disappointed. This isn't the way I imagined he would behave now that we are finally alone.

So, I take matters into my own hands, climbing across his lap, and kissing him with intense need.

I need him to know I'm ready for this, and I bask when I feel his excitement beneath me. I grind against him, but I want more contact. I reach for the hem of his shirt, but he grabs my wrists.

"Jenna." He says my name like an oath that he is trying to keep.

I lean forward to kiss his neck, then gently suck and nip his ear lobe.

He moans, and I surge with feminine confidence, but that's short-lived as he rolls me off him, so that I'm sitting and he's standing over me. He's breathing hard, as am I, but it's not arousal I see in his eyes, it's something else entirely.

"No." He says, and I sit up, thinking I've made a mistake. *Stupid virginity.* "No?"

He walks to the railing and leans over but I'm starting to catch on. He didn't plan on having sex with me tonight, he's turning me down, *again. What's wrong with me?* I'm shocked, hurt, embarrassed, and pissed off. I stand and wait, not sure what to do.

"It's our first date, J."

Yup, definitely pissed. "Whose fault is that!"

He turns and faces me. "You're not serious."

I take a step forward, challenging him with my arms crossed over my chest.

"What was I supposed to do? Have your father come after me, again?"

"My father? What are you talking about?"

He snickers. "Yeah, why don't you ask him about that."

"What does that have to do with now?" I put my hands on my hips.

"I'm just making sure I don't cross the lines anywhere. I would think you'd respect me for that."

"Well, I sure as hell know this isn't how any other first date of yours would go if you were with someone else."

His posture tenses and he folds his arms over his chest. "What's that supposed to mean?"

"I toured with you for a year Mark. I've seen you with other women. You wouldn't have made it through dinner."

"Yes, and they weren't a..." He stops himself.

"Say it." I glare at him, my hands are fisted at my side. He doesn't speak. "Say it, Mark, they weren't what? A teenager? A kid? A virgin?"

His face is furious, then softens. "Yes. They weren't eighteen years old and inexperienced."

I'm holding back a river of tears, and the dam is about to break free. "Oh ok, so it's not only my age, it's my virginity *and* lack of experience. God, I really wish when I was back home, that I had taken care of this and not inconvenienced you. Maybe I'll just go find someone now to take care of it." My heart is racing, and I storm back into the house and run barefoot to the front door.

"Jenna! I'm sorry, stop! Just stop." He runs to catch up to me.

"Just take me home." The dam has broken. I'm crying, and I don't want him to see me like this.

"I love you, Jenna. I didn't love any of them."

I look up at him through glassy eyes. It's the first time anyone other than my parents has said that to me. "If my age is always going to be an issue, I can't see you anymore."

He stares at me so long I don't know what to say or if I should move.

Finally, he speaks. "So that's it. Just like that."

I nod. No matter what, I will always be six years younger. Maybe in a few years, it won't make much of a difference, but it obviously bothers him now.

He stares pensively at me. "Fine. You win." He lifts me easily and throws me over his shoulder.

I kick and flail. "What are you doing?" I yell as he crosses the house toward the bedroom.

"I'm treating you how you want me to." He pushes the bedroom door open, throwing me down onto the bed, then pulls the cord on the lamp next to the bed, and a soft glow fills the room.

I watch in awe as he removes his shirt, then undoes his belt buckle before sliding down his pants.

His body is lean and muscular, and the myriad of ink across his torso and back is *so* damn sexy.

I lean up onto my elbow and lick my lips, admiring him from head to toe. I don't get to admire him too long before he grabs my hands and pulls me up to my feet.

"Turn around." He says, spinning his finger in a circle.

I willingly comply turning around, my back to his front.

His fingers graze my neck as he reaches for my zipper, sending sparks shooting out all over my body as he unzips my dress and it falls to the floor.

I turn around to face him and stand there, exposing my black lace lingerie that I snuck into the pile of clothes that he bought earlier when we were shopping.

He raises an eyebrow and looks at me with a hunger I've never seen before. His cock is hard already and I blush when he slides his boxer briefs down and it springs free. His body is a truly a work of art, I've never seen anything so beautiful.

I run my hands over his chest, down his stomach stopping before his cock.

His hands cup my neck and he takes my mouth again, his tongue gliding across mine, as his other hand works to remove the lingerie. "This is nice, Jenna, but I want you naked."

I nod and help him, I'm completely impatient. When I'm finally naked, he lays me back gently. I lie still as he climbs over me, his arms stretched out on each side of my head, and although I put on a brave face before, I'm a little nervous now in the moment.

"You're a spoiled brat Jenna," he says. I swallow hard and lift my chin leaving my neck exposed, my pulse is beating out of control, so much so that he can probably see my veins throbbing. "But I'll be damned if you think anyone else is touching you." Then he kisses my lips roughly, our teeth clash and he nips my bottom lip before pulling away and continuing his assault on my neck, nipping and sucking so hard that I'll surely have marks.

I grip the comforter tightly as he licks over each nipple, alternating between licking and sucking. The sensations shoot straight down to my pussy and I'm already very wet.

He doesn't stop, or give me a break, he continues his journey south, moving lower, kissing over my ribcage, down my stomach and licks a circle around my navel. I'm squirming uncontrollably because I know where he is going and I'm a tightly wound ball of excitement and nerves.

I arch my back when he flicks his tongue over my clit, it could be seconds or minutes I have no idea as I writhe and shudder, and goosebumps cover my skin. My orgasm goes on and on, his warm mouth is exquisite and overwhelming, and he doesn't stop. "You're so damn perfect J." He grips my thighs.

I twist my fingers in his hair, my body quickening again as he licks and sucks me and I'm chasing another orgasm when he stops abruptly, making me groan in frustration.

"Don't stop, please don't stop." But he does, standing to pull a condom out of the bedside table and I watch as he rolls it onto himself, then climbs over me, tenderly moving a piece of hair off my forehead. He kisses my lips softly. "You're sure?"

I nod for yes. *A million times yes.* "I want it to be you."

"J, I won't be able to stop."

For the love of God, for a bad boy persona on stage this man is way too chivalrous.

I want to be clear, so I look him straight in the eyes. "Fuck me."

He smiles and laughs, kissing me again, before obliging my

request. He spreads my legs wider until I feel him at my opening. I close my eyes as he inches in. It's tight and uncomfortable, but not unbearable.

I suck in a breath and he stops. "Look at me." He commands.

My eyes snap open. That's when I see it, he loves me, he's in love with me and I recognize it in myself the way my heart swells.

He starts again gently, our eyes are locked as he pushes all the way in. My body expanding, until he hits my end. "You ok?"

I nod assuring him and he thrusts slowly over and over until the discomfort turns to pleasure and I rock with him. Meeting each thrust as he claims my mouth, our tongues swirling as he thrusts faster, hitting my clit each time, and I know that the orgasm that's brewing will be a powerful storm.

"That's it J. Come for me."

Then I do, breaking our kiss so I can cry out, my core clenching around him and within seconds he follows me, grunting and cursing as his body shudders over mine.

He slides off to lay next to me, he leans up on his elbow, his head in his hand. We're both quiet as I close my eyes and focus on breathing.

It was completely and totally perfect, everything I had hoped and more, I'm sated and fulfilled.

His fingers draw tiny circles up and down my stomach.

"J?"

"Hmm?" Sleep is quickly pulling me under.

"Spend the night with me."

I turn into him and kiss his jaw. "I don't think I could move even if I wanted to."

He lifts the blanket over us, and pulls me even closer to him.

"I meant what I said before. I love you Jenna. I think I loved you from day one. I'll give you all of me, always, I promise."

I smile against his chest. "Good, because I promise to never make it easy."

He laughs and kisses me. "I have no doubt about that."

31

"Second quarter sales are down." Jamie frowns as he reads the current numbers in the round table meeting. The board of directors look just as dismal.

"We need more live events." I speak up knowing we will be ok because every label has its ups and downs. "We just need something fresh."

Jamie looks at me then around the table.

"Acquisitions should be monitoring YouTube and Soundcloud. I'll tell them they have carte blanche to set up meetings." I shut off the projector and am about to call the meeting adjourned when Jamie speaks again.

"One more thing." Jamie says.

I look over to him, this must be something new, we've hit all points on the agenda already.

"I got a tip a little while ago and I think we need to consider all options. Sunrise Records is no longer representing Jenna, I say we—"

"No." I cut him off. *Is he out of his mind?*

"Mark, it's not just about you. We have to do what's right for the label."

I stand and head toward the door, pausing. "If Sunrise didn't want to take a gamble, why on earth would we?"

"That's what we do!" He argues.

He's blindsided me with this, but I won't call him out in front of the board. "Jamie, can we talk about this, in private."

He nods slightly and frowns. "I'm asking the board for approval to meet with her and make an offer."

I lower my head in defeat knowing the board will approve it.

"Mark, these numbers are dismal. We need someone already established." One of the directors says and the room seems to buzz in agreement.

"Ok, well for the record my vote is no." I storm out and head to my office, slamming the door behind me. A violent storm of emotions brewing inside of me.

Jamie knocks then enters a few minutes later. "Mark, I'm sorry, but we need her."

"Why do we need her? We've been fine without her." I walk to the cabinet that holds the strong stuff, it's only eleven in the morning, but I need something strong enough to cut through Jenna.

"That was then, this is now." Jamie follows my lead and throws back a shot.

I hold the glass pointedly at him, while I'm deciding if another shot is necessary. "You went behind my back." I accuse.

"You know this is the right thing to do. If you took your head out of your ass for a second and put aside what happened a month ago you would agree."

"I'm not delusional Jamie, I knew she wasn't coming back to me just because she slept with me. I knew we weren't going to live happily ever after, but I don't need my entire life interrupted by her."

He nods as if he understands, though he couldn't possibly. Sleeping with her opened new wounds, her leaving again opened old wounds.

If I don't choose self-preservation this time, I'm going to be an empty shell of a man. Hell, maybe I already am.

"I can't be a part of this. I'm choosing myself this time." I grab my keys and leave him standing there.

—————

I DRIVE EAST toward Santa Monica. The weather is perfect, and traffic through downtown is steady, but I'm able to reach the restaurant in forty minutes.

I'm ten minutes late, but she won't mind. I pull into the lot and see she is out front patiently waiting.

"Hi, baby." Marissa greets me warmly with a big kiss that I return with equal fervor.

"Hungry?" I ask, grabbing her hand and she smiles widely.

"Starving." She has that wicked gleam in her eye.

"Good, let's go." I hold her next to me, she smells like musk and sandalwood and it's perfect because it's nothing like Jenna.

We're seated right away and order Sushi off the lunch menu. It's a popular lunch spot but most of the rush is over and the place is emptying out.

I called Marissa the week after I slept with Jenna, profusely apologized for standing her up, and asked her out on a real date, which ended with me in her bed.

This is just causal, my plan to have some fun, clear my head while I get over Jenna and surprisingly, the past few weeks have been a nice change of pace.

I'm definitely not in love with Marissa, but I do genuinely enjoy spending time with her.

We're just finishing lunch when I see a mob of photographers lined up on the sidewalk outside of the restaurant.

This spot is not usually a hot spot for the paparazzi so I can't help but wonder who has brought out the vultures.

"Who is it?" Marissa asks me with piqued interest.

I shrug knowing that whoever it is probably isn't welcoming the attention that they are getting.

Marissa gasps. "Mark look!"

I turn in the direction Marissa is looking. "Fuck." I see who she is pointing at and who is the cause of all the attention outside.

I'm out of my chair and outside in seconds before I can stop myself. "Back off!" I yell and push people out of my way until I'm right in front of her. She's as surprised as I am, that once again, we are in the same place at the same time and the cameras flash faster as they realize the coincidence too.

I take her hand and pull her safely out of the mob and into the restaurant.

"Hi." She says and laughs nervously, she's obviously uncomfortable.

I eye her skeptically as she lifts her shades and rests them on top of her head, and avoids making eye contact.

I stand dumbfounded that she's here, that I'm here, that the universe is obviously a mysterious force not to be reckoned with.

"Thanks. I haven't needed to be rescued like that in a long time. I should have planned that out better." She finally says as she fixes a strand of her perfect hair.

I'm about to ask what she's talking about when Marissa grabs my arm and squeezes it.

"Oh my God, Jenna. I'm a big fan." She squeals.

Jenna looks from Marissa holding me, to me, and back to Marissa again.

I see the minute her disposition changes from shock back to celebrity mode. It's microscopic but I see it.

She holds her hand out. "Well it's nice to meet you uh..."

"Marissa." They shake hands quickly but all I can focus on is Marissa holding onto my arm. I want to push her hand away, but I don't. "I hope this isn't awkward." Marissa giggles.

"Awkward?" Jenna raises an eyebrow.

"You know, seeing Mark with someone else."

I feel like I'm having an out of body experience. Jenna smirks and I catch her eyes, as she notices the ring that's still around my neck and I know that smirk, she's about to eat Marissa alive. I have to shut this down.

"Marissa, we really have to get going." *I need to get out of here.*

"Ok, ok. Mark has a whole evening planned. He's such a romantic." She slaps me on the chest and runs back to the table to grab her purse.

"Wow, she's something. Good for you." Jenna says through a tight smile. I inwardly cringe at her condescending observation while she pulls out her phone and types something.

"Why are they following you? Did I miss something?" I ask more out of concern than curiosity. She waves her hand like it's not a big deal.

"I'm giving them what they've always wanted."

Now, I'm really curious. "Which is?"

"Me, uncensored." Her expression scares me, it's almost sadistic. Like she's sacrificing herself for the greater good of the paparazzi.

"What the hell does that mean?"

Marissa comes back just before Jenna gets to answer.

With a wicked gleam in her eyes, she replaces her sunglasses. "Enjoy your date night." She turns and leaves, a black SUV is waiting for her at the curb.

I want to run and ask her what she meant but the driver takes off quickly. I quickly pull out my phone, open my Twitter app and look at what's trending. "Son of a bitch."

"What is it Mark?" Marissa asks beside me.

I look down at Marissa, who I forgot was still standing next to me. "She's writing a tell-all book."

32

"Ok, cut! Cut!" The director yells, and everything stops. "Everyone, take five!" He shouts. The director is Dick Emilio, and he's top-notch, everyone whose anyone wants him for their music video.

I stand with my hands on my hips as he walks over to me.

"Jenna, doll. What's the problem? You're missing steps. We rehearsed this."

"I'm sorry, I just can't concentrate right now, and these stupid platform shoes are heavy." I'm whining. Max isn't around, Mark is away, and it's four in the morning. The last thing I want to be doing is filming this music video.

"I got this," Randy says as he comes up to us, he pats Dick's shoulder and tells him to give us a minute for a pep talk.

"Here, try this." He hands me a bottle of amber liquid and shrugs. "It's faster than coffee."

I take the bottle and down as much as I can in one swig. The liquid burns and makes me cough. Then I take one more for good measure because I'm tired and want to get this over with so I can go home.

He nods approvingly and tells Dick we're ready.

Dick nods. "Ok, everyone, from the top."

The music starts, and again we dance the choreography that we've been rehearsing for the last week, some days we rehearsed for eight hours, so I know the steps I'm just exhausted and unmotivated.

I can already feel the effects of the alcohol and my feet glide across the floor a little more easily. We're dancing in a warehouse, set up like a maze, so there are cameras above us as well as up close for the headshots, and I make sure I look where I'm supposed to. My outfit is overly suggestive. I'm barely covered in short jean shorts and a crop top that's slit down the middle, exposing from my cleavage down to my stomach, and two little pieces of tape are all that's holding me in.

The choreography is just as risqué as I shake and shimmy, hoping the double-sided tape holds, while Anton, the male love interest in the video, chases me through the maze.

We've been up close and personal in rehearsal, and I was fine, but now that we are actually filming, my nerves are on overload.

At the end of the video, Anton is supposed to finally catch me, and we do this sexy little grinding dance where I lift my leg up onto his hip. This is where I've been messing up, right before we get to this part.

This time though, I hit my stride. The buzz is in full swing, and when Anton grabs me from behind, and we sway to the music, I'm sure it's the sexiest I've ever looked, and when I turn into him and we get to the grinding moves, I know we are nailing it.

He dips me and pulls me back into him, and our faces are so close our noses are touching, we're both panting, and we pause in an intense moment staring into each other's eyes.

"Cut! Cut!" Someone shouts.

"Shit," I mumble because I know we did the scene perfectly, and I'm about to yell at Dick when I realize it's not him yelling cut.

I hear a commotion and yelling and see Mark rushing onto the set. He makes his way through the maze and over to where Anton and I are standing—now far apart from each other.

"What the fuck are you doing?" He pushes Anton's shoulder, and

Anton stumbles back from the force. He regains his balance and pushes Mark back.

It quickly becomes a shoving and yelling match, and I scream as a crowd of people comes over to break them up.

Mark grabs me by the wrist and pulls me out of the maze and into the back of the warehouse until we are out of earshot. Randy follows behind us until Mark turns to him and gets in his face. "Not now." He grunts.

Luckily, Randy retreats, but I watch Mark nervously because I've never seen him this way. His face so contorted.

He drops my hand. "What the fuck was that?" He asks harshly.

"That was you interrupting filming after a twelve-hour day!"

"Anton isn't getting paid to seduce you, or is it the other way around? I smell the alcohol, Jenna."

I scoff and give him the middle finger. "The video is supposed to be sexy, Mark, it's called acting! Do you want me to put on a nun outfit and prance around?"

He rolls his eyes. "You look cheap. It's not a good image for you."

"Fuck you. Why are you even here?" But he doesn't get to answer because Dick comes over to us.

"Mark, what's the problem?"

"I don't like the video, it's distasteful and who picked out this... costume?"

"Jenna did," Dick answers him, and Mark glares at me.

"I'm not a baby. This is what's hot right now." I say defensively.

"You're not a whore either, but yet, here you are."

His words sting. I cross my arms over my chest to cover myself.

"Mark, listen, we don't have time to re-shoot, we don't have time to redo any choreography. Jenna and Randy were on board. Now, we only have the warehouse for a few more hours, and we've already lost considerable time since *someone* kept forgetting her steps. So, can we just get on with it?"

Mark closes the gap between them, his posture is stiff, and his arms are folded over his chest. "This is the last time you will work on her videos."

"Good, because the next time you walk onto my set and call cut, I'm going to lay you out." Dick turns back to me. "He's going to kill your career." He storms off, yelling to the production crew to reset.

I look to Mark, hoping his expression has softened, but I think it's even more intense now. "We're not done, we'll talk about this later." He turns to leave.

"No," I say firmly and drop my hands down to my side, balling my fists and squaring my shoulders. He stops and turns around. "We won't. Don't ever embarrass me like this again." I turn on my heel and head back onto the set.

Four hours later, I drop down onto my bed. I sleep most of the day, and when I wake up, Max is in the kitchen, making us food.

"Mark, fuck up today?" Max asks.

I grab a beer from the fridge and pop it open. "He embarrassed me during filming today, why?"

He hands me an iconic blue bag with the words *Tiffany and Co.* on it. "He came by earlier, asked me to give this to you." I peek inside the bag and pull out a handwritten card, and a Tiffany pouch.

J,

I'm sorry about today, I lost control. I realize that our relationship is a conflict of interest since I should be throwing you to the wolves to make money off you for the sake of the label. Sex sells, I get it, but I can't sit back and watch, while you become a distasteful version of yourself. I hope that you keep in mind how protective I am over you and what image you want to portray in Hollywood. I love you, please don't lose yourself.

Love, Mark

I PUT the card down and open the little blue felt pouch. Inside it is a sterling silver diamond J pendant on a necklace. I hand the card to Max and take the pendant over to the computer.

I sip the beer and stare at the computer screen while I sit and wait for the dial-up. Listening to the rings and static sounds as it connects.

Max sits next to me on a bean bag chair. "What are you going to say?"

"I'm not sure. Something along the lines of, I won't let it get that far."

"You know he's not wrong. It's dangerous here, and he's already saved you from a lifetime of porn movies."

I roll my eyes and open up AOL instant messenger, he's not online. So I click to email him instead. I have the message almost ready to send when he signs on and immediately messages me.

Braveheart: I'm sorry

Jcutie123: Thank you for the necklace.

Braveheart: I fly out in the morning...

Jcutie123: Have a safe flight.

Braveheart: How long are you gonna be mad at me?

Jcutie123: How long will you be gone?

Braveheart: J...

Jcutie123: Mark...

He doesn't answer. I sit back and delete the email I was about to send because it sounds desperate and I don't want to come across as anything but in control.

Instead, I message him again.

Jcutie123: Makeup sex? I brought the costume home...

I wait ten minutes. No answer. So I close AOL and power down the IBM. If he wants to be like that so be it.

Max puts the pendant around my neck, and we hang out on the couch talking. A few hours later I'm dozing off when I hear the buzzer.

I'm not expecting anyone so I ignore it and let my eyes close again hoping Max will answer it, which he does.

He shakes me lightly. "It's lover boy. I buzzed him in."

I stand, groggy from sleep and hang out in the open doorway watching Mark as he walks down the hallway toward the apartment.

He stops in front of me and I pull him inside and down the hallway to my room where I sit Indian style on my bed.

"J, I know I messed up today, but you drive me crazy. You're mine, I can't see other guys look at you like that."

"Why didn't you answer me on AIM?"

He sits down next to me, lifts his shirt over his head, then grabs my hand and puts it over a freshly inked tattoo on his left peck.

I study it and look up at him. "What is it?"

"Anam Cara—Celtic, for soulmate." He uses my finger to trace the outline. "Your heart and mine, it means unconditional love." I run my fingers over the raised skin, studying the double hearts that are intertwined. One upside down, linked with the other that is right side up. A red infinity knot ties the two hearts together through the middle.

"I love it." I say honestly.

"It's a reminder for both of us, that I'll always wear your heart and you'll always see mine is in the right place. I promise."

33

"I'll stalk her on social media."

I switch the phone to my other ear, swipe tears off my cheeks, and try not to sound like I'm crying. "Lily, we're not seventeen, she didn't steal my prom date."

She sighs. "Jenna, don't tell me you're not upset about this. You just slept with him."

"God, I hope you're alone. We both needed closure, obviously now he's finally able to move on. Besides, I'm the one who left. I'm pulling in now." I hang up, throw my phone into my bag, and check myself in my compact.

It's obvious I've been crying, and there's little I can do to hide it before I go inside.

Lily pounces on me as soon as I walk in the door. She's talking excited and follows me from room to room, ignoring the fact that my face is red and blotchy, and my eyes are puffy from crying.

"Ok, so, media requests are blowing up. Record labels are fighting over you. Jamie from Heartbeat Records called. You *are* a genius, talk about taking lemons and making lemonade." She says excitedly.

"Yes, well, today, everyone wants to make money off me. We'll see how long it lasts."

She heads to the kitchen and starts making us some tea.

I received a certified letter a week ago that the label wanted to part ways, saying they didn't feel my project was 'where they wanted to go' at this point in time.

I wasn't even worthy of a friendly call to get the news.

Max would've told me I had three choices, do nothing, write a whole new album, or, I could do something completely unexpected.

So, I channeled my inner Max and fought dirty, deciding to do someone completely unexpected.

I called a friend of mine, Angie, who has been writing celebrity biographies for decades. Angie has been dying to get me to write a book for years, she's even offered to help by ghostwriting some parts.

I've never had any desire to talk about my life, but seeing Dr. Wild has made me realize it's time to finally tell *my* story, and it won't hurt to help me become relevant again.

I knew there would be some buzz about the press release, but I wasn't expecting the frenzy that has ensued.

Lily hands me a cup of tea and sits next to me. Still frantically answering emails and managing my social media.

"Lily?"

"Hang on. Oh..." She says as she frantically scrolls on the iPad.

"Is that a good, oh?" I ask curiously.

"Um..." She hesitates.

"Oh, boy. Tell me." I demand.

She hands me the tablet, and I read the email. It's a cease and desist letter from Mark's attorney, basically saying that I cannot publish any book without Mark's review and express permission.

"What a smug asshole. How does he know that I had any intention of including anything about him?"

"Well, you were." Lily points out bluntly.

"Why do you say it that way?"

"Because you can't have one without the other. People want to know. They were fascinated with you two. My Mom even cried after your divorce."

"Lily, I need to ask you something." I pause a minute. "With Tom gone, I need a manager. Someone who can handle me. I need you to hire a new assistant. I want you to be my manager."

She shakes her head adamantly. "Jenna, I... I don't know if I can do that."

"Why?" I ask increduously.

"I don't want to screw anything up."

"You pretty much do everything anyway. Max didn't know everything when he started. Come on, let's go."

"Where are we going?"

"To meet with my lawyers, and then I'm going to do something stupid."

"JENNA, WE SHOULD *NOT* DO THIS." Lily is pacing next to me as I charge through the parking garage. "The lawyer specifically said not to..."

I stop and face her. "Lily, please. You know I never do what I'm told, either come up and support me or wait here." I don't wait for her to answer.

"Ok, tough girl." She swings her braids over her shoulder and catches up to me.

We barge through reception, the same girl is at the desk as the last time I was here, but I don't address her, and I head right for the elevator.

"Ms. Foster! You can't go up. I was told not to—"

"Call security then." The elevator door opens, and Lily and I get on. I quickly push the buttons to close the door and push the number for his floor.

"Girl, you are something else." She stares amused at me.

I'm glad I don't have time to answer because the door opens, and I make the trek down the hall quickly before I get stopped by security.

I don't knock because I don't care what I'm interrupting. I only care that he's trying to derail me.

He's on the phone when I barge through the door. I'm breathing heavy, my blood is pumping and the adrenaline coursing through my veins makes me dizzy.

He hangs up and stands.

"Why?" I ask him as he walks over to the minibar. He nods, briefly acknowledging Lily, who is still standing by the door.

"That was security." He says casually.

"I don't give a shit about your security. Why are you being difficult? Jamie told me you don't want me under the label when you, yourself, offered it to me weeks ago." I shout.

He calmly pours himself a drink. "Drink?" He asks, lifting the glass to his lips.

"That's very low, Mark."

His blue eyes are frigid as he stares back at me. "You're right, that was extremely insensitive." He puts the glass down on the table.

"Is this because I left your hotel room? You're punishing me?"

"I'm not interested in being part of your self-destruction."

I walk toward him, our eyes are locked, and the tension is palpable. "What is it that you're afraid I'll say?"

"Write about yourself, but leave me out of it, or be prepared for me to shut it down." He's changed since the night in the hotel, just like someone flipped a switch. The affection now replaced with disgust.

I look at him skeptically, realizing what this change of heart is. "I hurt you."

There's a knock at the door, behind Lily. *My time is up.*

"Everything ok?" The security team comes in and waits for Mark's direction. He puts his finger up for them to wait.

"You finally got what you wanted, Jenna." He walks back to his round desk and sits behind it. "You wanted me not to care. This is me not caring. You wanted me to move on. This is me moving on. Don't come back."

His words clench my heart. I feel the stab of pain as the metaphorical knife twists in my heart, as the security guard puts his hand gently on my arm. I quickly pull away and walk to the door stopping to stare at him one last time.

"For the record, I never would've defamed you or what we had."

He doesn't say anything, he doesn't even look up at me.

I'm barely out of the building when I realize what just happened. Weak in the knees, I stumble, almost falling.

Lily grabs my arm to steady me and eyes me warily. "What's wrong, Jenna?"

I gasp and cry out. "Sleeping with him, I just realized..." I choke back the grief and regret my decision to leave him that morning. "He's over me."

"Why is that a bad thing? You divorced him."

I shake my head, the world is spinning. "I made the biggest mistake of my life."

She stares at me, puzzled. "What? Divorcing him?"

We could start splitting hairs there, but what difference does that make now.

"Sleeping with him, it broke him, but it fixed me. I'm still in love with him, Lily."

34

JENNA - AUGUST 1998

I'm lying poolside, in my skimpy bikini that barely covers anything. The sun is frying me to a crisp, but I don't care, it feels too good.

The radio is on and multiple stations have been playing my single. It's still so surreal to hear it.

I lean over and take a sip of the wine cooler I've been nursing for the last hour. Max is asleep under the umbrella next to me. I poke him and he wakes startled.

Mark has been away for the weekend and he didn't care if Max and I stayed at his house, so here we are. He's due back later tonight and I can't wait to see him, we've been in a good place despite both of us on the road.

"Let's get some takeout." I fan myself with my hand. Maybe I am getting too much sun.

"What do you want?" Max asks, rolling over.

"Chinese?" I suggest.

He nods and I jog up to the house climbing the stairs two at a time because they are hot. I pull out the menus, place our order and hang out in the air conditioning for a little while, lounging on the couch.

It's only a short time later that the doorbell rings and I pop up to get the food. I pop my shades on so I won't be recognized. I expect to see the delivery guy behind the door what I don't expect, is my parents to be staring back at me in disbelief.

"Mom, Dad, what are you doing here?" I ask astonished they are here.

"Jenna..." Mom is staring at my bikini or lack thereof, but my Dad is focused on the hickeys that cover my neck and my breasts.

He pushes inside and starts to look around for Mark. "Where is he?"

"Dad he's not here." I say trying to run damage control.

"Jenna, he's not keeping you here against your will, is he? You're not his sex slave, are you?" My mom asks whispering the last part as her hand goes to her neck mortified.

I laugh at her, she's always so dramatic. "No, Mom, I'm not here against my will, but I wouldn't mind the latter." I say amusedly.

"Why are you doing this to us?" She cries, and I can't help but roll my eyes exasperated.

"Doing what to you?"

"You look like a prostitute." She looks me up and down once more.

"Oh my god." I flop down onto the couch. "It's a bathing suit. I wasn't expecting company."

"Are you living here?" My Dad shrieks obviously peeved that I'm here playing house.

"No, of course not." *Not that I would mind that.*

"You definitely look at home."

I shake my head, not understanding why they are so upset that I am here. "It's my boyfriend's house. He said I could stay here while he was away. Why is this such a big deal?" *I'm an adult!*

I hear the balcony door slide open and closed. "Jenna? What's taking so long?" Max comes in and stops when he sees my parents. "Mr. and Mrs. Foster." He says shocked.

"Max, is Jenna living here?" My Dad has his arms folded over his chest.

"No," He shakes his head. "I mean, she stays here sometimes."

Great, here comes my Mother's temper tantrum and lecture on sex and living together before marriage.

The doorbell rings again and Max answers it this time, paying the delivery guy, and retreating to the kitchen with the food.

"Jenna..." My Mom looks at me once again with disgust.

"Mom don't, I don't want to hear how I'm going to hell for fornicating before marriage."

She dabs the corners of her eyes.

Max returns and sits in the chair opposite me while my Dad stares me down.

"Jenna, for the love of God, go put a shirt on and when are you expecting Mark back? I would like a word with him." Dad questions.

"This is ridiculous." I walk past him, jogging to the bedroom. I pull out one of Marks white t-shirts from his drawer and slip it over my head. I can hear my Dad still questioning Max, so I head to the kitchen to make a plate of food and then drop back down onto the couch.

Everyone stares at me.

The four of us stay like that, staring at each other until long after the sun sets. I start to doze off when I hear the front door creak open, making me jump.

Max is sleeping on the chair and my Mom is crocheting on the other end of the couch, while my Dad paces the living room.

"J?" Mark calls out to me. My heart is racing because this isn't going to end well, Mark and my Dad don't get along as it is, and I've been dreading this moment for hours.

"In here." I call back, from the living room. I close my eyes and try to breathe deeply as I hear his footsteps arrive. I open my eyes and he enters the living room obviously surprised to see our visitors.

"Hello?" He says, cautiously looking from me, to my parents and back to me.

I stand but Dad yells for me to sit down.

"Mark, a word." Dad motions for Mark to follow him into the kitchen.

Mark doesn't move. "Jenna? What the hell is this?" He ignores my Dad and looks to me for an explanation. He's pissed. *Beyond pissed.*

"This, is about what you've done to our daughter." Dad now stands just a few inches from Mark, his temper also flaring.

"What are you talking about?" Stepping forward, now face to face with my Dad.

"You know damn well, McGinley. You've isolated her from her family, she's marked up like a leopard, drinking, and sleeping here more than her own apartment, according to the landlord."

"You do realize she's an adult right?" Mark stares him down.

"She's our daughter, I think we realize how old she is. You're using her for God knows what, she hasn't released the album that was supposed to be out already under *your menial* label, and you have her holed up here while you're out doing whatever it is you do."

I stand quickly to diffuse the situation. "Dad, seriously, I was just here suntanning."

"Look at your body!" He grabs my t-shirt and tries to rip it over my head, but Mark stops him.

"Get the fuck out of my house. Now." He yells, his hands pushing my Father.

"Mark. Please." I go over to him pleading with him not to make things worse, but he completely ignores my pleas.

"No, I want them out, now. You can stay if you want, but I'm calling the cops if they're not gone in five."

"I told you that you were no good for her. That you would ruin her." My Dad throws back at Mark.

"Dad!"

Mark and my Dad are toe to toe again. Max sits up wide awake now and jumps up to stand between them.

"You're the one who has been selling her out. Pushing her into Hollywood, hoping for a payday for yourself!" Mark yells, his face bright red in anger.

My mom speaks up for the first time. "How dare you! Her father has nothing but the best intentions for her."

Mark turns toward her. "You keep telling yourself that, Maureen.

Is that why he set her up with Randy who has been trying to push her into porn since day one."

She stands and goes to my Dad, waiting for him to dispute Mark's claim. "That's not true. Frank tell him."

My Dad is silent which speaks volumes.

"Dad? You knew?" I'm mortified.

"Jenna... I heard rumors about him, but we had a good relationship, he said he would keep you away from all of that."

I feel sick to my stomach, my hand rests over my mouth and my Mom's hysterical cries make me want to lash out, but Mark beats me to it.

"I'm the one here with her, protecting her from the vultures. If it weren't for me, Randy would have her in Ensenada, strung out on Coke and in more porn than you could ever imagine."

Tears stream down my cheeks. My own father already knew that it was a possibility that Randy would try to get me into pornography and still he hired Randy as my manager.

"Jenna, please, just listen." Dad begs, his eyes softening. Reminding me of when I was a child and just his little girl.

"Just go, and don't come back." I storm out of the room and head for the bedroom. Max follows. I sob uncontrollably because Mark didn't tell me my Dad knew about Randy, and because my Dad isn't the person I thought he was. *Fuck Hollywood.*

I sob for hours, realizing that I lost my family to fame. When I finally can speak without my voice cracking, I call Randy and fire his ass.

35

"I'm focused. I think writing the book is helping." I adjust the iPad to fit my face in the little frame, so Dr. Wild can see me. She's been checking in on me every other day.

"Good. You're doing so well, and although your reconnection with Mark didn't turn out how you had hoped you didn't resort to your addiction. I'm proud of you, Jenna." I can't help but smile. "Ok, well, I'll see you next week for your regular session."

I nod and hit the red X, then turn back to my computer.

I tap my fingers over the keys. They fly over them as I finish writing the memory of what severed my relationship with my parents. Fresh tears coming to my eyes as if it just happened.

It took a long time for me to talk to my parents again, but things were never the same.

I didn't trust my Dad, and I saw my Mom for what she was, a religious zealot who hated my lifestyle and was always condemning me.

Initially, I was mad at Mark that night for how he treated my parents. Once I learned that my Dad knew about Randy trying to push me into porn for quick, easy money, I realized that Mark and Max were the only ones I could trust to take care of me.

After I fired Randy, Mark hired me the best of the best, a whole management team. Wesley "Wes" Brooks, a seasoned professional who was hired to be my manager. A move that I know truly set my career into motion. Mark may have always pushed me when I didn't want to be pushed, but he always took care of me.

I stare at the screen. It's been two months since I saw Mark in his office. I haven't seen or heard from him or his lawyers since they asked to see the final draft of the book.

My heart still aches, and when I close my eyes, I still see him looking at me like I was no one special. Like I was nothing to him. *Is that how I looked at him? Is this how he felt when I signed on the dotted line?* It's awful.

"Jamie is here to see you." Lily stands in the doorway, interrupting my melancholy thoughts, and waits for me to answer.

I close my laptop, grab my cup of coffee, and head out to the foyer, putting on a happy face. "Hey, Jamie! What's up?"

He gives me a big hug and kisses me on the cheek. "We need to talk."

I nod and motion toward the balcony, I have a feeling I'm going to need fresh air for this one. I settle on my lounge chair, and he sits on the other end. "So, what's going on?"

"You know I've always thought of you like a sister. I thought you should know what's going on. Mark's ex or not, the truth is the label needs you.

Mark aside, the board is unanimous about bringing you on board. I need to know where you stand, have you considered all your options?"

I should have figured this wasn't a friendly visit, it's a negotiation. "Jamie, I have to be honest. I don't think I should sign with Heartbeat. I feel like I've caused enough damage. Mark is..." I think how to finish that sentence because Mark is done with me and saying those words hurt too much. I know he doesn't want me there, and I don't know if I could handle him not supporting me.

"Mark told me what happened."

I nod, of course, he did, Jamie and Mark are like brothers. "So, you know that I slept with him and left him again."

"I do. And I think he's thinking with his heart, not with his head about this."

I stare out at the ocean. "I think you're wrong, Jamie, because where I'm concerned, Mark doesn't have a heart anymore."

"Help me fix it then."

I shake my head. I know I've already done too much damage. I can't fix it. Dr. Wild tells me I have to move on. Not hold onto the past. *Easier said than done.* "After five years, all it took was one night for me to realize I'm still in love with him. I wouldn't know where to start. Besides, he's moved on."

Jamie looks at me in disbelief. "Wait. Say that again? You're in love with him?"

I nod solemnly.

He sits back and mulls over what I just told him. "You guys are a fucking disaster." He laughs.

I laugh. "Thanks."

He leans forward, resting on his knees. "I'm serious, and Jenna, I wouldn't be so sure he's moved on. I know him, Marissa is a distraction."

"A distraction with big boobs and long legs." I think Jamie might just be wrong about this.

"I think I know how to fix this." He says abruptly.

I raise my brow at him. "Fix it for who?" *Mark, me, or the record label?*

"Hear me out."

"I'm listening." I sip my coffee that's cooled off and set it back on the table.

"Jealousy." He says, as if it's obvious.

"I'm not jealous—" I protest, but he cuts me off.

"Not you... him. It drives him crazy, seeing you with someone else. Like, when you dated that guy a couple years ago, he was miserable and took it out on everyone."

"That was then. Do you hear yourself? Where am I supposed to find an eligible bachelor that will agree to play games to make my ex-husband jealous."

He looks at me with a wicked gleam. "You're looking at him."

36

JENNA - SEPTEMBER 1998

"Here, try this." Max hands me a shot glass full of amber liquid. "What is it?" I sniff the contents and try to guess.

"Southern comfort with lime."

I shrug and throw it back, then make a pucker face.

It's my nineteenth birthday. I haven't seen or talked to my parents since Mark kicked them out, and I'm not handling it well.

Mark is trying to make me forget that fact by throwing me a huge birthday bash with all our friends.

The house is full of people, but I feel so alone.

I don't understand this feeling that's pretty much constant lately, but the alcohol numbs it considerably, so I keep drinking.

"One more," I say to Max, and he pours it into the glass. I swallow the amber liquid and slam the glass on the counter.

There is booze covering every square inch of the counter and people blowing cocaine off the toilet seat down the hall.

This is how Hollywood parties.

I hop off the counter and stagger through the house to find Mark. I know I've had too much to drink, things are spinning, and I'm trying not to fall.

"Jenna! Over here." Jamie calls me to the couch. He's sitting with people I don't even know, but it's probably a good idea for me to stop moving, so I do. I grab the arm of the couch and sit down carefully. "You don't look so good." He laughs. He's drunk too.

"Where's Mark?" I slur.

"Who knows." He throws his hands in the air and slides closer to me, the room is really spinning now. I lean my head on his shoulder and close my eyes. The spinning gets worse, faster. I squeeze my eyes shut. "Come on, he's probably upstairs. I'll help you." He stands carefully and pulls me to my feet.

Together we stumble up the stairs with his arm around my waist. My stomach is about to revolt, and I dry heave halfway up while my vision goes in and out.

Finally, we make it to the bedroom, but I'm nearly useless to carry my own weight, and I feel Jamie lifting me and carrying me toward the bed.

He tries to lay me down, but we stumble and fall back onto the bed, he lands on top of me. He's laughing and struggling to get back onto his feet, but I'm just trying not to throw up.

I close my eyes and put my arm over my forehead. I don't know how much time has passed when I feel a hand move over my breast, groping me. It's sloppy and not what I'm used to from Mark, but I can't move. I say stop, at least I *think* I do, before I feel lips on my collarbone, traveling up my neck and I just know this isn't right. I know it's not Mark, but I'm powerless. I can't even open my eyes, I'm dead weight.

The bed shifts. I feel my shirt being tugged up.

Another pause in time... the world goes black, then I hear a commotion, yelling, and the bed shifts again, and I feel myself being turned onto my side.

Then there's nothing but darkness.

"Jenna." I hear Mark. He's calling my name, but I'm still somewhere else, and I try to claw at the light. "Wake up, J." He urges.

I groan and open my eyes. The light hurts, my whole body feels weird, but I somehow force myself to sit up.

"Good. You're ok. Now I can kill both of you."

I lift my knees to my chest and put my head in my hands. My throat is dry and feels like I swallowed sandpaper. "What are you talking about?" I whisper hoarsely.

"Look at me." It takes me a minute until I am able to focus on him, but when I do, Mark is standing, but leaning over me, his face is enraged.

"What's wrong?" I sit up all the way now and put my arms around his neck.

He pushes my arms back down.

"Mark?" Fear slices through me.

He stands up straight and puts his hands on his hips. "You want to tell me why I had to beat the shit out of my best friend last night?"

I'm at a loss, and obviously playing catch up here. "Jamie?"

"Jesus! Jenna! Yes, Jamie." He yells.

"I don't know, I give up. You tell me."

He leans over me again. The anger is rolling off him in waves. His eyes are bloodshot, and now that I get a good look at him, I'm sure that he hasn't slept. "You were passed the fuck out, and he was on top of you, three seconds away from putting his dick in you."

"What? You're crazy!" I stare in horror at him.

"Pants down and all Jenna! I'm not crazy!" I leap out of bed, almost landing on my ass.

I shake my head. "I don't believe you."

"Well, maybe if you didn't blackout, you would remember. Tell me, how did you get upstairs? Did you ask Jamie to bring you up?"

I'm quiet as I dig through the fog to try and remember. "No, I was looking for you. Jamie offered to help me. Where the hell were *you*, and what were *you* doing? How about that, Mark?" I stand with my hands on my hips.

"Oh, no. Don't dare turn this around on me. I wasn't standing over a bed with my pants around my ankles that's for damn sure."

"Are you seriously accusing me of bringing Jamie up here to fuck him in your bed?"

"That's what it looked like to me."

I don't remember everything that happened, but I know deep

down in my heart that I didn't willingly let Jamie do anything to me. "I didn't feel right, I was looking for you," I say finally.

He sits on the bed and rubs his temples, saying nothing.

"Fine. Don't believe me." I run down the stairs and grab my keys and purse and don't stop until I pull up outside my apartment.

I tell Max everything, even though he already knows most of it and feels awful that he wasn't there to intervene. "Someone must have slipped you a roofie." He says after I tell him how I felt, and we spend the rest of the day sleeping.

Three days go by without any word from Mark. I'm falling into a deeper depression, which I have now identified as the overwhelming heavy feeling that has been hanging around, and I don't know how to pull myself out of it.

Things get even worse when Wes tells me I have to fly out to New York last minute for an appearance on a daytime show, and that I have back-to-back performances at several malls along the east coast to promote my single.

The trip is awful. I'm moody, and everyone walks on eggshells around me. Even Max winds up flying back without me because apparently I'm "unbearable" to be around.

A week later when my driver pulls up to my apartment, I yawn as I walk like a zombie up the stairs throwing my bags just inside the door.

I gasp when I see Max, Mark, and Jamie sitting on the couch. I flinch when I look at Jamie, who has two black eyes that have turned a myriad of nasty colors, and his nose looks broken. Mark looks at me stoically then rests his arms on his knees as he leans forward, clasping his hands in front of him.

Jamie is the first to speak, he points to his face and stands. "Trust me when I say I totally deserve this, Jenna." He explains, but I don't move or speak. I wait for someone to tell me what the fuck is going on. "Jenna, I'm really sorry. I never meant to... I was really fucked up, and I almost..." He chokes on his words, so Mark speaks up.

"You almost raped her." Mark finishes for him.

I swallow hard. Watching as Mark stands and paces, and it's obvious that he has made everyone uncomfortable.

Jamie nods. "You're like a sister to me, I would never hurt you, the drugs—"

I cut him off. "Jamie, I don't remember anything." I close my eyes, thankful that my memory of that night hasn't returned.

"I told Mark what I did. Obviously, he handled it with me, but I wanted to apologize to you. I don't want to lose my friends over this. It was all me, Jenna, you didn't do anything."

I nod and look from Mark to Jamie, scared that the band is in jeopardy because of this. "What now?" I ask innocently because I don't know where we go from here. We are all always together, and things have never felt more awkward.

Mark walks over to me and brushes his thumb over my cheek. I'm sure I look like hell with no makeup on, dark circles under my eyes, and a lingering hangover, but his touch comforts me, and I lean into his hand.

Mark's eyes bore into me. "The two of you are not to be alone together. Got it?"

I cross my arms over my chest, his tone with me still feels accusatory. "Fine."

"And no more parties, you shouldn't be drinking anyway." He admonishes me.

I throw Max an angry look because I just figured out why he flew home, he's a nark, and I've never been so damn angry at him.

"Ok, *Dad*." I don't wait for a reply, I storm into my room and lock the door like the disgruntled teenager that I am.

37

JENNA - AUGUST 2015

"You look amazing." Jamie pecks me on the cheek as we step out of the limo and he grabs my hand, squeezing it gently.

I'm wearing a black short sleeve, silk shirt, that has a gold zipper down the front exposing my red lace bra, skin tight leather pants and black stilettos.

The goal for the evening is to not lose my cool or sobriety. We are at a launch party for one of the artists the label is representing. Mark will be here, no doubt with Marissa in tow and I may have told Jamie I'm not jealous but it's hard not to be envious.

Thankfully, Jamie and I were always close enough that this just feels like I'm hanging out with an old friend and it's not weird when he wraps a hand around my waist as we head into the private club.

I hear a few people commenting as we walk past. Most are surprised that I'm here, but I know everyone is dying to know *why* I'm here.

"Jenna!" I hear Olivia before I see her, she runs up and gives me a huge hug then holds my shoulders so she can look me over. We used to be good friends. After the divorce was final, we split ways because it became too awkward. "You look great!" She smiles from ear to ear.

"Thanks. You do too! Congrats on your promotion. I always knew you could handle more than the front desk."

She smiles warmly at me and we go on with mundane small talk until Jamie politely excuses us.

"Ready?" Jamie whispers.

I nod and shiver because I'm bristling with nervous energy. This could be dangerous.

Dave sees us and heads over. "Hey Jenna!" He kisses both my cheeks and steps back, analyzing Jamie holding me too close and the placement of his hand on my hip. His eyebrow goes up, but he doesn't otherwise comment. "Jamie, Mark is looking for you."

Jamie nods as we simultaneously see Mark at the bar, Marissa is next to him. I look at Jamie nervously, but he smiles and pulls me forward.

Immediately I switch to celebrity mode, putting on my nothing-can-hurt-me mask in place, and hope that my confidence on the outside absorbs on the inside.

Mark turns and sees us before we get to the bar, but people keep stopping us every couple feet. I stop to take pictures with several of them before we finally make it over to him.

I see the confusion in his expression. He'll never expect what's coming.

I say hi to Marissa but she's completely clueless, and too busy sipping on a martini, that my presence doesn't bother her in the least.

"Ok, I'll bite. What's going on here?" Mark squints as he looks at both of us. "You signed her?" He asks.

Jamie puffs out his chest and suddenly it's battle of the alpha male. "Much worse than that. She's my date." Jamie is brave. I fear for his life right now.

Mark stands and glares at me as he looks me over head to toe. I see everything he isn't saying behind those glacial blue eyes, but I don't flinch, I don't even blink, I'm not sure I'm even breathing.

"How long has this been going on?" He's asking me but I can't answer, so Jamie does.

"Why don't we go outside and talk, before we draw attention to ourselves." Jamie suggests as people are staring at the 'Jenna and Mark reunion' and surely, we will be on social media in a matter of minutes. Marissa finally catches on and perks up, but Mark walks out leaving everyone behind.

I look at Jamie worriedly, but he winks at me.

We follow Mark out to the courtyard, my heart is racing. I just can't help it, I'm worried. I don't want anyone to get hurt. Jamie grabs my hand and squeezes for support. Thankfully we're the only ones in the courtyard.

"You expect me to believe my best friend and my ex-wife are dating, out of the blue?"

"Jenna and I have been friends a long time, we're just having fun."

Marissa brings up the rear, we all turn to look at her.

"Riss, give us a couple minutes, ok?" He says the nickname so sweetly.

I want to vomit. I want to run and hide and cry and drink a bottle of vodka but more than all that, I want to go back in time five years.

She turns and heads back to the bar, already drunk and stumbling and I suddenly think maybe Jamie is right. Mark would never have let me walk away stumbling. He would've taken care of me, maybe he's just tired of being the caretaker for someone.

He paces the courtyard. "Is this your grand plan for me to sign her?" Mark's angry voice snaps my attention back to him.

"Mark, you know we don't need your signature to write her a Contract. The board unanimously agreed to sign her." Jamie pivots on his heel, watching as Mark paces.

"What's your game then?" His eyes narrow at us.

Jamie shrugs. "You're with Marissa. I didn't think I was overstepping."

"Ok, well I hope you will be very happy together. She can write all about it in her book." He heads for the door.

"Mark, wait." I cry out. It comes out desperate and he has no reason to but he stops and turns back. I look at Jamie and he nods, understanding that I want to talk to Mark alone.

Jamie squeezes my shoulder and heads back inside the club.

"What?" His tone is cold, but I move closer, standing inches from him, but now that we're alone, I don't know where to start.

"You're killing me." I start with that because that's the emotion that floats to the top.

"I'm killing *you*? Are you serious right now." I know he's remembering that night Jamie almost raped me all those years ago. Everyone forgave him and he did a stint in rehab. Nothing of the sort ever happened again, but Mark was funny with me and the guys after that, they knew I was off limits. Always.

"Please, don't look at me like that." I beg.

"I knew it didn't mean anything to you, but God Jenna, you could've said goodbye."

I'm about to tell him it was a horrible mistake, but I look at his chest, the ring around his neck is gone. It's over. He's finished with me.

I start to cry because that's what I do when I'm frustrated. "I know. I know that and I wanted to. I just didn't—"

"Now this with Jamie? I don't even know who you are anymore." He ignores me.

"I could say the same thing. Since when don't you have my back?" I say between sobs.

His body language is closed off, his posture is stiff. "I guess we screwed up one too many times. That night was a mistake and it changed everything." With his hands in his pockets he retreats inside, leaving me in the courtyard.

I sit down at the table. There's a half empty beer bottle. I lift it to my nose and inhale. It's heaven in a bottle. *Just one sip, Jenna. Just one sip.*

I lift it to my lips and tilt it back, just before the liquid gets to my lips, I throw it across the courtyard, the glass shatters into infinitesimal pieces everywhere and so do I.

THE SCRAPE of the curtains opening and the light shining through them is too much. I turn over and cover my head with the pillow.

"Time's up, get up and get packed we're leaving." Lily says, rushing around the room.

I see Lily is executing her right to boss me around now. "I guess you ordering me around means you decided to be my manager after all?"

"Jenna, you have been in bed for three days, you have to put this pain and suffering to good use. Plus, I found an amazing opportunity for you, but it requires you to not look like... that." She draws a circle around me with her index finger.

"What opportunity?" I ask genuinely interested.

"Grab your cowgirl boots, we're going to Nashville."

Ok... That was not what I was expecting. "Come again?"

"Ok, so Jace Walker, you've heard of him, right? Well, he's looking for a duet partner and Jenna I've heard you sing country, you would be perfect. So... I called his manager and Jace said yes, he wants to meet up with you right away."

"Jace Walker?"

"We need to get out of here, this isn't healthy. You and Mark, L.A., you need a change of scenery. Come on, get up." She grabs my hands and pulls me out of bed, and I shuffle into the bathroom.

I don't let her know it but she's right, it's not healthy. The past three days in bed have been me trying not to binge drink. The addiction is trying to swallow me right now and I'm doing the best I can.

One sip is all it will take to bring me down.

I shower and primp because I haven't since the night of the launch party with Jamie and then I check my phone, there's several missed calls, including my Dad and Jamie. Then there's several texts from Jamie asking if I'm ok and where I am. I turn my phone off, pack a few bags and head down to find Lily.

"Ready?" She asks and I smile because I am welcoming this opportunity with open arms.

I can't wait to leave.

We land in Nashville a little after three in the afternoon. It's hot and humid. We stop at our Airbnb to unload the luggage and then head straight to the recording studio to meet with Jace and his manager.

"This is so cool. I can't believe you're really here." He gives me a quick hug.

Jace is taller than I imagined. Six feet of long legs in blue jeans and cowboy boots. He's a couple of years younger than me and very handsome.

"I can't believe I'm here either. It's been a long time since I've collaborated." I admit nervously.

"Here, sit down. You need a drink?" He hands me a sheet of music with lyrics and takes a seat opposite me at the microphone.

"Just a water, thanks."

He lifts his guitar onto his leg, and strums a few chords until his manager, Will, returns with our waters. "Ok, so it goes like this." He strums and sings, and the song is great but I'm nervous about our chemistry. Singing a duet is all about chemistry. "You want to try it?" He asks.

I smile. "Let's do it."

Lily and Will leave the booth and Jace and I stand, facing each other in front of the mic. He smiles at me and it makes me relax. *Just have fun.* I remind myself.

We get through most of the song before the producer corrects us and tells us to start from the top again. We start and stop two more times. The third time we make it through the whole song and Jace lets out a long loud whistle.

"Girl, that was amazing. What do you think?" He asks, his hand gripping my shoulder.

"I think it was great!" And it was.

"So, you'll do it then?"

I look over at Lily and Will who are deep in conversation. I take a deep breath and then realize I have nothing else to lose.

"Yes, absolutely."

He whistles and hollers, clapping his hands loudly. "Alright! This calls for some celebrating."

38

MARK - OCTOBER 1998

"Here." I hand her a sheet of music and sit on the balcony, as I hold my guitar on my lap.

"What is it?" She raises her eyebrows, immediately interested in whatever has changed my mood. It's been so long since we've had a carefree moment, and seeing her excited about something makes me smile, which is so rare these days.

"Something I wrote." I start playing the music which I already know by heart. "It's a duet."

She looks upset. "A duet? For who?"

"For us."

She shakes her head. "I've never done a duet before."

I put my hand over the chords to stop the sound. "It's not much different, instead of one person singing, two people sing concurrently, sometimes one verse at a time, chorus together." I'm being a smart ass and teasing her.

She fakes a smile. "Ha, ha."

"Come on, let's try it." I start playing the chords again as she looks over the lyrics.

"Ok. I guess." She shrugs her shoulders.

I start from the beginning, and she sings the first verse about being lost and alone. We sing the chorus together about fighting for the one you love and falling hard, and when the last verse floats from her lips, I know exactly what we need to do. We need to record this for her album.

"What do you think?" I ask, hoping that she feels the same way that I do.

"It's good."

"Just good?"

"What do you want me to say, Mark?" She stands and walks back inside. I follow her. She turns to face me, her eyes glassy. "You want me to sing a duet with you about love, but we're in a bad place right now."

"I know, J. Just give me time. I know I haven't been the same with you. I just... I just keep seeing it."

She puts her hands on the kitchen counter, her arms straight out, and hangs her head. "I don't know how many more times I have to tell you. I didn't do anything, I was drugged." I nod, knowing that I have to get over this, that it wasn't her fault she got roofied. The song was supposed to be therapy for me. I grab her and gently turn her, so she's facing me.

"I want to record the song with you." I rub my thumb across her cheek.

"I want you to look at me like you used to."

I push her hair over her shoulder and pull her close to me. "I love you, you know that, but if I ever see another man put his hands on you, I *will* kill him." I mean every word before I capture her mouth in a soul awakening kiss.

I slide her tank top down off her shoulders and plump her full breasts in my hand before I lift her up onto the countertop.

She runs her fingers through my hair, and I stand between her legs as they hang off the counter. "I don't want another man to touch me. I'm so grateful I don't remember anything from that night. Jamie is a good guy and all, but he's not you." I relish in her words, I miss us, the way we were, and I don't waste another second, I unbutton her shorts and lift her so I can slide them down. They drop to the floor.

My fingers grip her hips, and I slide her to the edge of the counter. I trail my fingers across her soft, smooth skin till I reach the apex of her thighs and slide my fingers under her nondescript panties.

She moans as I glide across her wet slit making her lean back on her elbows, her head falls back, and her hair fans out behind her. She's a vision, and I only live to please her.

I stroke her teasingly, over and over before plunging two fingers deep inside her, curving them until I hit that spot that makes her writhe against my hand. She moans as I pump inside her, my thumb pressing against her clit until she's panting and exploding around my fingers.

I want to come inside her. I want to climb on top of the counter and claim her as mine, fuck like an animal. Instead, I lick my fingers and grab her hand to help her hop down.

She wraps her arms around my neck and kisses me. Her eyes still hooded from pleasure. "Take me to the bedroom." She whispers. She wants more.

I kiss her lips, over each eye, then the tip of her nose.

"No."

She looks up at me, worrying her lip between her teeth. She thinks I don't want to have sex with her in the bedroom, maybe that's partly true, but the song is intense, and I want us to feel that intensity when we record it.

"We're bringing our sexual frustration to the studio."

She smiles and leans against my chest. "Let's go then."

I quickly chat with the engineer, Ross, a longtime friend, who has already set up all the equipment and loaded the prerecorded instrumental music that I gave him.

I grab my guitar and head into one isolation room while Jenna goes into another. We need to record separately to achieve optimal quality, but we can still see and hear each other. I tune my guitar, and I feel the heat of her stare through the glass, and I question this idea to record instead of taking her to bed.

"You guys ready?" Ross asks us, and we both nod, our eyes lock on each other. The music starts, and she's strong through the whole song, even though we're unrehearsed, and she's never recorded this way before. She's a natural-born performer, and her talent comes across at this moment that I've thrown her into.

Ross asks us to do certain parts over again, and then we do the whole song one more time, everything about the song makes me want to rip her clothes off and claim her.

When Ross finally says we're good to go, I rush into the other isolation room, pulling Jenna out of the studio and down the hall to a janitor's closet.

I push her against the wall and kiss her as my hands roam and push clothing out of the way. She grinds against me and unbuttons my jeans sliding them down. We're frantic, the adrenaline coursing through us, and she pulls her mouth away briefly as I lift her so I can slide into her, moaning at the way I'm filling her.

Then she pulls my mouth back to hers and its pure kinetic energy and need as we propel each other to orgasm, exploding together, and once she pulls every last drop from me, she drops her legs, her feet barely touching the floor as she still holds me around my neck.

"I want it to be like this, always." She says between ragged breaths.

I nod. "I love you," I say reticently. I can't say much else because if I fall anymore in love with her, surely it will destroy both of us.

39

MARK - AUGUST 2015

"Yes, I'm aware. Just have the band cut it again." I hang up and stare out the window. I turn at the sound of someone knocking at the door. It's Jamie. I turn back to the window. Things have been awkward, to say the least, since he brought Jenna to the launch, but we are partners, so I'm trying to be the bigger person. "What's up?"

"She's gone, she hasn't called or responded to any texts."

I know he's talking about Jenna because he's been worried for days.

"I wouldn't worry about it. She's a big girl."

He leans against the couch and folds his arms. "It's been a week, Mark. She could be in rehab or a drunken binge, maybe something happened to her."

I had considered all of this already. My adrenaline peaks and then drops again. "She has Lily." *This is all part of their game.*

"Mark, come on, dude."

I spin around to face him. "Don't dude me! Did you sleep with her? You know she's always been off-limits, no matter what."

He doesn't answer right away.

"Of course, I didn't sleep with her." He sighs. "What happened in the courtyard? What did she say to you?"

"That I was killing her."

He doesn't say anything and part of me thinks he already knows how our conversation went. I pull my phone out and google her. Nothing new comes up.

Then I check her social media accounts and find a photo of her from a few days ago. "I told you she was fine."

He comes to stand next to me at the window, and I hand him my phone. "Fine is a relative word. She's in a bar." He observes.

The picture is of her and someone I'm familiar with, Jace Walker, a popular country singer. They're smiling and having a good time at a bar. He has his arm around her shoulders, and the caption reads 'making music with this pretty lady.'

"Looks like your date is pretty close to Mr. Walker." I say dryly.

He drops my phone onto the desk and leaves.

I close my eyes and rub my forehead before looking at the picture again. Silently hoping she hasn't turned her back on sobriety. More than that, I hope I'm not the reason for it. I put my head in my hands and rub over my eyes.

I have meetings lined up for the rest of the day, and I'm tempted to cancel them and go find her. Enough of her games. If she had something to tell me, then she should have when I gave her the chance. I can't concentrate, so I tell my assistant to clear my schedule, and I take the rest of the day off to think.

Marissa is away for the week with the production company, which is a welcome absence right now. I need some time to myself. So, I change and head out to the backyard to sit out by the pool when my phone rings, it's Jamie.

I'm not in the mood to deal with any more of his crap, so I let it go to voicemail.

With everything that's been going on, I've been bad about going to the gym, so I jump into the pool deciding to swim laps until my body is begging me to stop, and I'm gasping for air.

Lifting myself out of the pool, then dropping into a lounger to lay in the sun, drying off. I must doze off because I wake to someone standing over me.

"Good job, asshole." Jamie throws something at me.

I sit up and wipe the fog from the nap away. "What now?" I stand and put my towel around my neck, reading what he threw at me. I skim it quickly, but Jamie has me beat.

"She's going to sign with Halycon records. Lily called you four days ago to negotiate, but you didn't return the call."

"Halycon? In Nashville?" I ask confused. *Why Nashville?*

"Yeah, courtesy of Jace Walker and their duet, she's a country sensation. This dropped this morning."

He plays the track on his phone.

"Fuck." Deep down, I knew we needed Jenna to bring the business back. I honestly didn't see her going outside the box on this one. I just assumed she would come home to Heartbeat, whether I was on board or not.

"If the label goes under, I'm holding you personally responsible." He stands with his hands on his hips.

"I'll call her." I can get her to come back.

He shakes his head like he's yelling at a child. "It's too late and good luck calling her, you're the reason she's running. You lost your professionalism, she flat out told me she wanted you on board. She couldn't handle that you wouldn't sign her, support her. God only knows why she's still in love with you."

"What are you talking about."

He pushes my shoulder. "Get your head out of Marissa's ass! Jenna's still in love with you."

"That's ridiculous! She left me, twice." I throw the papers onto the chair.

"You overwhelmed her with the truth. She didn't know what to do."

I replay that night in the hotel over again. "She never should have doubted me. I always took care of her."

"Enjoy your day off, asshole." He storms off and slams the door, and I can't help but think how ironic it is that the last time Jamie and I had an argument, it revolved around Jenna too.

I drop down on the chair and lean over with my elbows on my knees.

If Jamie is right, if Jenna still loves me, I've been a complete asshole to her. She may have deserved it, but I still took it too far.

An idea comes to me, if I can make it work, I can save the label and hopefully make amends with Jenna. I rush inside and get to work.

40

I 've only been in Nashville for a few weeks, but it's been a non-stop whirlwind promoting the single I collaborated on with Jace.

I'm having fun, and it's been the best few weeks I've had in a long time.

Nashville is breathing life back into me one day at a time, and I haven't had time to think about Max or Mark and Marissa or even Jamie, who is still reaching out to me, but I'm sure it's more about getting me to sign with Heartbeat than to see if I'm ok.

I wound up taking a meeting with Halycon Records. Jace is recording under their label, and although they were supportive with a great offer to sign me, Lily and I decided it's in my best interest to release a country album independently. Under my own label.

I love the idea that I'll have free range to record the kind of music that I want to, and I won't be tied down to one path.

I'm doing what I want to do. I'm following this journey with my heart, and no label is going to stifle my creativity.

Jace has been a big help and very supportive. Actually, everyone here is very supportive. I've already had several songwriters approach me, and my lawyers have already set the legal stuff into motion.

Since I'm committing to being in Nashville for the long haul, I decided that I should have some roots here. Jace offered to show us around town, and today we are touring houses with him and his realtor.

"Jace is here!" Lily yells from the hallway. Right now, Nashville feels more like home than L.A. has in a long time. I look out the window just as Jace is getting out of his Range Rover, he looks up at the window and smiles at me.

I bound down the stairs, and meet Lily at the front door. "You sure you want to buy a house here? The bugs are ruthless." Lily swipes at her arms and shivers.

"It's your fault I'm here so...." She slaps my arm and pushes me toward the door.

"You know, girl, if I didn't know you, I'd say you're actually happy."

"I *am* actually happy," I say defensively.

"Hallelujah, it's a miracle. Here, I got you a little something, for your birthday." I look at her, surprised as she hands me a small gift box. "Don't tell me you forgot your birthday."

I shrug my shoulders. "I haven't really had any reason to celebrate it."

I open the gift box and fold back the tissue paper to reveal a silver charm bracelet with a guitar that says Nashville, next to it is a heart charm with a J on it, tears fill my eyes.

"I love it. Thank you." I slide it onto my wrist and admire the gift.

"Don't get sappy on me." She says as we walk out the door onto the porch, where Jace is waiting patiently.

"Hey," Jace says in that low country accent that makes goose-bumps form all over my skin.

He opens the doors for us in true gentleman fashion and before long, we are driving into the posh suburban neighborhood of Frank-lin. It's nothing like the craziness of L.A., and the further we explore, the more in love I am. We see several houses and then break for lunch before we head back.

Jace and I have a live performance tonight at Centennial Park to promote our duet.

My hair and makeup team take several hours to get me show-ready, and by the time we're supposed to take the stage, my nerves are frantic, like electrical wires swinging from a utility pole.

I don't want to screw this up. I'm here for a fresh start, and I haven't performed live like this in so long. Let alone a whole new genre.

The MC announces us, and Jace takes my hand as we climb the stairs leading to the stage. He looks over at me, baring a dazzling white grin before we walk out. The crowd claps and cheers.

I'm wearing a knee-length white dress, Jean jacket, and brown cowgirl boots. It's the most comfortable I've been in years.

The crowd is already fired up, and the music starts right away. I take a deep breath and exhale, calming my nerves.

Jace sings the first verse in his deep, timbre voice, then we both sing the chorus about unrequited love and heartbreak, wanting to be somewhere else in life.

I swear the song was written for me. If my life were a movie this would be the theme song.

We sound amazing. My voice is strong, I give it my all, and I'm breathless yet, smiling when we finish.

Jace gives me a huge hug. We bow and hold hands as we walk off the stage.

Fans are coming up to us for pictures and autographs, the president of the label looks pleased, and other singers are coming up to compliment us, it's a magical night.

I head over to Lily, and she gives me a hug. "You were really great." She hands me my phone.

"Thanks."

"Hey, Jenna, look at this." Jace shows me his phone, we're trending.

I clap and squeal with delight.

Jace leans in close. "I'm gonna get a drink, you want water?"

"Please." Jace knows that I'm a recovering alcoholic. I decided it was best to tell him on the first day after we met. He was super understanding and even offered not to drink in front of me, I told him it wouldn't bother me if he did. I'm in a good place.

I walk off, through the park, it's beautiful with its southern charm and sunken garden.

I stop to look at one of the monuments until I hear footsteps behind me. I spin around thinking it's Jace with my water but it's not Jace.

My heart flutters when I see him and a mixture of excitement and regret tears through me. He stops, standing right in front of me, his face is unreadable. "You were flat out there." I cringe at his words, not that I haven't heard him say them before. My lips part and I'm momentarily speechless. *What the hell is he doing here?*

"Screw you." He's here to rain on my parade. I start to walk away but he grabs my elbow.

"You should have said that to me twenty years ago."

"What do you want?" I pull my elbow from his grasp.

"You weren't flat at all. It was perfect."

I nod and cross my arms over my chest.

He points down to my feet. "I see you traded in your flip flops for some boots."

"More like traded in grief and sadness for happiness. Did you come here to ruin that?"

He shakes his head. "No. I don't want to hurt you."

"Where's Marissa?" I look around expecting to see her nearby.

"She's on tour."

"Oh. Well, if you're bored the next show comes on at nine. You're not going to bring me down here. You made things very clear in the courtyard." My blood is pumping too fast.

"I'm not here to bring you down. I came for your birthday." He walks a few steps and picks up a bouquet of flowers from a blanket that I hadn't noticed before.

He hands them to me, and it takes me a second before I take them from him. "Thanks, but it's just another day."

"There's something else." He points to the blanket and I follow him over.

I look at him and then back to the blanket.

Max and I had a birthday tradition we started in our early teen years, we would eat popcorn and watch the movie *Sixteen Candles*. We did this every year on our birthday's and we never missed one. That is until now.

Not only does Mark have popcorn but he has the movie setup on an iPad.

"Wow, I don't know what to say." I shake my head in disbelief, silently wishing that I wasn't reminded of this tradition with Max.

"I just thought it might help today."

"Actually, I hadn't thought about it."

"Oh." He's disappointed and I suddenly feel like someone punched me in the stomach, grief is rolling in and sucking me under.

I see Jace walking toward us. "Why are you really here, Mark?"

"I just thought you might need someone today who understands." He says compassionately.

I look down and kick the dirt around, not answering and thankfully Jace approaches. "Hey, I've been looking for you." He hands me my water.

"Yeah sorry, I went for a little walk. Jace, Mark. Mark, Jace." I introduce them quickly.

Jace holds his hand out to Mark, who takes it and shakes. "Mark McGinley, I'm a big fan, it's nice to meet you man."

"You too." Mark's tone is clipped.

"Am I interrupting something here?" Jace points to the blanket. Mark answers "yes" at the same time I answer "no."

Jace laughs. "Ok, I'll give you guys some time. Jenna, I'll catch up with you later."

"Don't count on it, it's Jenna's birthday and I have plans for her."

I look over at Mark with fury and rage.

"Jenna! You didn't you tell me it was your birthday."

I lift my hands. "We've been busy working, it slipped my mind."

He laughs. "Such a workaholic." He kisses my cheek and takes off the same way he came.

I turn on Mark. "What the fuck was that? We don't have plans and I'm not watching that movie with you." I point toward the blanket.

He nods. "What's going on with Jace? Are you sleeping with him?"

I growl and storm off. I seriously think Mark has lost his mind.

He jumps in front of me, so that I have to stop.

"J, wait." My eyes linger on the chain around his neck, the weight of the ring hanging between us. *Why is he wearing it again?*

"I don't know what you're doing here, but you need to go home."

41

J enna left me standing in the park last night, not that I didn't expect that after how I left her in the courtyard. But I have the upper hand now that I know how she feels about me and I'm not going away that easy.

Lucky for me, I'm friends with a few people in Nashville and I was able to find out Jenna is recording today, and I don't think she's signed a contract with Halycon just yet.

I'm not sure what she has up her sleeve, but my plan is to catch her when she's done for the day.

It's not a great plan, but it's all I got.

Right now, I'm scouting new talent which is part of my two-fold plan to save the label, first, bringing the label to Nashville and second, winning Jenna back.

I hop from place to place, watching artist after artist. Music City is music twenty-four-seven and there's no shortage of talent.

The girl on stage is playing guitar, while she belts out an original tune. She's young, maybe eighteen, pretty enough and playing a cafe spot at ten in the morning, just waiting for someone like me to come along and notice her.

Someone who will ruin her by making all her dreams come true.

Someone like me, telling her how she must change in order to make it.

Right now, she's filled with hope and dreams of what's to come. She's free to come and go, no life on the road, chained to a record label who stifles the talent they discovered in the first place.

She thinks she knows what she wants, but until it's a reality and you're burned by the fame you won't know that you can't handle it.

Every time I see a young girl like this it makes me think of Jenna.

If I never pursued her, she would've stayed in Jersey, married some kid from high school, had three kids and a house with a white picket fence.

Maybe she would never have become an addict.

Or maybe she would've ended up in Hollywood anyway.

Her father was right, I ruined her. I ruined her, despite all the things I tried to shield her from, she still got burned.

The girl finishes her set. There's light applause from the few people in the cafe. She steps down the two stairs and grabs a cup of coffee from the counter.

I walk up to her casually and silently hold out my business card, she reads it quickly and looks up in surprise.

This is the start of the decline of this relationship. "You have forty-eight hours if you're interested." The clock is ticking for this girl, in forty-eight hours I'll move on and she'll be forgotten.

Maybe I'm in the business of stealing souls for a reason, maybe I'm no better than Jenna's Dad thought, but I'm going to make things right.

My phone chimes, and I leave the girl at the counter. It's a text from my friend at the studio letting me know Jenna just left. I quickly head out of the cafe. I'm just down the street from where the studio is and I get there in five minutes.

I see her. She's alone in one of the downtown shops. I start to cross over to her, contemplating what I want to say when I get there, but I'm too late.

Jace gets there before I do. I watch as they talk a second and then with his hand on her back, they head a few doors down the sidewalk to a restaurant.

She was waiting for him.

My heart sinks, and I start to feel like I'm on a wild goose chase, and that Jamie was wrong.

I head back the way I came and head into another cafe with blaring musicians. If I can't save things with Jenna, at least I can save the label.

I WAIT hours for some sign of Jenna around the city. The sky is darkening in the horizon and I'm about to give up when my phone chimes. It's a text from Jenna.

Are you still here?

I answer immediately.

Where are you?

She pings me her location, I'm not far.

Be there in ten.

I thank the universe which has always worked in mysterious ways for us and set off in her direction.

She's sitting on a bench outside the museum. Her soft brown hair is curled around her shoulders, her tan legs are bare in a jean miniskirt and she's wearing a low-cut black silk tank.

Jealousy cuts me like a knife that Jace might have watched her put this outfit on after their lunch date.

She sees me and stands. I kiss her cheek and make sure we are alone.

"I'm glad you were still here." She has no idea how much her words affect me. She points to the Musicians Hall of Fame Museum. "Wanna go in? I knew you would appreciate seeing it."

"I'd love to." I grab her hand and we start to walk inside. We walk with a private tour guide for the first hour, then he lets us wander privately. The museum is closed and it's an honor to be here.

"So, what did you do today?" She asks, turning near one of the exhibits.

"Scouting."

"Ahh, you're in the right place. Don't you have people to do that for you?"

"Yeah, but I just lost a contract for a big act, so I'm in the dog house." I wink at her, but she looks sad and lost.

"Listen, I was entertaining all opportunities, but I'm actually—"

"No, it's my fault. I was being stubborn."

She nods her head and we continue walking toward the exit.

Just before we get to the door, I pull her to me and wrap my arms around her. "Did I ruin your life?" I drop the bomb.

She squirms a little in my hold, she's uncomfortable. "Why are you asking me that?"

"I want to know if you think I did. The book... that's what I thought you would say. It's bothered me for a long time, something your Dad said to me years ago."

"I ruined my own life, and yours I suppose." Her eyes drop to the floor.

I tilt her chin up. I'm making her sad which wasn't my intention. "I never should have come for you at your graduation. I should have let you go."

She swipes an errant tear before it has a chance to fall. "I was so glad you came."

I close my eyes. When I open them, I see hope in her eyes, it gives me an idea. "Let me take you out. We should go dancing."

She laughs. "You don't dance like that."

"Sure, I do."

She shakes her head. "I don't think Marissa would be too pleased with that." I laugh because I'm amused at Jenna's blatant jealousy.

"True, maybe Jace won't like it either."

She puts her hands on her hips. "What's that supposed to mean? He's just a friend."

"Ok, come on country superstar. We're going dancing." I pull her out to the street, and we walk hand in hand the few blocks to the Honkey Tonk I found earlier.

It feels so good to have her in my arms, dancing closely, we are carefree and laughing, it's been too long and when she pulls me over to a small booth I'm not ready to let her go. I take a seat next to her and put my hand on her lap.

"Damn, my feet hurt." She complains.

"Quit crying, Foster." I get a smile then she orders herself a water and me a whiskey.

"Where are you staying?" She asks innocently, but none of my thoughts are innocent.

"Why don't you come with me and find out?" She gives me a look that says no way, but I don't think it would be that hard to convince her for real. "The Hermitage."

She nods knowingly. "When are you leaving?"

I sit back and put my arm around her shoulders. "Are you trying to get rid of me?"

She slides out of my arm and turns to face me. "I'm still trying to figure out what you're doing here."

If I don't say it to her now, I'll lose her to Jace or someone else.

"I want you to come back to me J."

42

JENNA - MARCH 1999

"You should wear this." Max holds up a revealing leather top and short skirt.

It's been six months since the thing with Jamie.

Things haven't been the same between any of us, and to top it all off, I haven't been in the same place for more than twenty-four hours in months.

Mark and I are back to being distant now that we are on separate tours, and I don't even know if he feels the same about me since the night we recorded our duet.

But I don't have time to even think about it too much or do anything about it.

The frenzy since the release of my debut album has been maddening. I'm playing sold-out arenas, and we have dates booked for the rest of the year.

I'm always tired, and I can't go anywhere without people following me or taking my picture.

Thank God Max has been on the road with me. I can't imagine doing this alone every night, and thankfully there were enough funds in the tour budget, that I hired him to be my stylist just so he could travel along with me.

"No, something glittery." I rub my temples, I have a headache brewing, this has been on and off for weeks. Migraines so bad it's hard to get out of bed, let alone perform with lights and loud music.

Wes had a Doctor see me on one of our tour stops who prescribed me a cocktail of pills to keep me going and reduce my stress level, but the headaches are relentless.

"Jenna, everyone is wearing glitter. You don't want to be like everyone else."

I lay down and cover my eyes. The only thing that helps is sleeping pills and lots of them.

"Fine. I'll wear whatever." He sits down next to me.

"Did you take your pills today?"

"Yes. They're not helping." I groan.

"Maybe we should go see someone else."

"No, I'll be ok." I hear Wes outside the door. He knocks before he comes in.

"Why isn't she ready yet?"

Max tells him something I can't quite make out. The pills make me indifferent. I feel like I have no emotion when I'm not on stage playing the part of a pop star.

"Jenna? Do you want me to find a doctor?" Wes asks, and I shake my head no. "Can you go on?" I shake my head, yes, and I stumble to get up on my feet. He grabs my hand and pulls me up. "I promised Mark I would take care of you, if you need something, you need to tell me."

"I'm good." I pull off my shorts, pop a handful of caffeine pills that I wash down with some vodka, and stand there as Max dresses me.

When I'm finally ready, I'm jittery and restless. "Breathe, Jenna," Max whispers beside me.

I kill it on stage, I'm energetic and personable, and the audience goes crazy. It gives me a rush, and I'm good until I walk off stage, and collapse in Max's arms.

I wake in a hospital room.

Max is standing by the foot of the bed, talking with a doctor. I squint and sit up, and they both look at me.

"Jenna, you blacked out." Max explains as he sits next to me on the bed.

I groan, my head is pounding.

The doctor tells me I have exhaustion, dehydration, and the cocktail of pills I've been taking aren't supposed to be mixed together.

"It's ok we'll get you back to normal." He tells me.

I take comfort in his words and close my eyes and sleep.

They pump me full of fluids, give me sleeping and anxiety pills, and a day later, they send me on my way. When we get back to the tour bus, there's a black SUV parked, and I see Wes standing outside with someone. I can't see who it is until we pull closer, and before Max comes to a full stop, I jump out of the car and run.

He's faster than me in my weakened state and gets to me first. "J." He holds me tightly, and I sag into his arms like a spineless jellyfish as he walks us over to Max.

"You're supposed to be taking care of her!" He yells to Max.

Max slams the car door, walking over quickly. "How can I do that when Wes has someone pumping her full of pills?"

Mark points his finger at Max. "If you can't watch out for her, you shouldn't be here."

"Tell me again, when was the last time you were here to take care of her?" Max rebuts.

"Guys. Stop. I'm ok." I don't need them arguing, it only makes everything worse.

"Let's go." Mark pulls me toward the SUV, helps me inside, and speeds away from the tour bus.

"Where are we going?" I ask, but he doesn't answer me, he just drives, and ten minutes later we pull into a hotel parking lot.

"You need a good night's sleep." We check-in under a fake name, get our room key, and once we are in the safety of our hotel room, I come undone. I don't know if it's the way he's looking at me like I'm a different person or the fact that he's here with me, but I hysterically cry and collapse in his arms.

"I'm sorry, I didn't mean to make you mad."

"I'm not mad, J. I'm worried. You're too skinny, and no one is taking care of you." He carries me to the bed, where he holds me for hours.

I fall asleep at some point and wake, feeling extremely well-rested.

"I love you." He whispers against my forehead as I stretch and yawn. I kiss him slowly, then faster until I'm climbing astride him, he helps me out of my clothes, and we make love for hours. He kisses and caresses every square inch of my body before carrying me into the shower, he washes me tenderly.

"I hate to go Jenna. I don't want to leave you." He says full of melancholy.

"I'll be ok." I'm trying to reassure both of us. Our twenty-four-hour hiatus is over, and we both have to get back to work. "I needed this. I didn't know where we stood anymore." I look up into his blue eyes. I see the pain in them, matching my own.

"I'm still barely talking to Jamie if it makes you feel better."

"No, it doesn't. He's your best friend. You need to stop this. We have to all move past it."

He hangs his head. "I know." He pauses a moment, then continues. "I want you to know, without a doubt, I want you. I'm in love with you. It's just so damn hard to be away from you like this."

I'm reading between the lines, and I prepare myself for the bad news that he's about to deliver. "You think we should sleep with other people while on the road?"

He slams the faucet off and grabs each of us a towel. "No. No fucking way. Why would you say that?" He climbs out of the shower, wrapping a towel around himself and then one around me.

I shrug. "I thought that's what you were about to say."

He pulls me to him. "No. Absolutely not. That's it, I'm getting you a cellphone. We need to talk more."

"Ok." I agree. My heart soaring that he doesn't want anyone else.

"You are mine. No one better touch you but me."

I nod. "So, I have your word then too?"

"You have better than that, Jenna. I'm going to Marry you."

43

JENNA - SEPTEMBER 2015

I hear him, but I'm having trouble comprehending the magnitude of his words. "Come back to you?" My voice is shaky.

"Yes."

"In what capacity?"

He turns to me and takes my hands in his. "I'm trying to fix things between us."

My heart is racing, and my palms start to sweat. "Fix things how?"

"I want you J. Not how we used to be, but an improved version of who we are now. I want you to be mine again." He says with a gleam of hope in his eyes.

I blow out a breath. This conversation is overwhelming. Yes, I'm in love with him, but I wasn't expecting this after the recent events and how he's been treating me.

I shake my head. "You're with Marissa." I hate myself for sounding jealous. I hate that I *am* jealous.

He grabs my hand. "Actually, I'm not. I flew to Austin before I came here to tell her that it's over. I told her I was coming to you."

"Mark, I'm here now, in Nashville. I need to be committed to this. I can't get distracted." I pull my hand out of his grasp.

"I know and I want to be here to support you."

"Well, I'm not sure how you will be able to do that while I'm on tour."

"That won't be for a while. You're still in the early phases of recording. I can fly back and forth."

I shake my head. "I'm not talking about *my* tour. I met with Jace today, he's already on tour and he asked me to be a guest opener for him. I said yes, our first tour date is a week from now."

He has a myriad of emotions run across his face. "You're going on tour with Jace." His expression is a mix of shock and disbelief.

"Yes, it's a great opportunity."

He sighs and rubs his brow. "I'll make it work. Tell me you want me Jenna. Tell me there's hope. Fight for me."

I look down at my nails, toying with the polish that's starting to chip. I look up, he's waiting for me to answer. "I want you."

He smiles wickedly and leans in to kiss me, but I'm vaguely aware that people have noticed us, and I turn my cheek.

"Take me home." I whisper in his ear and I anxiously count each minute that it takes to pay and walk back to my rental.

We barely make it inside the door before he pushes me up against the wall and kisses me into oblivion. His hands roam over my body and I tug at his hair. I freeze when I hear feet shuffling and Lily clearing her throat. We both turn to look at her.

"Hey, Lily." Mark says in a most charming voice.

"Did I forget to mention Lily's staying here too."

"Oh, don't mind me kids, I'm just heading up to bed." She winks at me and heads for the stairs. I laugh and hide my face in Mark's shoulder.

"Do you want me to go?" He asks and I slide my hands under his shirt. I imagine the warmth of his body against mine, undulating in that sweet sensual rhythm that only happens with him.

He can't leave me. "I want you to stay." I say sure and even.

"Good, because I wasn't going to leave." He lifts me up in his arms and I wrap my legs around him. "Bedroom?" He asks.

"Down the hall, to the left."

He walks with me wrapped around him until we reach the bed.

He sits me down, and I waste no time shimmying out of my shirt and skirt.

"In a hurry?" He smirks, pulling his own shirt over his head.

I raise my eyebrow at him. "Are you complaining?"

"Never. I'll take you flat on your back any day." He pulls me to my feet, cups the back of my neck and leans forward to kiss me.

It's a soft, sensual kiss that's slowly working up to a frenzied rhythm. I push him back until his legs hit the bed. He falls onto the mattress and I slide his belt out of the buckle and with his help pull his jeans down. His cock stands tall in his briefs. I grab the waistband and he helps, lifting his hips so that I can slide them off.

I take him in my hand and pump him, his soft skin is warm in my hand and he moans in appreciation when I lean forward and swirl my tongue around his tip, teasing him before I take him down to the root.

"Jenna..." He warns. I know he's close, so I suck harder, faster, until he turns the tables and pulls me up so I'm sitting astride him. "Ride me." He whispers, and I do, pumping myself over him as his thumb presses against my clit. I'm frenzied with need, and when he pulls me forward to kiss me it's simple, but enough to send me over. I come apart crying his name and his cock twitches inside me, his body convulsing, as my core tightens around him.

We stay there like that, me laying on his chest as I catch my breath. I grab the ring that's reappeared around his neck, wrapping my fingers around it. He lightly strokes my back with two fingers leaving a trail of goosebumps. I look up at him and he kisses me on the tip of my nose.

It's the perfect moment for me to tell him, so I do. "I love you." I whisper to him, and he closes his eyes. It's hard to see his expression in the dark, but I feel him smiling.

He flips me onto my back, he's still inside me and I feel him growing hard again.

"I've dreamed about this moment for years, hearing you say that again. I died inside a thousand times believing it would never happen." He presses a chaste kiss against my lips. "Please, don't leave me again."

Tears roll down my cheeks, stinging the corners of my eyes. "I'm sorry that I doubted you. I'm sorry we lost five years."

He kisses the trail of tears as he slowly moves inside me, promising me over and over we will be alright.

THE SUNLIGHT FILTERING through the shades wakes me, I stretch and moan. My body aches in the best way.

Mark made love to me for hours after I told him that I love him. I'm sore and sated and renewed, as if I've had years of therapy in only one night.

I roll onto my side but I'm alone. Panic tears through me and I sit up quickly. *Did Mark leave me the same way I left him in his hotel?*

I spring out of bed, run to the bathroom to grab my robe off of the bathroom door and head down the hallway.

"Lily!" I shout. I'm not sure how she is supposed to help me but still, I continue to shout.

"Whoa, where's the fire?" I turn to see Mark in the kitchen. He has eggs in a pan and bread in the toaster. I rush into him and he puts his arms around me. "Lily had a meeting. She said she would be back later."

"I thought you left." I sound like a small child who got separated from her mother. He looks me up and down, a heated glaze fills his eyes.

"You were supposed to stay sleeping until breakfast was done." My stomach growls on cue at the word breakfast. I kiss him and head to the Keurig.

"Coffee?" I mumble and try to stifle a yawn with the back of my hand, my heartbeat returning to normal.

"Sure."

I pull two cups from the cabinet.

"Since when do you drink coffee?" He asks.

"Since sobriety."

"Ahh." He understands. I don't have to explain, but I do.

I shrug my shoulders as I brew each of us a cup. "I need a vice. Coffee is a lesser evil."

He nods and puts the food onto plates, and we sit across from each other at the counter. "I'm proud of you J. I know it's not easy."

I take a bite of my toast after dipping it in the yolk. I bask that Mark remembers my favorite breakfast, as simple as it is. "So good." I lift my phone to see the time. "I'm supposed to be at the studio in an hour."

"I'll walk you over. I have a lunch meeting."

We finish eating in comfortable silence. Then I quickly change into comfortable clothes for a long day of recording, throw my hair in a messy bun and we head out. Mark weaves his fingers with mine and I reluctantly let go to answer my phone. It's Jace. His husky voice greets me warmly on the other end.

Mark re-threads our fingers and I feel them tense as Jace and I talk about meetings, promoting the tour, and appearances together, all which Lily is handling, so I take this as Jace checking on me with a friendly call.

"It's all good." I say and we end the call.

"He wants you." Mark has always been jealous of other men, so I'm not surprised at the tone in his voice.

"Stop it." I smack his arm.

"No, I'm serious. He wants you."

"Don't start. He's just being nice Mark."

He holds his hands up in surrender. "We'll see."

I roll my eyes and thank the lucky stars that we've arrived at the studio.

Grabbing my other hand, he pulls me into him. "Have dinner with me tonight."

I smile because the answer is of course is yes, but I play hard to get. "Maybe, if you're lucky."

44

MARK - JUNE 1999

I walk down the gangway and walk quickly through the airport, trying not to garner any unwanted attention.

I've been flying to meet Jenna every chance I can, even if I only have a few hours. It's been keeping us both sane, and it gives me peace of mind checking in on her wellbeing.

This time we have a whole weekend in the Florida Keys. I know she's already there and I'm running later than planned.

I had to make a pit stop, and I'm trying to maximize every second we have together this weekend. So, I'm impatient as my driver loads my luggage, and I tell him to take me straight to the house. Thankfully, it's not that far from the airport.

My heart is racing the whole ride. I can't believe I'm this nervous as we drive down the private road and pull into the driveway. The house is set back from the road giving us plenty of privacy. I planned this entire weekend, it has to be perfect.

I tip the driver handsomely. He hands me my bags, and I stride up the walkway to the front of the house.

Inside, the house is exactly what I expected. A beach house painted in bright colors, large windows letting the natural light in, and flowers in a vase on the table by the door as the smell of the ocean fills the house.

What I don't expect is to see Max walking out of the kitchen with a pitcher in his hand or him in his bathing suit.

"Hey, did you just get here?" He asks me even though I'm holding my bags, and it's obvious that I just got here.

"Where's Jenna?" I ignore his question.

"Outside." I drop my bags, walk past him, and head outside. She's sunbathing in a skimpy bikini by the pool.

I stand in front of her, blocking the sun. She lifts her shades and squeals when she sees me jumping off the chair into my arms, but I push her away.

"Why is Max here?" I demand.

She looks at me, stunned because of my reaction to her. "I invited him. I didn't think it was a big deal."

My temper is flaring, I've never been so angry with her. "You didn't think it was a big deal?" I run my hands through my gel slicked hair, surely making it look crazy.

"No, you don't usually care, so I asked him to come."

I back away from her. "I do care. I didn't realize I was getting a package deal for eternity when I brought both of you to L.A."

She stands with her hands on her hips. "He's my best friend, and the only family I have, thanks to you." She shouts.

"Ok, well, I hope you two have a nice weekend." I head back toward the house.

"No, Mark, wait." She grabs my arm, and I stop. "You're seriously leaving?" Her horrified expression pains me.

"He gets you every day Jenna. You were supposed to be mine for the weekend." I can't see past my anger.

"Did you tell me that?" She stares at me incredulously, like I'm the one being unreasonable.

"Are you serious? I have to tell you that. You don't think I want you to myself for a long romantic weekend?"

"You're acting crazy." She yells at me, and I walk away from her, not understanding how she couldn't see this coming.

Inside, Max is standing in the kitchen. Jenna comes in behind me. I'm standing inches away from Max, who looks at us concerned with my obviously angry demeanor.

"Are you gay, or are you following Jenna around because of some puppy love infatuation?"

"Mark!" Jenna yells behind me. Max doesn't flinch or move a muscle.

"It's my fatal error for not telling Jenna specifically I wanted her alone, but now I'm starting to think there's something wrong here if you didn't realize it either."

Max puffs out his chest, the hurt evident for only a second before he recovers. "You know. I really don't know what she sees in you." He walks off, but I cut him off in his path.

"Jenna told me you were gay, are you or not?" I ask once more, wanting a clear answer.

"Jenna, I'm leaving." Max sidesteps me, but I take one more stab. "You spend too much time together, it's not normal."

He ignores me and stalks toward the bedrooms.

"That was horrible! I can't believe you just did that, he's my best friend!"

There's no future for us if we can't get any time alone. "Well, J, you have to choose him or me because I'm not into this threesome thing we have going on." I'm not backing down this time. I've been dealing with this for way too long.

"That is not fair."

I nod because she's making her choice, and since I'm the one who brought this up, I have to be ok with that choice. "Tell him to stay. Enjoy the weekend." I grab my bags in the entryway and head back out to the driveway.

She follows me out. "If you leave, I'm done with you. You're being such an asshole."

I turn back. I don't know why I do, but my legs are faster than my brain. "This asshole, was going to propose to you. I'm so glad I know how you feel now." I don't want to throw it in her face, but I can't tell which way is up right now.

I walk down the driveway until I'm out of sight, then I call a cab that takes me back to the airport. A flight separating us by three thousand miles.

The gulf between us has never seemed wider.

45

JENNA - JUNE 1999

Max is on one side of me, and my bodyguard, Big Mike, is on the other. My stomach is twisted in knots because Mark flew home yesterday and hasn't answered any of my calls. *I told him I was done with him.*

I screwed up royally this time.

I had called Jamie after Mark left, hoping that he had told him where he was going, but he didn't, and none of the other guys knew where he was until this morning.

I've been trying to get back to L.A. all day, but bad weather is keeping me grounded.

I'm in my best disguise with my sunglasses on, but people are still staring, and the longer that I sit here, the worse it will be.

My mood is anything other than friendly, and I'm liable to lash out if anyone approaches me.

In twenty-four hours, I've managed to ruin the two most important relationships in my life.

Max agreed after a lengthy conversation that we need to put some distance between us, and if I continue my relationship with Mark, he doesn't know how we can continue being friends.

"I was tired of following you around anyway." He said after we had been up most of the night arguing.

He said I threw money at him, so he stayed on, but he was tired of life on the road.

It breaks my heart to admit it, but he feels more like my babysitter these days than my best friend. That's not how it was supposed to be.

Finally, our flight is called for boarding, and Max takes his coach seat, which he insisted on, and I take mine in first class next to Big Mike.

When we land at LAX, Max leaves for the apartment, and Mike takes me to Mark's house. We have a few hours left to hash out the weekend, and I plan to do just that.

I ring the bell twice. He doesn't answer, so I use my key to let myself in. I walk through the house, but there's no sign of him.

Then I see him on the balcony with a note pad in his hand.

He's writing, and it looks productive. I don't want to interrupt him, but we only have a few hours before I need to be in Toronto.

I slide the balcony door open. He turns but doesn't acknowledge me.

If he's surprised that I'm here, he doesn't show it.

I kneel in front of him and put my head on his lap.

"I'm so sorry." I cry because I can't help it, the tears just keep coming. I'm extremely emotional, and the past several hours of holding it in at the airport are finally releasing. "I love you."

He puts his pad down onto the bench, grabs my arms, and pulls me to stand with him. I didn't have a plan for him kicking me out, but I'm not leaving here without saying what I came to say.

"I'm sorry too." He surprises me by apologizing, and I look up at him.

"Why are you sorry? Everything you said was right. Max and I do spend too much time together. He's not living his own life following me around. I fucked up inviting him to the Keys, I wasn't thinking." He listens to my whole spiel, sighs, and drops my arms.

"I don't think I'm right for you, Jenna. I want much more than I think you're ready for. Maybe it's the age difference, or maybe we're just incompatible, but someday you will regret being with me."

The tears stream steady now at his proclamation, dread settles in my gut. "No. Don't do this." I shake my head and dig my nails into his side. I'm gasping for air, and it feels like I'm suffocating.

"You'll be fine, J. Go, and be nineteen, I sure as hell did, and I want you to have that too, no regrets."

I nod, even though I couldn't disagree more. I suck in several deep breaths as he walks me to the door. My life feels like it's over.

He kisses my cheek, and I feel like I'm going to be sick because this isn't what I want. I want him to scoop me into his arms and make me feel safe.

But I know he's not going change his mind, not right now. He just needs time to come to his senses. A Wave of nausea hits me again, worse this time. I turn to go, but I don't make it. Dizzy and light-headed, I collapse into darkness.

The next few hours in the ER are a blur of people fussing over me and asking me a million questions.

My eyes are red-rimmed from crying, and Mark is sitting in the chair next to the bed, not talking or looking at me, and I'm pretty sure the nurses think we had a physical altercation because they keep whispering and staring.

"You don't have to stay," I whisper.

He looks up at me and stands, leaning over the bed he bends to kiss the tip of my nose. "Just relax." He whispers.

I look around, making sure no one will hear us. "I want to marry you, I do. Please don't break up with me, I already gave everyone up to be with you."

He leans down lower over me, staring intently at me. "That's the problem, I don't want you to feel that way. I'm just selfish when it comes to you. You're so young. I don't want you to give anything up to be with me."

I lean forward to capture his mouth, praying he returns the kiss.

"Ms. Foster." The Doctor interrupts, and we both turn to look at him. "First, I just want to say it's an honor to be your physician today, and I have some good news. You're going to be just fine. All your bloodwork came back fine, but, you are severely dehydrated."

"Is that why she passed out?" Mark asks.

I look at the doctor, who I see is holding something back. I close my eyes and blow out a breath.

"Well, some women do have fainting spells during pregnancy, it's not ideal, but I think if she drinks more water and rests more, it shouldn't happen again."

"Pregnant?" Mark repeats and the doctor nods.

"Yes, about eight weeks. Congratulations." The doctor hands paperwork to Mark and leaves. I just stare at the wall in shock, because how did this happen?

"Jenna?"

I just stare at him because I have no words.

"Where were we eight weeks ago?" He thinks out loud.

I still can't answer him because a million other thoughts are clouding my brain, like how much I've had to drink and how many caffeine pills I've been taking.

I hop out of the bed and grab my date planner from my bag, furiously flipping back to eight weeks ago.

Mark had come to visit me in Georgia on a twenty-four-hour stopover.

That's not what I'm looking for though, I flip back to the previous week and then the week before that. "Fuck." I canceled my birth control doctor appointment and never rescheduled.

He's watching me, and looking intensely at me waiting for me to explain. I can't tell if he's angry or not.

"I forgot about my shot. I canceled and didn't reschedule."

He leans down in front of me, puts my planner back in my bag and pulls me off the floor.

"I'm sorry, I—"

He kisses my lips, interrupting me, as he puts his hand over my belly. "This is amazing."

"Amazing? You were just breaking up with me a second ago for being too young, now I'm going to have a baby?" I'm borderline hyperventilating. "Mark, I can't have a baby."

He kisses me again, blocking all the things I want to say but can't because he is obviously over the moon with this news. We break apart.

"I want to go home." I say meekly.

"You got it. I'll be right back." He says and goes to handle getting me released.

What he doesn't realize is I don't mean home to his house or to my apartment. I want to go home to Jersey, because this is the worst thing that's happened to me since I left.

46

"How are you hanging in?" Mark's smooth voice hits me as I step out of my trailer and into the fog of production crews setting up our next stop.

"I'm fine," I say for the millionth time. It's the same conversation every time I step foot in a new city, he calls to check-in, and I tell him I'm fine a million times.

I *am* fine. This isn't my tour. I'm older and wiser and sober, and there's no drama.

Being on the road has been a welcome past time so far, and I promised Mark if it became something else, I would leave.

"I miss you, J." We only had a short time together in Nashville before I left, and we've only seen each other in person once and on FaceTime.

If only FaceTime had been around back in the day, maybe things would've been easier on us.

I hear someone calling me. I turn and see Jace waving me over. "I miss you too. I gotta go, they're calling me over for a soundcheck." I say regretfully that once again our time is cut short.

I end the call and head over. We're in some bumble town of Indiana, and it's hotter than average for this time of year.

"Hey, what's up?"

Jace waves as I walk up and leans on the back of a chair.

"Just wanted to make a suggestion." Will, Jace's manager, stands next to him and is the one doing all the talking.

"Ok..." My senses tell me the bottom is about to drop out.

"We're all in the business of selling records, right? Soon enough, you will be putting out a record, and we could all benefit from more exposure."

Where is this going? "Why don't you just tell me what you're trying to say nicely. I've been around the block. I don't need you to sugar coat it." I square my shoulders.

"When you sing with Jace, we want more sexual tension, touchy-feely that sort of thing. It's all about selling the song." Will says.

I look to Jace for confirmation that he's on board with this.

"Jenna, it's just a suggestion. I don't want you to do anything you're uncomfortable with."

I haven't told anyone besides Lily that I'm back with Mark, not because I don't want anyone to know, well really, I don't. Once everyone knows, it's hard to keep them out of my private life. Everyone wants the scoop.

"Yeah, sure. Just on stage, nothing crazy." I turn around and start walking back to my trailer. I close my eyes and start to text Mark this new development. I know he will adamantly shut this down, no matter what the argument.

"Jenna. Wait." Jace runs up beside me. "I didn't have anything to do with this. The record label—"

"It's fine. I've been used before. I get it, nothing personal, just show biz." I am actually hurt by Jace and this plan. I thought he appreciated me as an artist, not a toy.

"I'm not using you. I wanted to contact you a long time ago. I didn't think you would come out of hiding, especially not for country music."

"No one ever asked, and I wasn't in hiding. I was dealing with a mental breakdown." I walk away and slide my phone back in my pocket, deciding its best to see how tonight's show goes before telling Mark their sales approach.

Four hours later, I'm dolled up on stage with Jace, there's nothing too dramatic happening as far as touchy-feely goes.

I bat my eyes and smile. He grabs my hand, and I'm sure to the audience we look flirty and sexually attracted to each other.

The last note on the guitar fades in and out, Jace goes in for a hug as usual then we pull away and bow together. Everything is normal, I'm relieved. We turn to walk off stage together hand in hand. Unfortunately, I feel him tug on my hand too late. He spins me around, catches me in his arms and plants a kiss on my lips.

I panic and mold into him, melting into his kiss, so I don't cause a commotion or look crazy. The audience is clapping and catcalling, as he pulls me back up and pulls me off the stage.

"What the fuck was that?" I push at his chest.

"I know, I'm sorry. It just came over me." He says innocently.

"Jesus Christ, Jace." I walk off in a huff. My heart is racing, I'm shaking and my palms are sweating as I sprint back to my trailer.

Lily is sitting with her feet propped up when I push open the door and slam it making her jump. "What? What happened?" She rises off the couch at the sight of me.

"Did you know about this plan?" I point my finger at her.

"What plan?"

"Jace and Will's publicity stunt. They told me before the show to be more touchy-feely, and then Jace kicked it up a notch by kissing me on stage. That's gonna go over well with Mark, by the way."

"Oh, hell, no." She storms out, and the door slams behind her.

I take my phone and set it on the table, staring at it like it's going to explode.

I'm scared to check my social media pages, so I sit down and wait for it to ring because it will ring. It will ring, and it will be Mark, and we will have a huge fight because that's what we do.

How was it only hours ago that everything seemed perfect?

There's a knock at the door, interrupting my manic thoughts. I know it's Jace because it would be impossible for it to be Mark already.

I hold open the door but don't invite him in. "Lily is giving Will an earful. I'm not sure you want to be here when she gets back."

"I know I deserve that, but please hear me out." I step aside and let him in. "I just got carried away, Jenna. Obviously, I think you're a very attractive woman, but it won't happen again." He promises.

"Good. Is that all?"

He shoves his hands in his pockets and scuffs his boots on the floor, making a loud scraping noise. "You gonna be mad at me the rest of the tour?"

I smile and laugh at his demeanor, which is almost childlike. "I just might be."

He drops down on the couch, letting his head fall into his hands. I stare at him, not sure what's going on with him. "Is this lifestyle always so lonely?" He asks. Fame has hit him quickly too, I feel sorry for him. Nothing can prepare you for it.

I drop my arms, which have been crossed defensively since he walked in. I lean against the table and sigh. "It has its highs and lows, just like everything else. I think I would've had a better handle on it if I were older. Maybe I wouldn't have hit rock bottom so hard."

He looks up at me surprised. "You're such a successful artist, how could that be hitting rock bottom?"

I used to think about that a lot. As long as I had a lot of money in the bank, I didn't think about the damage I was doing. I measured my success in terms of money, and that got me nowhere. "Who defines success?"

"What do you mean?" He looks at me quizzically.

"Maybe your terms of success are different than mine. Everyone has a different definition of success, but no one who makes it says, 'I'll do this for free,' you do whatever you have to keep it going, at least, that's what I did. I wish I had looked at it differently back then." *Just have fun.*

He shakes his head as he stands. He takes my hand, and my stomach flutters nervously. "You're a good person, Jenna." He heads for the door. My phone lights up on the table beside me, I watch it as it almost vibrates off the table and onto the floor. He turns once more before he heads down the stairs. "Have a good night." The door quickly swings shut behind him.

My phone buzzes again.

I leave it on there on the table and wait for Lily to return, I can't wait to get the hell out of here.

47

MARK - OCTOBER 2015

I stop calling her a little after midnight.

The idea of hopping on a plane and beating the shit out of Jace is extremely tempting, and I'm not completely ruling it out yet. But if I've learned anything over the years, it's that my reaction will be the catalyst for how Jenna handles the situation.

And usually, that will end up with us in a huge fight.

So, if I go there and raise hell, I'll be the bad guy, not Jace.

I'll wait it out because I'm confident Jenna was not expecting that kiss to happen.

Jamie and Dave were with me when the video hit social media, and they saw exactly what I did. Jace caught her off guard.

Besides the fact, if there is something going on between them, I'll kill him. No one is going to get in our way this time. I'm not losing my second chance with her.

I pace the house for another hour in case she calls back, but at some point, I fall asleep in the living room chair, my phone wakes me at six A.M. I glance at it and see Jenna's face on the screen.

"Morning sunshine, you're up early," I say brightly.

"I traveled most of the night, and then I couldn't sleep. Listen, Mark, there's something I have to tell you." She cuts to the chase.

Here it comes, I take a deep breath and prepare myself for what-ever she's going to say, but decide to let her off the hook. "I saw it already." We're supposed to be different this time, a new Jenna and Mark, so I make it easy for her.

"You saw it already?"

"I did." I close my eyes and swallow over the lump in my throat.

"And you're fine? Or you're plotting murder? You don't sound mad." She's surprised.

"Is there a reason I shouldn't be fine? Is there something going on?" My pulse drums in my ears.

"Of course not. It was a publicity stunt, it was so awkward, I feel like an idiot that I didn't see it coming. It's their stupid marketing tactic to ramp up sales. How frigging long have I been in this busi-ness, I should have known better." She's upset and rambling on.

"Jenna. Breathe baby." *Be the voice of reason.*

"Baby? Mark, how are you so damn calm?"

I blow out a breath, trying like hell to keep my cool. "Do you want me to come there?"

"Of course, I want you to, but honestly, I don't, because I want to handle this. Mostly, I'm surprised you're not already here, killing Jace." I hear the trepidation in her voice.

"J... you know I want to bash his face in. You know I've always been jealous when it comes to you. I don't want another man putting a finger on you, let alone his lips, but I'm trying to do things differ-ently this time around. So please handle him, or I will." I say as calm as I can.

"I handled it already."

"Good. Oh, and J..."

"Yeah?"

"Next time I see you, I'm going to erase any trace of that kiss from your memory. You're mine, don't forget it." We hang up, and I run my fingers wildly through my hair.

If I have to keep seeing videos on social media of the two of them flirting, I might have to go offline totally. I don't want to hurt her new adventure, but I can't sit back and watch them looking cozy together either.

I look at my schedule for the next week to see if I can squeeze in seeing her.

"Shit." I groan. I'm completely booked, there's no way I can catch up with her. I'm about to text Jamie to see if he can handle any of the meetings I'm scheduled for, when the doorbell rings.

I toss my phone down onto the table and make the mistake of answering it, rather than looking to see who it is. Standing just on the other side of the threshold is Marissa.

She looks beautiful, glowing even, and as I look her over, I realize maybe in another lifetime I could've fallen in love with her, maybe we could have had something long term.

Maybe if I never met Jenna, she would've been a perfect match for me.

I warmly embraced my time with Marissa and her affection as a lover, but... she's just not Jenna.

"Hi." She says emphatically and smiles. "Is this a good time?"

"You could've called," I say coldly and lean against the door jamb, folding my arms across my chest.

My posture is stiff and uninviting, I can't give her the wrong impression.

"It'll just take a minute. Is Jenna here?" I don't know why but the hair on the back of my neck stands when Marissa says her name.

I ignore her mention of Jenna and move to the side and motion for her to come in. "What's going on?"

"I have some news." She puts her bag on the small table by the door and flips her long dark hair over her shoulder.

"Ok?"

She nervously switches her weight from foot to foot. "I'm pregnant."

"Congratulations." The word automatically comes flying out.

She laughs. "It's your baby, Mark. I haven't been with anyone else." I feel the earth shift, the axis tilts, or there's an earthquake. Whatever it is, the room is upside down, and this can't be a reality.

I keep my cool, even though alarm bells are going off in my head, and my legs feel like they are going to give out at any moment. "How is that possible? We used condoms, you said you were on birth control."

She shrugs her shoulders. "I guess nothing is foolproof, right?"

"I don't know what to say." I don't. I'm at a total loss for words.

"Obviously, I know that you were just killing time with me or using me to get back with Jenna, but we need to figure out how to co-parent—"

"You're keeping it?" I yell, making her jump. I'm outraged. Obviously, we took measures to prevent this for a reason.

"Of course, I am." She's shocked and hurt, and I know she had hoped for a different reaction from me, but I'm in shock, and I'm an asshole.

"Marissa, if I wanted to be a father, I would've been already. I'm not. I don't want to be. I hope you can understand that."

She swipes at tears under her eyes and grabs her bag off the table. "I thought you were different, but men are all the same." She reaches for the door, and I have a moment of humanity.

"Marissa, wait..."

She turns, and I go to her, grabbing hold of her shoulders. I hold her firmly in my hands. "I wasn't killing time or using you, it wasn't nothing. It just wasn't something sustainable for me long term. I've never stopped loving Jenna."

"I get it." She says through tears. "I get that I'm not Jenna, I just... I just thought I could give you something she couldn't."

She leaves me standing there, and for the first time since I found Jamie standing over Jenna, about to rape her, I have no desire to see Jenna, because even though I just let Marissa leave, I know I will do the right thing.

48

MARK - JULY 1999

"What do you mean she's not there?" I ask Wes over the phone. "Just what I said. She said she had to go somewhere, I thought she meant the store, but she had Big Mike drive her to the airport, and he came back solo."

"The airport!" I panic because she's without bodyguards and traveling alone.

"Yes, and before you ask, I tried to call her cell, but it's off." I run my fingers nervously through my hair, pulling on the ends as I try and think like her. *Where would she be going? Why would she run?*

"How many days did you say she has off?" I'm starting to put it all together.

"Three, the next stop was New Jersey." Bingo. *She went home.*

"I'll get her to the show." I hang up, throw some clothes and toiletries into a duffel bag, grab my keys, and run out the door.

She's already had too much of a head start, and it's almost midnight when I pull up in front of her house.

I know I won't be greeted warmly, especially at this hour, so I pull away and spend the night at a seedy motel near the beach. In the morning, I'm up and out just after sunrise and drive back to the house, pulling into the driveway. My adrenaline is pumping full force, and I quickly climb the small set of stairs and ring the doorbell very confident that she's here.

"What are you doing here?" Frank answers hastily.

"Where is she, Frank?" I'm not taking any shit from him.

"She's sleeping. Pregnancy makes a woman tired." *Shit.* She told them.

"I'd like to see her." My voice is calm, but I'm one second away from losing my shit.

He steps out onto the porch, and Maureen steps out of the kitchen and stands on the other side of the door.

"We will take care of her from here. I think you've done enough."

Is he serious? "Done enough? What's that supposed to mean?"

"How about having her on the road all the time, so your little record company gets rich off her, while you screw around. Uh, let's see what else, taking her away from her friends and family and now knocking her up." He rattles off a bullshit list.

"She's going to be an unwed mother." Maureen sobs behind the door. "My grandchild will be a bastard."

Fuck this. I push past them both and call out her name. "Jenna? Jenna!" I get to her room or what I imagine is her room because I've never been here before. I was never welcome.

"Mark?" She croaks. She's on her side half asleep, I cradle her in my arms.

"Come on Jenna. Let's go." I start to lift her up, but she pushes me off her and sits back down.

Her Father's frame fills the doorway, and I sit down next to her on the bed.

"J?" I look at her worriedly.

"I'm sorry. I just wanted to go home." She explains.

"She's done with you and the tour. Shove it up your ass, McGinley. She's home now, and that's where she's staying." Her Father once again buts in.

"Fuck you, this is my baby too, and she's not staying here."

He steps further into the room, about to pull me out. "Maureen, call the cops."

Jenna starts to cry. "Dad, just give us a minute."

He eyes us warily before retreating to the hallway, leaving the door open.

I pull her to me and hold her tight. "Why on earth would you come here?"

She shakes her head and swipes the steady stream of tears off her cheeks. Her breathing is ragged. "I'm tired all the time. I feel like shit all the time. And I'm alone all the time. I can't take it anymore. I have no friends, no family, you're not around and now this." She points to her stomach.

I close my eyes and swallow her unhappiness. "Jenna, you have to be honest with me. We are in this together."

"It doesn't feel like we're together." She whispers, and I hold her as her body racks with sobs.

"What do you want? What's the plan while you're here?" I ask trying to hold it together. I'll give her whatever she needs.

"I don't know. I just need a break. I need to think about things." I pull back to look at her.

I read between the lines, realizing what she's not saying. "You don't want the baby?"

She cries harder and shakes her head. "I'm not in a good place, I can't even take care of myself. I've been hooked on caffeine pills and chasing them with copious amounts of vodka just to get through each day, on top of the cocktail of meds."

I put my head in my hands and lean over. She's trying to detox here. I'm worried about her and the baby. "Please just come home with me. We will give it all up, live a normal life. Fuck being famous, let me take care of you. Please don't let them brainwash you." I beg.

"Sir?"

I look up at the officer standing in the doorway.

"Step out, please."

I kneel in front of her. "J, please don't make me leave without you," I beg her.

"I love you. Just give me a few weeks to wrap my head around this." She's still sobbing, and I cup her neck and pull her in for a kiss.

"It's time to go." Hands grab my arms from behind, pulling me to my feet.

"Call me when you're ready to leave, I'll come back for you," I say hoping she will change her mind any second.

Her Mother and Father walk behind me and the officer leading me to the door. Maureen is holding rosary beads, tears stream down her face as she says a prayer for each bead.

"Don't hold your breath for her to call you," Frank says as he puts his arm around Maureen, pulling her close.

I don't acknowledge them. I don't acknowledge their animosity toward my unborn child or me.

Instead, I walk down the path to my car and acknowledge my own shortcomings for not seeing Jenna's addiction, for not knowing just how much she was struggling.

I spend the next two weeks at a hotel not far from Jenna's parent's house. I'm confident she will call, and I want to be close when she does.

I cancel her upcoming tour dates, and Wes and I do damage control with the media. Then I call Max and make amends, flying him back to Jersey so he can be with her. At least she has someone there who really cares for her well-being, and thankfully he calls me every other day with updates, so I know what's going on.

I'm tortured in sleep, and I spend every waking second making moves for our future. I put an offer on a house near the water that I know she will love here in Jersey. If she wants to stay here, then I will make the move. I'll give it all up.

By the end of the third week, my patience is wearing thin, I'm beyond frustrated she hasn't called by now, and my patience is dwindling.

It's a little after three in the morning when my phone rings. I answer quickly and sit up, expecting it to be Jenna, but it's Max.

"She's asking for you." His gravelly voice says into the phone.

I rub the sleep out of my eyes and thank the universe.

"Ok, I'm on my way." I get up quickly, already putting clothes on.

"Mark," His tone changes, it's solemn, and I can hear him holding back emotion. "We're at the hospital, she's cramping and bleeding."

I run into the hospital ten minutes later. My adrenaline is through the roof, and I've never gotten anywhere so fast in my life.

Her parents and Max are standing outside the room, her Father sits when he sees me, obviously displease that I'm here, and her mother totally avoids my glare.

"What happened?" I ask Max as I try and steady my breathing.

"She woke up this way."

I put my hand on the knob, but he grabs my arm.

"She doesn't want to see anyone else but you."

I nod. "I'll let you know what's going on." I take a deep breath and step inside, closing the door behind me.

She's sitting up crying, and when she sees me, she kneels up on the bed and cries harder. I climb onto the bed and hold her, and she grabs onto me tightly, like she's falling.

I don't know what to say, so I just hold her until she calms enough to talk.

"They don't know what happened." She murmurs. I kiss her hair as I listen.

"I didn't want this." She continues. I wince thinking she's talking about the pregnancy. "I've spent the last couple of weeks falling in love, and it's gone, just like that." She snaps her fingers.

I pull back to look at her, I see the grief, my heart constricts.

"And do you know what my parents said?" Anger rolls through her tears. "They said it's an act of God, that he answered Mom's prayers. She prayed that he would take this baby, that I won't get pregnant by you again."

I try and remain stoic, unaffected by this news. "You don't believe this happened because of that, do you?"

She leans over the bed to reach the tissue box on the table. "I don't know what I believe, either she's crazy, or I am. But Mark, I swear to you that I was in a good place about this baby." She holds her hand over her stomach "I told everyone I was calling you tomorrow, well

today. I was just so exhausted before, I didn't know what I wanted."
She blows her nose and rubs her eyes.

I sit quietly. I'm overwhelmed with emotion, but I shove it down
and hold her hand as she talks because what she's feeling supersedes
anything I'm feeling.

"I hate them. I'm sorry I ever came back. You were so right. They
were trying to brainwash me."

I rub her back and hold, and an hour later, she finally falls asleep.
I sneak out to talk to Max, who tells me her parents went for breakfast. I'm grateful for that as I recount all of what Jenna just told me.
He dries each tear before it has a chance to fall and I listen as he tells
me things about her Mother, things I didn't know, including her
history of mental illness. I briefly question if her Mother did have
anything to do with the miscarriage, beyond prayers.

He pats me on the back and tells me I should take her far away
from here before he heads down the hall.

Back inside the room, I hold Jenna's hand and promise her more
babies through my own tear-filled eyes.

That's the first time I break my promise to her.

49

"Hang on, let me grab my purse." Lily and I are celebrating with a shopping spree that the first draft of my book is complete and in the hands of the editors.

She hangs by the car while I run inside my trailer. I jump when I see the silhouette on the couch. He stands and I gasp, leaping into his arms.

"Oh my god! What are you doing here?" I kiss his lips and he holds onto me like that for a minute before releasing me, he sits back down. "What's wrong?" I ask.

"Come here gorgeous." He pats the seat next to him and I giggle like a teenager and straddle his lap instead.

"I don't think it's fair, you get better looking with age. Do you know how long it takes for me look like this?" I say truthfully and he laughs then kisses me again, but his demeanor is tepid.

He's different somehow. It's been a busy three weeks for both of us, with me wrapping up the book, and the tour dates I signed on for, at the same time he's been expanding the label into Nashville.

"I need to talk to you. I've waited long enough."

I groan, because I know whatever he has to tell me isn't good. I feel it rolling off him and I try to prepare for impact. "I don't want to know. Whatever it is just fix it. I love you and I want to be with you no matter what."

He moves me off his lap and paces the floor. "Remember you said that a minute from now."

"Girl, what is taking you so long—oh..." Lily comes in and abruptly stops when she sees Mark. "I'll just wait outside." She gives me a wink and closes the door.

I laugh. "You were saying?"

"Our relationship and the universe never seem to be on the same page. I don't know why I thought this time would be any different."

My heart rate kicks up a notch. "Don't say that, we deserve another chance." I get up and put my head on his chest and link my arms behind him.

"I just want you to know how much I love you." I pull back and look into his face, which is riddled with varied emotion.

"Ok, Mark, you're scaring me."

He rubs his thumb over my lips. I press his hand against them and kiss his palm.

He looks at me with so much love, I want to stay in this moment forever, but it doesn't last. He pulls the rug out from under me. "Marissa is pregnant." I stare at him unmoving, for fear has me frozen and my heart thumps wildly against my chest. "She says it's mine."

I step backward like I've been burned and turn away from him. My head and my heart are warring over emotions.

"You were still sleeping with her?" I ask.

He turns me gently back to face him. "No, the last time was two weeks before I came to Nashville for you."

I count the weeks in my head. "Thirteen weeks?"

"Fourteen." He corrects me.

I close my eyes, this has to be a nightmare. "And you're sure it's..."

"We used protection and she told me she was on birth control, so I don't see how. My lawyer is handling it now. I'm sure you can imagine, my reaction wasn't exemplary and she's no longer speaking to me directly. The court will make her comply with my request for a paternity test." He says confidently.

I move toward the window. "I don't know what to say."

"Jenna, the ball is in your court. You tell me what you want."

"What I want?" Turning quickly, I face him then step away.

"This doesn't have to be over. This wasn't supposed to happen." He reaches for me.

"This doesn't have to be over? In what world, do you think I could watch you raise a baby with someone else?"

He drops his arms in defeat. "The same one you said a minute ago, where you love me and want me no matter what."

"That's not fair." I didn't know it was this.

"Life isn't fair J. I didn't think life was fair when you divorced me, and you didn't think life was fair through five miscarriages."

My blood is boiling. "Don't you dare." I point my finger at him, and he hangs his head.

"We can make this work J, and you know it."

"You know what I think. I think the only winner here is you."

"How so?" He asks, exasperated.

"You get it both ways. I say fine, we will make it work then you get me and the baby you've always wanted and then I'm the third wheel, in the middle of you and Marissa." I'm really trying to be rational.

"You would never be the third wheel."

I shake my head as images fill my head. "You say that now. What about birthday parties, graduations, all those milestone moments you're going to want to be there for?" I hear my voice getting louder with each syllable, the hysteria of reality is setting in. Rational goes out the window.

"So, I'll do the right thing financially, but not be involved." He counters.

"You can't do that. You know what it's like to not have a Father in your life."

"Then tell me! Tell me what you want me to do!" He shouts and tears prick my eyes.

"I want you to pick the baby. I want you to have that, because being with me forever is not guaranteed. We've screwed up before and I don't want to be the reason that you miss out on being a Father." By the time I get it all out I'm sobbing and shuddering.

He grabs my wrists and pulls me to him roughly, capturing my mouth in an all-consuming, gut wrenching kiss before he backs away. "If you change your mind, you know where I'll be."

50

"You're starting to burn."

I slide my shades down onto the bridge of my nose. "I don't burn, I turn red first, then I brown."

Mark laughs. "Ok, that's the definition of burning. Rollover, I'll rub some lotion on you."

I smile slyly, but I turn over. "I think you just want an excuse to touch me."

"Jenna, I don't need an excuse." He's so right. He's had me dozens of ways over the last four weeks, some days we didn't even leave our cabana, and I've enjoyed every second.

He spreads my legs and kneels between them as he unties the string on my bikini top and rubs suntan lotion over my hot skin.

"Do we have to leave?" I ask hoping that we can stay in the paradise that is called Aruba forever.

"No, we can stay a little while longer."

I smile at his answer. "Then what?"

He massages my shoulders with the lotion, and I close my eyes. "I think you should go back to writing music." He says it to be inspiring and motivational, but I shake my head.

"I don't think I'm ready for that." *I'm not ready for that.*

"Then, just take time off." He agrees.

I shake my head. "We've already been off for a month." I turn over and take my top all the way off.

He smiles wickedly at my breasts. "So what J. You needed a break." He lays over me. "I'll take care of you. You just worry about healing."

He never fails to amaze me.

"I love you," I say, and he leans forward to kiss me. Kissing always leads to more, but I'm ok with that, and I push down his board shorts, and lifts his hips as he helps kick them off.

His fingers stroke my sex over my bathing suit bottom. I'm instantly wet for him, and he knows it. It doesn't take much for him to arouse me, and I press my clit against his erection.

He pulls away suddenly, breaking our passionate kiss. "Marry me, J. Be mine. Don't make me wait anymore." He's watching my face intently for my reaction.

"I'm already yours." I run my hands over his tattooed chest, tracing over the hearts that are intertwined by a red ribbon.

He sits up and grabs his board shorts, carefully taking something out of the Velcro side pocket. "I'm serious. I want us to belong to each other. I want everyone to know you're mine. I need this, J." I look up to the gorgeous Azul sky, and for a minute, I think that he's just caught up in the moment until he grabs my hand and holds out a dazzling rock in front of him. "Will you marry me?"

I sit up and smile through thick tears and nod my head emphatically. "Yes." I choke out the word.

He's beaming as he slides the three-carat princess cut solitaire on my finger, then pulls me to him. Crushing me against his chest, whispering promises to take care of me forever while we make love on the lounge chair until the sun sets, and my growling stomach can no longer be ignored.

"You like it?" He asks, as I hold my hand in front of the candle that's illuminating our dinner for two.

"I love it. I'm glad it's finally on my finger, how long have you been carrying it around?"

"Long enough. It's been one thing after another, the timing was never right."

Not after I ruined his last attempt to propose. I frown, remembering how things always get in the way of us. I look up and watch the palm trees swaying lazily in the ocean breeze. "I don't want to wait," I say decidedly, and he looks up at me, confused, so I keep going. "I want to get married as soon as possible. I don't need a huge wedding."

"Isn't that every girl's dream?" He cuts into his steak as I press my fork over each piece but not actually eating anything.

"Maybe. But they don't have to contend with the paparazzi."

"What do you have in mind?"

I sit back and watch as the light dances off the diamond. "A small wedding, just our friends. We should do it here."

"What about your parents?" I love him for asking, but he's lost his mind.

I lean forward and put my elbows on the table, resting my hands under my chin. "No. Absolutely not! They can read about it in a magazine."

"Jenna... I know what just happened, but down the road, you might regret not inviting them."

I stand abruptly. My chair scrapes loudly against the concrete as I push it back. "Then, there is no wedding." I start back toward the path that leads to our cabana.

"Wait, J." He runs after me.

I keep going until he grabs my elbow and spins me around.

"Do you think that I really care if you don't invite them? Trust me, I don't, but if you wanted to invite them, then I would deal with it."

"No. What parents wish horrible things on their child, let alone an unborn baby."

His expression softens. "Come here. They won't hurt us ever again." He wraps his arms around me and leads me back to our cabana, where I fall asleep in the safety net of his arms.

The next morning an entire wedding team descends upon the cabana to help me plan. Mark handles calling our friends and making their travel plans with the resort, and in less than forty-eight hours, we have the entire thing arranged for the day after tomorrow.

"Mark?" We're lying in the hammock, on the porch. "Do you believe in God?" I ask, tentatively.

"I don't know. I think there is some spiritual being, something bigger than all of us. Why do you ask?"

"My mom is so crazed that I think it scared me away from religion. I was just wondering what you thought."

"I used to be really angry about my parents dying so young. I blamed God for a long time, so maybe I'm not the best person to ask." He confesses.

"I'm sorry about your parents. I wish I could've met them. Hopefully, they would've liked me." I imagine what his parents were like.

"They would've loved you." He kisses the top of my head, and we fall asleep like that under the stars.

<hr>

"I can't believe you're getting married today." Max dabs his eyes with a handkerchief.

"I am so glad you're here. I've been a horrible friend lately."

He waves his hand like he's swatting a bug. "Don't worry about it, I knew you would come back around. Besides Mark and I made up, it's all good."

"Everything will be different. You won't be my roommate." I say forlorn.

"Like you were there so often." He laughs, and I playfully smack his arm.

Hair and makeup work on me as Max and I sip mimosas and reminisce on our childhood, my first encounter with Mark, and the fun times that we've had on the road.

The conversation is so light and happy that I momentarily forget about the miscarriage, the grief associated with it, and the fact my Father won't be here to walk me down the aisle. Even though I vehemently didn't want him here, it's still casting a shadow on this day.

"Jenna," The door opens a crack, and the wedding planner peeks her head in, I wave for her to come in. "Will you be ready in five?"

"I'm ready now." I stand in a gorgeous Max-approved white dress with a deep V neckline. The top is covered in beads and lace, and the bottom is all tulle that flows gracefully as I walk in my strappy, white peep-toe heels. My hair is pulled half up with an exotic flower pinned behind my ear.

"Alright, well, let's get you married."

Max goes ahead of us, and I follow her down the hall that will lead us out toward the beach where there is a canopy and hundreds of flowers placed strategically among our closest friends.

No one else is expecting us to get married, so there won't be any uninvited guests.

I pause at the door. My breathing quickens, my pulse is racing.

"Ok, they're ready." The planner says I hear the piano and violins, but I can't move.

I'm frozen.

"I—I just need a minute."

She whispers something I can't make out into a microphone on her blazer. I hear the music stop.

I bend over and take a few cleansing breaths before I start hyperventilating, and in a few minutes, the nerves pass, and I focus on breathing normally.

"Ok. I'm ready." I say, recovering.

I hear the music restart. I put on my celebrity smile and exit gracefully through the doors as I walk toward the man who loves me more than anything.

Our friends are seated except for Jamie and Max, who are standing on either side of Mark.

When Mark sees me his eyes glitter, and I know he's holding back tears, he doesn't take his eyes off me, and I feel safe as I continue down the aisle.

He's wearing tan linen pants, an untucked white collared shirt, and he's barefoot. He looks insanely handsome, and I can't believe he's all mine, well almost.

When I'm finally in front of him, he gives me a once over, and the corners of his mouth turn up. The way he's looking at me makes me bite my lip. I feel his stare between my legs.

"You look... gorgeous." He whispers seductively.

I smile and wink at him. "You don't look so bad yourself."

The officiant starts, and we join hands as we say our vows. Mark goes first.

"I spent so many years wondering if there was someone out there for me, but no one ever caught my attention. Then you showed up, and I was mesmerized by you, and I knew that all those years I was waiting for you.

I'm so glad you showed up, J. I love you more than I thought humanly possible, no one can hurt us, and I promise, that you will be first, always."

I swipe at an errant tear that has escaped, despite my best efforts to contain it. I clear my throat, and every word I had memorized now seems insignificant at this moment. So, I wing it.

"I thought you hated me. When we first met you were so cold and indifferent toward me, and it was like that for so long, that I wanted to leave, but I didn't want to prove you right, that I was just a bratty kid. And if anyone told me that years later, I'd be standing here with you, like this, I would've said they were crazy.

But then you gave in, you changed, and you let yourself fall in love with me, and I failed you so many damn times, and I'm so sorry.

I don't ever want to fail you again, so I promise to be the strong person you think I am. The person that's only strong when you're by my side. Thank you for loving me."

He drops my hands and pulls my hips to him as he kisses me tenderly.

The officiant clears his throat and hands each of us our wedding bands, and we take turns sliding them onto each other's fingers.

I look down at my hand, and I'm beaming like a beacon of light in a storm. I feel grounded and secure for the first time in a long time.

An hour later, Mark is leisurely leading me around the small dance floor for our first dance.

"Look at your ring," I whisper to him. He slows but doesn't stop as he looks from me to the band on his finger. "Inside." I clarify.

He stops and slides the ring off his finger, turning it until he sees the inscription.

"I'm yours forever." He reads out loud before slipping it safely back onto his finger. He pulls me close and holds onto me tighter than ever before as if I will float away.

51

The liquid burns on the way down. I'm not proud of myself right now, but I let it slide because I did a good deed.

I gave a child a father, when all I really wanted to do was be selfish and say pick me.

I take another swig from the bottle and hold it up. It's almost empty. I know I'm over doing it since I haven't had a drink in so long, but I don't care. I'm weak. I'm desperate. Desperate to numb, desperate to forget. No session with Dr. Wild will fix me right now.

After Mark left, I told Lily we would go shopping another time, that I didn't feel well.

Then I came back to the hotel, ordered a bottle of vodka from room service and am currently drowning any semblance of a feeling that pops up.

There's a knock at my door. "Dammit." I get up and stagger over to the door, looking through the peep hole.

I swing the door open. "Hi."

Jace stares at me like he's never seen me before. *I must look like hell.* "Everything ok?" He asks and I hold up the bottle of vodka.

"It is now." I hiccup and cover my mouth and a fit of giggles ensues.

"Jesus, give me that." He takes the bottle from my hand and sets it on the table. "What are you doing?"

I shrug. I don't know what I'm doing. "Ruining my life."

"Any reason why?" He asks, treading lightly, unsure of what to do.

I shrug again and sway. Jace grabs my arm and pulls me over to the couch.

"I got back together with Mark." I explain.

"That's great! When?"

"A few months ago."

He looks at me quizzical.

"I didn't tell anyone. It was a secret." I whisper.

"So, you're drinking because..."

I scoff as if I expect him to already know. "He got Miss Perfect pregnant."

He removes his hat and runs his fingers through his hair. "Oh boy, and Miss Perfect isn't you, is it?"

I shake my head wildly back and forth. "It's my fault anyway." The words come out slurred but I'm sure they make sense.

"I can't wait to hear this one. How is it your fault he got someone pregnant?"

"Before we got back together, I told him to move on. He did, or at least thought he did and BAM!" I slam my hands together. "Now she's pregnant, despite birth control and condoms."

"That doesn't give guys much hope huh?"

I look up at him trying to figure out if he's joking or not. I reach for the bottle again, but he swipes it before I can get my hand around it. "I just need one night, please. I will stop tomorrow."

He shakes his head. "Come on cowgirl. I'll put you to bed." He helps me up and I hold onto his shoulders.

"Jace, please. I gave myself one night to lose it. I've gone on a bender before and then didn't drink for weeks. I need this, it hurts."

He's not giving in. "Nothing you drink tonight, will make it hurt any less tomorrow."

Dammit. I know he's right. I groan and climb into bed dropping sideways onto the pillow.

He sits next to me on the bed and leans against the headboard.

I turn and look up at him confused. "You're staying?"

"I'll make sure you don't choke on your own vomit."

"I don't think you have to worry about that, I'm a champion."

"Wow, that's something to brag about. I'll just stay till you fall asleep then."

I roll my eyes but don't argue. "Why did you come by anyway?"

"We'll talk tomorrow, it's not important."

I sit up defiantly. "Tell me. I'm curious now." He sighs and rubs his eyes.

"I was going to ask you to go with me to the Country Music Awards. It's a little short notice, but I'm up for male vocalist of the year. It would be good for you but obviously, I didn't know you were with Mark." He looks at me apologetically. "Or not, but don't worry about it."

"I'll go." I say because I don't have anything else to look forward to and Jace has been good to me since the scandalous on-stage kiss.

"Don't answer now, it will just be an alcohol induced commitment." I lay back down and clutch the pillow tightly.

"I'll still say yes in the morning."

"Ok, cowgirl."

"JENNA. JENNA, WAKE UP." I hear whispering over the throbbing headache. I sit up on my elbow and look at Lily who has three heads right now. "What are you doing?" She's still whispering, which I'm grateful for at this moment but not understanding why. She points behind me. Jace is next to me in the bed on his side with his arm draped over my hip.

"Oh." I sit up and he stretches and rolls onto his back. "This is not what it looks like." I defend myself quickly.

She stands with her arms folded over her chest. "Jenna Foster, what did you do?"

I slide out from under the covers and pull her over to the living room area. "This looks a lot worse than it is. I may have been a bad girl, but I didn't sleep with Jace. Well not in the traditional sense obviously."

"Explain."

"Marissa is pregnant. Mark is the father. I freaked out. Drank a lot of vodka. Jace took the bottle away. Put me to bed, obviously he fell asleep. The end. Now you're all caught up."

She looks like she's going to hit me. "I can't believe you were drinking!"

"That's what you take away from this?"

"Yes, you were almost sober a year!" She throws her hands in the air.

"I know Lily, I'm aware. But I am human." I drop down on the couch.

"Ok, go back to Marissa." Her voice softens and I tell her everything Mark told me. She sighs disappointed. "So now what?" She takes a seat next to me.

"I told him to choose the baby."

She glares at me. "Why on earth would you do that."

"Uh, what choice did I have?"

She shakes her head emphatically. "You chose for him."

I scoff. *Like I wanted to give him up all over again.* "No," I continue to argue. "I gave him the greatest gift."

"Your love is his gift."

Is she always this relentless and argumentative? "Lily, I love him enough to let him go."

"That doesn't sound like love, it sounds like a selfish choice because it's too hard for you. You think you're being selfless by choosing for someone else but it's not, it's running, when he can have both."

I glare at her. I need to make her understand. "No. I can't watch the love of my life raising a child that's not ours. Maybe if I could have children I would feel differently. In my eyes she has the upper hand."

"Upper hand? The child holds all the cards. She will always be the other woman and now, the only thing she has is a baby and a father who doesn't want her."

"Don't be so sure about that." I wallow in self-pity.

She stands and heads toward the door. "Jenna, circumstances in life don't give you a pass to be selfish. You could make it work. This was an excuse for you to go back on your sobriety. And for the love of God, get Jace out of your bed. With your luck, Mark will see him here. Oh, and your video appointment with Dr. Wild is today." She leaves and slams the door.

I rub my temples, the hangover headache is settling in.

"You think she believes you?" Jace startles me.

"Oh, hey." I swipe self-consciously at my face and hair, surely, I look like hell. "Believe me about what?"

"Us not sleeping together."

I shrug. "Sure."

He leans against the wall. "She's right though."

"Excuse me?" I stand defensively.

"If you really love him, make it work."

"That's easier said than done."

He shrugs his shoulders. "I don't know either of you that well, but I see how he looks at you."

I look down. "Sometimes things work out for the best."

He nods sympathetically. "I'm gonna take off, you need anything?"

I shake my head and walk him to the door. "My answer is still yes by the way."

He grabs the nearly empty bottle of vodka and opens the door. He winks and smiles, a heart melting smile. "Ok cowgirl, see you later then."

52

"The last two months were heaven," I tell Max as we lay on the L shaped leather sofa in Mark's—now my—living room.

"I bet it's nice not having to face reality."

I look over at him and sit up on my elbow. "He still hasn't called?"

Max had been seeing someone who subsequently hasn't called him in over two weeks.

"He won't. He was still in the closet."

I make a pouty face at him and lay back down. "I think I'm going to go on the road with Mark, their new tour is starting soon." My voice sounds devoid of emotion, which wasn't what I was going for. I'm trying to sound cheery and happily married.

Max knows me better than that.

"Why? Don't you want to do your own thing?"

I think before I answer him. I was fine—no, more than fine while we were away, but now that we're here, I can't help but feel melancholy, and I'm not sure if it's because Mark has been busy or just because we left paradise. "Being here, I feel locked away. I can't go outside alone, and if I go out, I take the chance of someone noticing." I hold up my left hand and spin the diamond to where it should sit on my finger.

"Are you regretting it?" Max wonders aloud.

I sit up and head to the fridge, pulling the bottle of vodka out of the freezer. "Regretting what?"

Max sits at the island while I pour each of us a glass. "Getting married."

"Of course not." I say quickly, maybe too quickly.

"Then why are you hugging a bottle of Grey Goose at eleven in the morning?"

I sigh loudly and blow out a breath. "Mark thinks we should try for another baby. He thinks we should move on from what happened."

"And..."

We clink our glasses together.

"I just can't get past it. I'm numbing with vodka. I wasn't expecting to get pregnant, and yes, initially, I was unhappy about it, but I think that's why I'm having such a hard time now." I admit.

"Maybe you should see a therapist. Talk it out, I'm sure a lot of women go through these feelings."

I take a sip from the glass. "Honestly. It's easier not to talk about it. I'll get over it soon enough."

He shrugs. "Ok... If you say so." He stands. "I'm gonna get out of here, I have an interview at the studio today."

"I could just make a call, you know, then you wouldn't have to interview." Max wants this job more than anything. I could get it for him by simply calling.

He nods. "I know, but I want to make it on my own."

I know that feeling better than anyone, but still, I shrug because I want to help my best friend. "Ok, suit yourself." I walk him to the door, kiss his cheek, and once he heads down the driveway in his beat-up Honda, I run back to the kitchen and dial the studio manager from the cordless phone. *What good is being famous if I can't help my best friend out?*

I hang up just as Mark comes in. "Hey, beautiful."

"Hi," I say with a smile because he's home much sooner than I thought. "You're early."

He wraps his arms around me, and I inhale him, the pheromones intoxicating my senses. "We have plans."

"Oh?" I kiss his neck, hoping that we're on the same page and we will land in bed.

"We're going out." He announces.

I tense and back away, my posture is defensive as I put my hands on my hips and stare back at him incredulously.

He's appalled by my reaction. "We're not caged animals, Jenna. We can go out."

I storm off into the bedroom and slam the door.

Mark follows behind me. "Why is it every time I say we're going out, you act like I'm a leper and you can't be seen with me."

I slam things around the room and pace the floor. "I don't know, why don't you ask Jerry. He's ruined me ever being comfortable with you in public." The rumors about us are overwhelming, invasive, and I'm paranoid.

"J, that was years ago and a much different situation."

"You came up to me on that beach, and I stuck up for you. You let me flounder."

He rakes his fingers through his hair. "What did you want me to tell him? That I was ten seconds from taking you back in the house and having sex with you, an intoxicated, underage teen—who, by the way, came onto me."

"Yes, because you were a prick to me!"

He starts laughing uncontrollably.

"What?" I shout, but he only continues in his fit of laughter, which makes me even madder. "Seriously?" I start toward the bath-room, but he grabs my arm.

"No one has ever said that they wanted me because I was a prick to them."

"You're an asshole."

"An incredibly handsome asshole?" He grins and pulls me into him, and I soften. "You're mine, J. I want the world to know it. I can't control what they will write about us, but you can be sure that I will take care of you."

Damn him. He breaks me down every time. "What should I wear?" I concede to his plan.

He kisses the tip of my nose. "Whatever you want to wear while bowling."

"Bowling?" I stare at him increduously.

"Problem?" He asks, but I smile affectionately and flirtatiously at my husband because I'm about to kick his ass.

"I'm a novice, you may have to help me."

He throws me down on the bed. "I think I can handle standing close behind you and teaching you the fine art of bowling."

"Great. Now make love to me." This is where we excel. No matter what the fight is, we come back to each other here, between the sheets.

"I thought you'd never ask."

An hour and a half later, I step out of the shower and put on a tight-fitting t-shirt and a pair of jeans. I throw my hair up into a messy bun and lightly apply some makeup while I replay our fight over in my head. It gets me thinking about something Mark said, and an idea hits me, and for the second time today, I run to the phone.

Wes picks up on the third ring, and I ceremoniously tell him the favor I'm in desperate need of and then skip down the stairs to where Mark is waiting for me.

Luckily, we get into the bowling alley undetected, despite this being a popular celebrity spot. We stop and talk to a few people we know and then head to our lane. Mark quickly learns that I am not a novice bowler, and I start trash talking. We are laughing and carefree, and I'm having a great time.

"You never cease to amaze me," He kisses me tenderly after I beat him at a third game. "Is there anything you aren't good at, Mrs. McGinley?"

There's a list miles long, but I let him fantasize about my abilities while I run to the ladies' room.

A gentleman is standing next to the men's room. I just know he's a photographer, but he doesn't appear to have a camera on him. I play it cool and head into the bathroom.

By the time I come out, the man is gone, and I quickly head back to Mark. It's now or never. I grab Mark's shirt on each side and pull him to me. "Take me home," I whisper flirtatiously enough, so he gets the hint, and within five minutes, we are heading toward the exit, where I already know we will be swarmed with sleuthing paparazzi who got a tip a few hours ago about a newlywed celebrity couple.

The moment the door opens, the onslaught begins. Mark quickly pulls me toward the car, but I grab onto his arm to slow our pace. He glances at me nervously, but we don't speak. Instead, I stop and turn, flashing a tooth baring grin while holding up my left hand. The flashes of the cameras and a swarm of questions surround us.

Mark grabs my hand and pulls me close, settling his hands on my hips. He kisses me quickly before we run off to the car, getting in quickly and speeding off before anyone can follow us.

Once we are out of sight and far enough down the road, he turns toward me at a red light. "What did you do?"

I smirk and shrug my shoulders. "You said you wanted the world to know and that we couldn't control what they write about us. I just wanted to make sure we had a little input. I pulled the band-aid off."

He laughs and shakes his head. "See, you never cease to amaze me." I smile and he grabs my hand, bringing it to his lips and tenderly kissing my knuckles.

"I hope I never disappoint."

53

"This is the one." I step out of the dressing room in a pale pink, beaded gown that flows down to my feet, the dress is sheer except for the bodice, which barely covers the top of my thigh. The sleeves are long and it's fitting in all the right places and I just *have* to wear this one.

We're back in Nashville for the award ceremony and I've tried on close to thirty gowns and despite the selection, I haven't felt right until this moment.

"Damn Girl." Lily says behind me. I lift my hair up and then let it fall around my shoulders. "Leave it down." She says.

"I'm actually nervous." I shake out my hands.

"Well you better squash those nerves because hair and makeup are on their way."

"Ok unzip me." I turn so she can help me, then I sit on the couch while I wait for the beauty team. I grab my phone and open my contacts. My finger hovers over Mark's name but instead I press my Dad. It rings five times before he finally picks up.

"Jenna." He says adoringly.

"Hey Dad."

"What's up sweetie?"

I twirl a piece of my hair around my finger. "I'm getting ready, T-minus four hours to red carpet."

"I'm so happy you're performing again. You were born to be a star."

I roll my eyes. He always says that. "Dad, I have to ask you something. It's for the book and it's something I've always wondered. I want to be honest and transparent."

"What is it?" He asks hesitantly.

I take a deep breath and blow it out slowly. "How come you never liked Mark? I guess specifically, what couldn't you get past?"

The other end is so quiet I check to make sure the call didn't drop. "Jenna..."

"Dad... just give it to me straight. Was there a reason? Did he do something?"

He sighs. "Mostly, it was the age difference. His persona didn't help, the things I saw in the magazines about him being with a different girl every week, I held everything against him. I was over-protective of my little girl and I just didn't think he was right for you. He stole a piece of your youth."

I consider his words. "You told him he would ruin me. Do you blame him for me becoming an alcoholic?"

"Honestly, no. I think the lifestyle was to blame. I never lived through it and I can't imagine the pressure everyone put on you. I never understood then that Mark was the one that kept you grounded."

My mouth hangs open. "Wow, that almost sounded like a compliment."

"Yeah, well, I don't think we will play a round of golf together any time soon, but I—I wish sometimes that things would have worked out for you and him. I know he took care of you and made you happy, most of the time. I just didn't understand it back then."

I smile and know that I need to ask the one question that's bothered me since the first miscarriage. "I know this sounds silly, but I always blamed the miscarriages on Mom, that she prayed for them so much that they happened. It always felt like there was a curse on me."

"Your Mom was sick, Jenna. I wish I had taken care of her, like Mark took care of you." His voice is thick, on the edge of breaking.

I blink quickly trying to hold back the tears. "Dad? What would you say if I told you that Mark and I got back together, but that it's a very complicated situation?"

"I'd say that I'm not surprised. He was always chasing you, every time you would run, he would find you, maybe he loved you too much. Remember something Jenna, nothing is perfect, but failure is better than fear."

I smile, my heart feels a million times lighter. "You just gave me a great idea. Love you Dad, I gotta go."

"JENNA! JACE! OVER HERE!" Photographers line the red carpet and Jace leads me through the chaos with his arm around my waist. It's been a long time since I attended an award show but it's very much the same, with the photographers and interviews and people asking what designer I'm wearing.

I don't want to take any attention away from Jace so when he's being interviewed, I step back.

He pulls me in to pose for picture after picture and people shout questions at us in hopes that we answer. Most are only interested if we are a couple.

I hate to give off the wrong impression, but I'm beaming, and it has nothing to do with the handsome man who has his arm linked through mine.

We take our seats and I squeeze Jace's hand for good luck. The show is great, I'm enjoying every minute, and when they call Jace as the winner for male vocalist of the year I stand and hug him, and he kisses my cheek.

When the show ends, I talk to a few other well-known country singers while I wait for Jace. My phone buzzes, I pull it out and head outside so I can hear Lily on the other end.

"You killed it with that dress. Social media is buzzing about it."

I laugh. "Well I'm so glad that I picked it then."

"That's not why I called. I just found out some very interesting information. Did you know Mark is living in Nashville?"

My heart is beating a million times faster than it should be. "Are you sure? How do you know?"

I can feel her tension through the phone. "He bought the house. Your house. As in the one you put an offer on two days ago."

I gasp. "Are you sure?"

"A hundred percent. I just saw the realtor and he told me. He asked if you were back together."

I see Jace out of the corner of my eye. "Lily, I have to go."

"Have fun at the after party—"

I hang up before she finishes and grab Jace's arm. "Would you be upset with me if I were a horrible date and ditched you."

He laughs. "Not at all, everything ok?"

"Yeah, there's just somewhere I have to be."

He winks knowingly. "Go ahead cowgirl."

I congratulate him again and head off to the waiting limo.

I google the nearest church and ask the driver to take me there. I stand outside and look up at the gothic exterior, doubting myself, now that I'm actually here.

Talking to my Dad before, the idea dawned on me that if my Mom thought her prayers were heard when she wanted something, then maybe I could pray for something and be heard too.

I ask the driver to wait for me and walk up the steps, pulling on the old-fashioned brass handle attached to the old white door that creaks open, the white paint peeling.

It's late and I'm obviously alone, yet I don't feel alone. It's been so long since I've prayed, but I kneel before the alter the best I can in this dress, just like Mom used to, then I take a seat in the first pew. I fold my hands, close my eyes, and say everything I came here to say.

The angry words, the sad words, and my hope for the future. I'm in and out in ten minutes, feeling renewed as if divine intervention could easily solve all my problems that quickly. I exhale a breath and climb back into the limo.

Fifteen minutes later, the driver pulls in front of *the* house. I step out into the cool November night, I shiver and pull the fur stole around my shoulders tighter. I turn and watch the limo as he heads back down over the gravel drive, dust floating up into the night sky. There's a black luxury sedan in the driveway, but the house is otherwise dark.

I walk the short distance to the front door and ring the bell. I'm nervous that Lily was misinformed when there's no answer. "Shit." I say, struggling to pull my phone out of my small evening bag when the door opens.

Mark stands surprised in the doorway. He looks extremely handsome in only a black t-shirt and sweatpants that hang daringly low on his hips, his hair is a sexy mess.

"You're here." I say in disbelief a little above a whisper.

On the way over here, I had several theories on why he bought the house, but I didn't truly believe that I would actually find him here.

"Are you happy or mad?" He eyes me carefully.

"Depends. Why did you buy the house?"

He steps onto the porch. We're mere inches from each other. "You always had good taste in real estate. Expensive taste, I should say."

I smirk and nod, I can't argue there. "Location, location, location."

"I promised to give you everything. I fantasized about us building something here, something unbreakable. That was obviously before I found out about Marissa and the baby. I guess I was hoping there was still a small chance."

I close the gap between us, pressing myself against him, I hold onto his shoulders. "I called my Dad today. I needed to fill in some gaps for the book. I asked him why he never liked you."

"Oh, this should be good." He says sarcastically and I see the surprise in his eyes as I move my hands lower wrapping my arms around his waist.

"He said you loved me too much."

He rolls his eyes and his arms encircle me tighter. "Is that even a valid reason not to like someone?"

"He said I always ran from you, that you were always chasing me. I thought he was crazy, but then I realized, he was right.

I always let failure and fear win and I *was* always running. I realized that's what I'm doing now and I'm tired of running.

I want you Mark, even if this is the hardest thing I ever do. I trust you to take care of my heart. So, I decided I would turn the tables this time. I would've gone to the end of the earth to find you tonight."

54

I climb over her sleeping body and tenderly kiss her lips. She stirs but doesn't wake, exhausted from the hours I spent inside her, but it's Christmas morning, and I can't wait to give her my presents.

I kiss her neck, over her collar bone, and gently caress her nipples with my fingers before taking each one in my mouth.

She moans, and her eyes flutter open. "You're a machine." She says but does nothing to deter me from her body.

"Only for you Jenna. Always, for you." I kiss over her stomach and down to the apex of her thighs, where I settle between her legs and lick her seam.

She sighs and moans, and before long, she shudders and sags against the mattress. "Was that my Christmas present?" She smirks.

"Maybe." I joke and reach over the side of the bed, grabbing the two small wrapped boxes from the table.

She sits up, and I hand one to her, watching as she eagerly unwraps it.

She gasps and lifts the glass ornament out of the tissue paper, holding it in front of her.

"Our first Christmas, 1999." She reads out loud and runs her fingers over the ornament couple holding tightly to each other as they kiss.

"I love it." She says hugging it, and I hand her the other box.

"This one is even better." I smile.

Again, she quickly unwraps the small box to find a cassette tape. She looks at me curiously. "A mixtape?"

"I've been compiling it for a while. Each song reminds me of you, of us, of how you make me feel."

"I can't wait to listen to it, but first..." She kneels and throws her arms around my neck and kisses me before she leans over and pulls something from her night table drawer. "I feel silly now. I wasn't as creative as you."

I kiss her back for good measure. I don't need a gift from her, she's the only thing I want.

She hands me a gold box. I slide the silver ribbon off, lifting the lid quickly and fold the tissue paper back to find a small square white envelope. I look at her, she's glowing with excitement before I flip it over to open it, pulling out a black and white square. My head snaps up to her and then back down to study it. "You're..." I'm scared to say the words.

She shrugs, like it's no big deal. "Yes."

"For real?"

"For real."

With tears in my eyes, I clutch her to my chest, and she sobs. I pull back and stare at the black and white square admiring the jelly-bean shape that is our baby.

"The book says he's the size of a prune."

I laugh and move to sit next to her, pulling her close to me. "He? Isn't it too early to tell?"

"Just a feeling."

I kiss her hair, and we fall asleep again until noon when the phone wakes us.

She leans over and answers. "Merry Christmas." She says, but it's reluctant. I sit up at attention and try to hear who's on the other end, but she doesn't give me any clues, and I can't hear.

"I'm sorry to hear that." Her voice is distant and cold, and she hangs up and stares into space.

"J?" She looks up at me, and tears drop down onto her cheeks. "What is it?"

"My Mom called me, on Christmas, to tell me Rocky died." *Shit. Her dog.* She swings the covers off and pads to the bathroom, disappearing behind the door.

I listen to see if she's coming right back. When she doesn't, I grab the cordless and dial the number to her parent's house. Her mother answers on the third ring.

"Maureen, it's Mark. Yeah, Mark, your daughter's Husband. Listen, I don't know if you've heard the expression, timing is everything, but maybe you could've waited till, I don't know, tomorrow to call Jenna about Rocky." I reprimand her.

She spews off some unintelligible reason for ruining her daughter's Christmas with the news of her dead dog.

"Don't call here again, she has nothing to say to you." I hang up and knock on the bathroom door, but she doesn't respond. I try the handle, and it turns, so I push it open.

I find her standing at the sink, splashing cold water over her face. I move behind her, letting my hands rest on her shoulders. She turns into me, and her shoulders heave as she sobs.

"I'm sorry, J. Tell me what to do."

She shakes her head. "I don't know. I'm all over the place right now. I'm sad and angry and..." She puts her hand over her stomach. "Hungry. Really fucking hungry."

I laugh then wrap her in her robe before pulling her out to the living room and onto the couch. I wrap a blanket around her shoulders and pop a VHS into the VCR.

We stay like that, sharing a stack of pancakes and bacon as *Home Alone* plays, me absentmindedly stroking her hair.

When the movie is over, I turn her head to me. "Do you want me to tell everyone not to come over?"

She shakes her head. "No, I'm not going to let anything ruin this. We've been looking forward to this for so long."

She heads into the bedroom to get ready, and I don't see her again until our friends start to arrive. She emerges from the bedroom in a gorgeous red mini dress that hangs off-shoulder, the three-quarter sleeves flare out at the elbows, and the bottom of the dress has ruffles that flow around her thighs. My eyes drop to the floor, to the silver sparkle platform heels that make my Wife four inches taller than normal. I'm completely enamored with her and jealous that I have to share her with our guests.

"Good thing, I'm tall," I say, which makes her smile, and I kiss her cheek. "You're glowing." I observe.

"I feel fat." She whines.

I place my hand over her stomach, and she looks at me worriedly. "Everything will be fine. I promise."

She nods, and we head into the living room to greet everyone.

We're seated at the table when Jenna stands and clinks her glass, all eyes go to her, and she's flawless standing there, I've never seen a more beautiful human being.

"I just wanted to thank you all for sharing in our first married Christmas together. This year has been extremely difficult for me, and I just want to thank all of you for being there and understanding." She swallows back tears, and I stand and hold her from behind for support. "Anyway, I gave Mark his present earlier, and I just wanted to share it with all of you, our close friends, before you see it on the cover of a magazine. I'm pregnant!" She blurts out.

Everyone erupts into a fit of clapping and chatter and hugging us both. The buzz around the room distracts our guests, and I grab Jenna, and we slip out onto the balcony.

She puts her arms around me, and I pull her close, breathing in her scent as the ocean rolls in the background.

"I'm still going on tour with you." Her tone is resolute.

I look down at her. Her jaw is set in a tight line.

"Are you sure that's a good idea? You exhausted yourself traveling last time."

"Yes, but I was the one performing. You'll be doing all the work. I'll be fine."

I step back and sit down on the sofa, clasping my hands in front of me. "You know I want you with me. I just want you to take care of yourself."

She crosses her arms over her chest. "I said I'll be fine."

"Ok," I throw my hands up because her mind is already made up, and there's no point in ruining our perfect Christmas. "Come on, let's go back in."

"Congrats, man!" Jamie slaps me on the back when we reappear and hugs and kisses Jenna on the cheek before Max pulls her excitedly into the kitchen.

I sit across from Jamie and lean over. "She still wants to come on the tour." Even just saying those words, this feeling of dread comes over me.

"She's fine. It was just a freak thing last time. Quit getting your panties in a knot." He jokes.

I laugh it off, and he punches me in the arm, but the intense feeling keeps me in a mood for the rest of the evening.

"You're acting funny," Jenna says as I put the last of the dishes into the dishwasher.

"Am I?" I dry my hands on the towel near the sink and lean against the counter.

"You don't want me following you on tour?" She questions.

"That's not it."

"Then?"

I could lie, I could act tough and brush this feeling off, but I can't where Jenna is concerned. "I'm scared," I admit and immediately feel relief sharing such a simple truth with her.

"Me too. But I think we can compromise." She runs her fingers over my arms. "I need you. You keep me grounded."

I shake my head. "How on earth can I say no to you?"

She smiles, and I'm done for, which was probably her plan all along.

55

MARK - NOVEMBER 2015

We're standing on the front porch, the air is chilly, and I lean my forehead against hers. I can't believe she's saying everything I want her to. Words that I damn well know, I could never say if things were reversed. "I wouldn't blame you for running this time. I could never watch you having another man's baby."

"If you asked me to walk away so you can be with her, I will, but I won't just leave this time."

I grab her hand and squeeze. "You know I don't want anyone else, baby or not."

She grabs the ring around my neck and spins it between her fingers. "Good, because I'm yours." She smiles wickedly, her hazel eyes shining in the moonlight.

I smirk. "You want to see your house or what?" She grins, and I lead her inside.

She skips excitedly through the wrought iron doors and stops in the foyer to take it all in. "Don't worry, I didn't make any changes." The house is empty, save the four-post bed in the master bedroom.

She drops my hand as she heads down the hallway and into the gourmet country style kitchen. Her energy is infectious, and I pick her up and spin her around quickly before sitting her on the countertop. She freezes when she sees a bottle of whiskey on the counter. She looks from it to me as if it's poison. "I didn't know you were coming." I offer apologetically and immediately move to pour it down the drain.

She grabs my arm. "Don't." She looks at me with fierce determination. I slide the bottle toward the back of the counter and scoop her up, her legs go around my waist, and I make a mental note to get rid of it later.

She links her hands around my neck as I take us to the first-floor master suite and set her down, so she's standing in front of me. "Turn around." As gorgeous as she is in this dress, I want her out of it. Now.

I tug the zipper down. The slight exposure of her creamy skin makes my dick twitch. I slide the shoulders down and let the dress pool to the floor.

She turns, and her arms encircle my waist, tears shimmer in her eyes. "I don't want to lie to you by omission. I had a little setback," She sniffles. "The night you told me, about the baby, I wasn't in a good place, and I gave in, I was drowning."

A setback. I nod. I'm extremely proud of her, but I don't want it to come out condescending, so I don't make excuses for her. "Are you back on track?"

"One-hundred percent."

"Good." I grab the back of her neck and pull her in for a kiss. She holds onto my biceps as my tongue explores her mouth, and I lift her onto the bed. She falls back, pulling me down with her, kissing me with equal fervor of need and want, matching my own.

She pushes at my shoulders until I flip onto my back so that she's sitting astride me and leans forward, gently biting my earlobe before she moves lower, kissing and nipping my neck, my nipples and down my stomach.

I groan when she stops, standing before me, and I lift my hips so she can slide down my sweatpants and boxer briefs.

My cock springs free, and I growl as she wraps her hand around me, lowering her mouth over the crown, swirling her tongue around the tip. Her mouth is so damn good, and my orgasm is building fast, but I'm not done with her, so I sit up and pull her on top of me.

She settles herself comfortably over me and rides my cock with such intensity. She's lost in the moment, and I'm in awe watching her.

Her body shudders, and she cries a feral sound, her climax rolling right into a second one. She calls my name, and hearing it roll off her lips is enough to send me over the edge.

She falls on top of my chest, both of us panting. I roll us over, so I'm on top, gently kissing the tip of her nose. She closes her eyes and swallows hard.

"I'm not done loving you," I say, growing hard inside her again.

"Good." And its hours before we fall asleep in each other's arms.

I wake to the sound of obnoxious noises coming from down the hall. I sit up quickly and realize I'm alone in bed. I check the bathroom, but there's no sign of Jenna, so I scoop up my clothes, throw them on and head out toward the noise.

There's a team of people working around the house. Some painting, some cleaning, and some delivering furniture.

I stop when I see her in the midst of delegating, wearing one of my t-shirts tied off at the side and a tight pair of her jeans, her feet are bare on the hardwood.

She looks authoritative, in control, yet relaxed, and she's absolutely breathtaking.

Lily is on a chair next to her, tapping away on a tablet.

I clear my throat because no one has noticed me standing there. She looks my way and nibbles her bottom lip with a sly smile before walking my way and wrapping her arms around me.

"I'm sorry if we woke you. I've already gone food shopping, made breakfast—which is now brunch—and obviously got started on some renovations." She waves her hand around the room.

"*You* made breakfast?"

She slaps me playfully. "Is that all you heard? You'll be sorry, my cooking has come a long way."

"She's right." Lily glances up at me from behind her screen. "She had a professional chef give her cooking lessons."

"See." Jenna laughs and sticks her tongue out at me. I pick her up and spin her around, and she squeals.

"Alright, love birds." Lily wrinkles her nose.

I put her down and peek around Jenna so I can see Lily.

"Jenna, we have work to do." Lily says, her gaze returning back to her screen.

"I don't think she likes me," I whisper to Jenna.

"What gives you that impression?" She looks at Lily over her shoulder.

"I don't know, maybe the death stare has something to do with it. Go work. I'll enjoy breakfast, or brunch, whatever it is now."

I kiss her cheek and head into the kitchen. I'm sitting at the island eating when Lily comes to fill her cup of coffee.

"You were right, her cooking has improved," I say, trying to spark up a conversation with her.

She fills her mug and puts the pot back down harshly. "Mark, I'm gonna level with you. I support this," She waves her hand toward me. "Relationship because you make Jenna happy. But I'm telling you right now, you hurt my girl, you're gonna deal with me. You got that?" She threatens me.

I smile, put my fork on the plate, and fold my arms over my chest. "Are you insinuating that I'm not being transparent?"

"No, I'm not. I'm telling you that if you break her, I will cut you down."

"She's stronger than you give her credit for. Besides, Jenna has all the power here, you should know that." I say meaning every word.

She crosses her arms over her chest like I'm not convincing her.

"Point blank, Lily, we are on the same side. I'm not going to hurt her, and I'm going to damn well make sure Marissa isn't going to."

She drops her arms and lifts her coffee mug. "Good. I'm glad we got to have this heart to heart." She walks toward the doorway, before turning sharply. "Oh, and one more thing. I was rooting for you this whole time."

56

JENNA - JANUARY 2000

"Where are we?" I yawn and peer through the curtains from the bus window. We've been traveling the better part of the last two weeks.

"Cincinnati." Mark tells me.

I nod and roll over. The bus is much bigger this time. The guys splurged a little for the new bus and it's worth it to be able to spread out and travel with them. "My flight leaves in a few hours." I pout.

"We had a deal Mrs. McGinley." He reminds me.

The compromise we settled on was two weeks on tour, two weeks off until I'm too far along to travel.

I throw the covers off and wrap my robe around myself. "I know, I know. I have a doctor's appointment anyway. Max wants me to record those couple of songs and besides, I need to start thinking about a nursery." I kiss him and head into the bathroom to get ready for my flight. I don't want to be separated but I do feel tired and some time being home is a good idea.

Two hours later Mark is kissing me on the tarmac in front of the private jet. I sleep almost the whole flight and when I pull up in front of the house, I'm exhausted and beyond ready to climb into bed.

I know Mark is on stage, so I call Jerry to give Mark a message that I'm home safe and then I sleep straight through the night.

The next morning, I call Max first thing and we make plans to record the songs and go shopping for the nursery later that afternoon.

"My pants are getting tight." I complain as we walk in disguise while browsing at a popular baby boutique near La Brea.

"You know you're only going to get bigger right?" Max points out, as if I hadn't realized that.

"I need to hire a personal trainer."

Max rolls his eyes. "What about this one?" He points to a cream-colored crib with a matching dresser, changing table and armoire, it costs a fortune, but I love it and I buy the whole set. *It's nice to have money.* "You don't want to wait for Mark?" Max asks me after I slide my card. I shake my head knowing Mark will love whatever I pick.

We make a few more purchases in the boutique and I buy some maternity clothes as well. I'm trying to keep everything on the down low, but I suspect the shop owner knows it's me.

We're a few blocks away from the boutique when I notice someone following us and I'm sure Max notices too when he whispers. "Lunch?"

"Oh my god, yes, please. I'm starving."

We walk arm in arm until we get to a cafe down the street, where we take our time eating and its hours later when we step outside. I look around and it appears whoever was following us has lost interest because they are nowhere in sight.

"Ok, I think we should work on those songs, missy. We were supposed to be doing actual work today." Max admonishes me and we head over to the studio Max works at and run through the songs without any music. "You said you wrote these on the road?"

"Yes, why? Are they bad?" I worry, biting my finger nails.

He shakes his head. "Not at all. They're really good. I like that they aren't so poppy." He says and grabs a guitar from its case. "Reminds me of your church days, voice of an angel and all that crap."

I laugh and he starts plucking chords on the guitar over and over. I close my eyes and listen to the melody, I feel the music, and I love the way the words flow and ebb to the beat of the guitar, like they were made for each other.

When we're finished Max writes down the music and I'm so proud that working here has given him new life, a purpose and he's learned so much in a short time.

"It's gonna be great." I say when he drops me in front of the house a short while later. I hug him goodbye, and then plop on the couch for some down time.

My Nokia rings, I quickly answer it. "Husband." I greet him.

"Wifey." His voice sends goosebumps all over my body.

"Where are you now?" I say saddened that I'm not there with him.

"Wilkes-Barre. Forget about me, I want to know how you are?"

"Great. I ordered furniture for the nursery earlier, you're going to love it. Oh, and I found an interior designer."

"See, I told you being home wouldn't be so bad." He's silent for a minute. "I wish I could go with you tomorrow." He says of missing my doctor's appointment.

I silently wish for that too, I'm nervous about the appointment but I play it off. "Me too, but par for the course when you marry a super-hot rock star."

He laughs and I'm smiling from ear to ear. "I'll call you after the appointment."

"Ok. I love you J."

"Love you too." I hang up and go to work on writing more songs and its hours later when my stomach growls, that I realize how tired I am and that I skipped dinner.

I grab a few crackers to stave off the wave of nausea that hits me, then crawl into bed on my side and wait for it pass. I wake the next morning with the mix of sunlight and nausea and I try to force down a couple more crackers while I get ready. *It's just nerves.* I tell myself.

I hop into my brand-new black BMW 328i that Mark insisted on and head for the freeway. Channel surfing the radio stations, and stopping when I hear Tainted Innocence's new single come on the radio. I giddily sing along knowing it's a great omen and that I shouldn't be nervous. *Everything will be ok.*

Surprisingly I make it to the doctors with a few minutes to spare and they usher me in through a private back entrance, and right into an exam room. I appreciate them being discreet because I'm not ready to share the news with the world just yet.

"Good Morning." The tech says as she takes a seat at the sonogram machine. "It's a pleasure to meet you, my daughter is a huge fan." I smile warmly at her but I'm nervous, my palms are sweating and I'm dying to see my baby on that screen.

"How old is she?" I ask trying to distract myself from the nerves.

"Fourteen. She wants to be a singer too. Ready?" She asks and holds the bottle of gel over my stomach. I nod and she begins, the gel is cold, and she pushes hard with the transducer over my skin.

I lean back tensely against the chair as the image comes on the screen, and so far, I can't make out a damn thing as she pushes and works the controls clicking buttons and taking images as needed.

"Ok, do you see that?" She zooms out, and I squint at the black and white TV monitor. "There."

Tears stream down my face, the outline of a baby is on the screen bouncing as the tech moves her hand from left to right.

"It's in there? Is it... ok?" I ask hopeful.

"Yup, everything looks normal so far. According to this you're sixteen weeks." My heart is pounding, and I say a silent prayer. She hands me a long sheet of sonogram images and after I meet the doctor who tells me everything is right on track. I head back out the private door, walking quickly to the car.

I see a man leaning against a car next to mine. He waves but doesn't say anything, so I just get into the car and drive away. I'm driving almost half an hour on cloud nine, when I notice the same man who was leaning against the car behind me.

I change lanes so he can pass but he follows behind me. I speed up and change lanes again and I'm either paranoid or crazy, because I'm pretty sure that this man is following me.

I floor it and weave in and out of traffic until I lose him, then drive past my usual exit to the next one just in case he has caught up. Thankfully, because of the traffic he's no longer behind me.

My heart is pounding against my rib cage and I hear the whooshing sound of my blood pumping in my ears. I exhale a breath that I'd been holding and pull over to call Mark in a McDonald's parking lot. He's so excited when I tell him about the appointment that I forget to tell him about the man following me before we hang up.

"It's all in my head." I say to myself and drive home.

The next week is spent meeting with Max at the studio, writing and collaborating with musicians, and putting music to my words. It's a productive week but I can't wait to meet up with Mark in Vegas.

I head home at lunch time to meet with the interior designer who has been in the house all morning with a small crew working on the nursery.

"Jenna, this is an honor and you have my word that no one will hear the news from me or my staff. We are very discreet." She assures me.

"I appreciate that."

"Come, you must see the amazing transformation, in such little time." She pushes the door open and it's like I'm standing in a completely different room than I was this morning.

"It's beautiful." The walls are painted a neutral cream color and stars and moons glitter on the walls and the ceiling, and it looks like something out of a nursery rhyme.

She claps her hands together. "Good, I'm so glad you like it. We'll be back tomorrow to finish up."

"Thank you." I walk her out, put on comfy clothes and order Chinese food before settling onto the couch to watch Sex in the City and I must fall asleep because I hear a noise and it startles me awake.

Slowly, I make my way up the stairs and into the bathroom. I turn sideways in the mirror. A huge smile forms on my lips as I notice the little bump starting to form. I pat my stomach happily and climb into bed.

The next time I wake it's three in the morning and I hear a noise and this time I know that I'm not imagining it.

I lean over and grab the cordless phone. I may be paranoid, but I'd feel better if the police came to check things out.

The floor creaks just outside my door. I dial 911 and put the phone to my ear barely getting out the words but somehow, I do, and I tell the operator that I think there is an intruder in my house.

She tells me to hide. I get out of bed quietly and go into the closet. My heart is racing, and I can barely breathe. The door to the bedroom opens. I'm praying it's Mark, that he's come home to surprise me, but I confirm it's not when I hear the intruders voice.

"I know you're in here." A male voice says.

I hear sirens not too far, but my luck runs out when the closet door opens and a hand grabs me and pulls me out. Screaming loudly, I try and break free, but his grip is tight. I realize I'm still holding the cordless phone and I use it to hit him in the head and quickly make a run for the door.

I'm at the top of the stairs when he recovers, and grabs hold of me again. "Not only did you marry him, you let him get you pregnant, didn't you?" He shouts.

I cry and struggle to get away but my foot slips off the top stair making us both lose our balance, and together we tumble down. Down. Down.

He's on top of me when the police break down the door and they struggle to wrestle him off me.

Everything hurts, and when the EMT rushes to my side, I tell him in the smallest voice that I'm pregnant. I grip my stomach and pray for everything to be ok.

57

"Dinner was absolutely amazing."

I smile satisfied that I've impressed him. I brush his cheek with my thumb as we sit on the couch, watching mindless reality TV. "I don't know if that's a compliment, you still sound surprised. I'm glad you enjoyed it, though."

He kisses my hair, and I turn my face so that I catch his lips. This is how the past few weeks have been. Lazy days, filled with love-making and doting on each other.

He pulls away, his fingers grip my chin. "I promise it's a compliment."

I lean back satisfied against his chest and curl my legs under me.

"You all packed?" He asks. Tomorrow starts a full week of east coast morning and late-night shows to promote my new single.

Lily and my newly hired team released the single on Soundcloud two weeks ago, and the requests started pouring in for appearances.

"For the most part." I link my fingers through his.

"I could still change my schedule around and go with you." He offers, as he has several times. Honestly, I would love for him to do that, we've been inseparable, living together full time, but I know he's too busy to rearrange his schedule.

"It's only a week. It will fly by." I say trying to convince both of us.

He pulls me closer, and we stay like that until we climb into bed.

The next morning Mark drives Lily and me to the airport, despite my arguing, Mark insisted that we use Heartbeat's private jet, and I get melancholy as he parks on the tarmac.

The crew grabs my luggage and Lily boards, giving us the chance to say goodbye.

He grabs my hips and pulls me close. I hold onto him the same way, and he stares at me so intensely. His eyes burn into mine, and I shiver under his glare.

"I love you, J."

I absorb what he's saying, what he wants, the future, the past. It's all there, in those four little words he utters.

"I'm so in love with you," I assure him and press my hand over his heart, where I know the tattoo of our linked hearts is.

He closes his eyes as if he's been waiting a lifetime to hear me say those words, and maybe he has. I've always loved him, I've told him countless times, but these last few months have been different. I am giving myself to him, my whole true self, when in the past, I always held back a tiny little piece, and I know he feels the difference.

I kiss him, baring no holds, my mouth claiming his, our tongues warring as passion spreads out from within, and since I can't take this any further here on the tarmac, I reluctantly pull away.

He leans his forehead against mine, breathless. "Don't get into any trouble without me." He pulls back and winks.

"I wouldn't dream of it." I back away slowly and then turn toward the plane, gracefully climbing the stairs and taking my seat next to Lily. Mark and I lock eyes until we can no longer see each other.

"Holy shit," Lily says next to me, I glance at her, finally coming down off the endorphin high.

"What?" I look at her like something is wrong.

"You two... you're amazing together. That was riveting, I have goosebumps."

I roll my eyes, sit back, buckle my seat belt, and prepare for take-off. "You wouldn't have said that if you saw what we used to be like."

"Well, you don't like to talk about it, what was it like?"

I lean back against the seat as the plane lifts off the ground. "Sometimes it was passionate," I point out the window like Mark is still out there. "Like that. Other times it was... a beautiful disaster. It amazes me that we were together as long as we were, well, minus the couple times we were separated. It was a rough thirteen years actually, mostly because I was difficult, now that I think about it."

"You? Difficult? I don't believe it."

I push her arm off the armrest and smile. "It wasn't easy, we were both traveling so much. When I needed him, he wasn't there, and when he was there, I was so busy being angry about the times he wasn't, that I didn't appreciate our time together. That multiplied with my raging alcohol and drug addiction, we were a recipe for disaster."

She nods. "Do you think you will get remarried?"

I've thought about that a lot, especially over the last couple of weeks, and each time the outcome I wanted was different, so I contemplate my words before I answer her. "Why does there always have to be more? I don't know if he will give me that piece of his heart again. I know I wouldn't if I were him."

"Come on, Jenna, you damn well know that man is a fool when it comes to you. He would marry you again in a second."

"That's the problem. Besides, I don't know why we need rings and a piece of paper. I didn't understand it the first time around. We know what we are to each other, gold and paper doesn't change that."

"Are you telling me that you didn't want to get married in the first place?"

"I'm saying that he needed the commitment, the legality of it. I always just needed him. For me, the pressure of being what the world thought we should be was too much."

"It's like Romeo and Juliette getting another chance. The world will be overjoyed." She says sweetly.

She doesn't know what she's talking about. The headlines swirl in my head, the press releases announcing our marriage.

'Mark and Jenna tie the knot in secret wedding.' 'Mark and Jenna wed,

dating before she was legal?' 'Mark and Jenna off the market, what do they even have in common?' 'Age is only a number for Mark and Jenna.'

Not that the headlines about our divorce were any better. *'After thirteen years, Pop Princess Jenna calls it quits.' 'Jenna says she's had enough' 'Power couple Mark and Jenna split amid affair rumors.' 'Jenna splits from rocker hubby as she looks for a younger beau.'*

"Trust me, no one ever thought we were Romeo and Juliette."

"You're not going to let them get in your head this time, right?" She questions.

I shake my head adamantly. "No way in hell."

She nods in approval, and I lean back and close my eyes.

We land in Boston shortly after eleven and head right to the studio for hair and makeup. The taping goes great, my performance is spot on, and I'm feeling great, that is until Lily pulls me off set.

"What is it?"

"This was posted a little while ago." She hands me her iPad like she is handing off a live grenade.

'Mark McGinley and girlfriend Marissa Russo are expecting!'

The caption is followed by a picture of Mark and Marissa at a bistro table having lunch. I question the authenticity of the picture, but I'm sure, without a doubt, it's Mark, and it must be recent because she's starting to show as the yellow circle and arrow over her belly nicely points out.

I hand Lily back the tablet and head back toward the green room where my purse is. She follows behind me.

I dial without hesitation and close my eyes in relief when he answers on the second ring.

"Hey, gorgeous." He answers.

I quickly text him the article. "Look at your phone." I hear him shuffle the phone and then sigh. "Where are you?" I ask.

"L.A." He answers honestly, but I can tell he didn't want to.

"Why didn't you tell me?"

"Don't assume—"

I cut him off. "I have to make assumptions because I'm reading headlines off of social media, and when I left, you were in Nashville."

"J... She called after you left, she wanted to talk about the paternity test, she doesn't want to wind up in court. I just didn't have a chance to text you about it."

I stomp my foot because it doesn't take long to send a text, and it feels like an excuse. "Fine. I have to go."

"Jenna, you said—"

"I know what I said. I just don't like it being thrown in my face." I snap.

"Ok. I'm sorry."

"I'll see you Saturday. I have to go." I hang up and toss my phone into my bag and stare into space.

Lily clears her throat. "Should I not show you anything else I come across."

I stare at her, shaking my head emphatically. "No, you should, I'm fine."

58

"Mark, phone! It's Max." It's eight in the morning and instantly the hair on the back of my neck stands when Jerry hands me the cell phone.

"What happened?" I ask Max. I know something is horribly wrong, he's sobbing, and I barely make out his words but the words I hear are gut wrenching. I choke on my own sobs and throw the phone against the wall.

The next seven hours are a blur.

We cancel our next three shows and the guys fly back with me because as much as I'm trying to put on a brave face, I'm over-whelmed.

Being this far from Jenna is making matters worse. It's taking too long to get to her.

When we get to Max's apartment it's late, Jenna is locked inside her old bedroom and I lay my head against the door.

"She won't come out, I've already tried." Max says softly, I turn to sit next to him, and the guys sit on the couch next to me.

"Tell me, everything." I already know the baby is gone, but I need to hear what happened.

He rattles off the details, his voice cracking as he does. "The guy was a deranged fan, he confessed to the police that he was following her for months. He got upset when he realized she was pregnant, and he followed her home after the appointment.

He was able to get in through an open window the interior decorator left open.

She's pretty banged up and bruised. What's worse the police were only two minutes too late." He sobs uncontrollably.

Jamie grabs my shoulder.

"Are they sure the baby..." I can't even say it and I swipe the tears from my eyes.

Max hangs his head, sobs still racking his body. "I'm sorry Mark. I know that doesn't make it better."

I stand and go knock gently on the bedroom door. "Jenna?" I call her but there's no answer. I need her. I'm raw inside and I know she's even worse. "Jenna, please let me in." I beg.

"Go away." Her voice is gravelly from crying.

I slam my forehead against the door. "J, please. Let me hold you."

"No. Just go away."

I punch the door, but she doesn't change her mind.

"Mark, there's something else—"

"I don't want to hear it." I storm out of the apartment, slamming the door behind me. I'm angry and desperate and I need a way to numb everything I feel.

The guys are seconds behind me as I walk into the bar and sit quietly throwing back shot after shot. I drink until I can't stand or see straight, and the guys have to carry me to the car.

Jamie comes into the bedroom around noon. The hangover is wicked and I'm hoping this was all just a bad dream. "Max called, she still hasn't come out." *Nope. Not a nightmare.*

"She's going to hate me. I sent her home, it took me too long to get to her and then what do I do, I leave her again." I gasp for air.

"Don't blame yourself Mark. This is a terrible, horrible, tragedy. That guy would've gotten to her no matter what, he was determined."

"Maybe. But I wasn't here, I should've been with her."

He shakes his head but lets me wallow in my self-pity. "Come on, we're surrounded by reporters. We need to get out of here. Let's go see if we can coax her out."

I shower and dress and then it hits me. The nursery.

I walk down the hall to the closed door and swing it open.

The room is beautiful, it's almost complete minus the furniture still in boxes. There is a hammer on the floor, and I fantasize smashing everything in the room to pieces, until there is just dust and debris and nothing that resembles a nursery.

I don't though. I just want to get to her, so I back out and lock the door.

When we get to the apartment, I resolve that I'm not leaving without her this time. I bang on front the door. Max answers and I head straight for her bedroom.

"I'm worried, she hasn't come out at all." He says solemnly.

I don't bother knocking. I don't bother talking to her through the door, I just walk up to the door and kick it in with all my might.

She's on her side, unmoving, no reaction to my intrusion, she isn't even looking at me her eyes are glazed over.

I panic.

My heart pounds as I rush to check her pulse which thrums against my fingers but it's way too slow. I cradle her in my arms and kiss her, a tear rolls down her cheek. *She's in shock.*

"I'm so sorry J. Please come back to me. Please, please, come back to me." It's almost an hour later when she snaps out of it and sobs hysterically as I hold her. I tuck her back into bed and she sleeps, and sleeps and the doctor confirms that she's in shock. He gives her a mild sedative and it's three more days before she emerges from the bedroom.

I rise from my makeshift bed on the couch as she takes a seat in a chair by the window without a word.

"J? Talk to me. Look at me, please, so I know you're in there."

She turns her head slightly as if she just noticed I'm here.

"Do you think it's going to rain today?" She looks back to the window and I look to Max for support because I have no idea what's happening.

He comes over and sits across from her.

"Jenna?"

She turns away from the window and focuses on Max.

"You look like shit. You need to eat and shower and stop acting like your Mother." He shouts.

She looks back out the window and then gets up and goes back into the bedroom, closing the door behind her.

"Should we call the doctor? Maybe we should go to the hospital." He says concerned, and we probably should but then again, it might work against us, she might be like this longer.

"I have an idea." I stride into the bedroom, pick her up and carry her out over my shoulder as I head into the bathroom. I turn the shower on, and she stands still as I undress her.

Her eyes stare straight ahead avoiding me. She's completely and savagely breaking my heart.

"You need to snap out of this Jenna, I'm not going to lose you too. You're stronger than this." I throw her into the shower, pushing her under the cold stream of water, shocking her.

She screams, an agonizing pained wail.

"Let it out Jenna. Scream. Cry. But you have to come back to me."

She shuts the water off and makes eye contact with me for the first time. The glaze in her eyes is gone, replaced with reality. Her chest heaves, she gasps for air and her knees buckle.

I catch her under her arms before she falls and hold her tight as her body shudders while she sobs. She's beyond frail from not eating and pounds lighter than she should be. I sink to the ground with her in my arms. "It's ok J, we're gonna be ok. I promise."

At this point, what's another broken promise, because I know we are far from ok.

59

MARK - DECEMBER 2015

"I'll see you Saturday. I have to go." Jenna hangs up, and I lean back in my office chair as the phone goes dead. The meeting with Marissa did not go well, and now Jenna is upset with me or rather the swift photographer who posted the article that Marissa is pregnant.

I steeple my hands under my chin deep in thought. Marissa wants to avoid going to court so that this matter stays private, and I don't disagree with her since I don't think there's any reason to drag everyone through the mud.

Yet, I want paternity results, and that's where the talk went sour, because I doubt her.

I head to a bar down the road to meet with the guys. Since I've been living in Nashville, we haven't really talked. I love living in Nashville with Jenna, I would put down roots anywhere with her, but California has always been my home. It's who I am.

"Come on, man, cheer up." Dave throws a napkin at me because I'm unusually quiet. "This will all work itself out."

"I'm glad you think so. I always gave Jenna shit when it came to other guys, and now, here I am having a baby with someone else. She said she can deal with it but—"

"You don't believe her?" Steve chimes in.

"I think sometimes it's going to be really hard." I take a sip of my beer.

"You're right back to where you wanted to be, no one thought you would be back with Jenna in a million years," Dave says before he shoves food into his mouth.

I look at Jamie for support or criticism. He shrugs, "I think she's full of shit."

I frown at him. "Jenna? Why would she go through all the trouble?"

"No. Marissa." He says blatantly.

I clench my jaw and raise an eyebrow at him.

"Tell me, whose idea was it to go to the outdoor bistro today?" He asks.

I see where he's going, and I can't say that I wasn't heading to the same conclusion after I saw the photo and the headline.

"So, you think she knows Mark and Jenna are blissfully happy, living in Nashville, and she's trying to do what?" Dave wonders.

Jamie looks from Dave to me. "I'm saying if it's Mark's baby, why isn't she more cooperative about a paternity test?"

"So, you don't think it's mine?" I chug the rest of my beer.

"I don't know, I guess time will tell, right?"

I throw my hands up. "I don't know what's worse, to be honest." Everyone is quiet. They understand what I mean. If this baby isn't mine, I lose another baby, yet, if it is mine, I'm bringing a child into a complicated situation with a woman that I don't love. "Well, this has been fun." I say disgusted with me situation. *Fuck the universe.*

I stand to go, and Steve slaps me on the back. "It's weird not having you around the office, man."

"Once the Nashville office is fully set up, I'll be splitting my time back and forth." I don't mention that it's to appease Marissa, who accused me of not having my priorities straight today.

It's late when I head back to my house, not the house I once shared with Jenna, but the one I purchased after our divorce. I send several texts to Jenna, but they all go unanswered, and once my head hits the pillow, I fall into a deep sleep. The morning seems to come faster than it should.

After packing some more clothes and personal items, I take an Uber to the airport, but I'm not heading back to Nashville. There's a lot of things I need to clear up. Jagged edges, that need to be dulled. So, I waste no time and head straight for my destination. I land in New Jersey by late afternoon.

The house looks the same from the outside. I pull in front of the driveway and push the button to turn the ignition off and sit solemnly for a few minutes, remembering the last time I was here and the fight that I had with Frank and Maureen.

My relationship with Jenna had hung in the balance, and then weeks later, she had the first miscarriage.

My presence won't be welcome here, but I press on, getting out of the car and striding up the walk to the front steps. My finger shakes as I ring the bell.

The door opens, and I'm face to face with Jenna's Father, only a screen door separating us.

He's older now, gray hair scattered around his head, with deep lines around his mouth and his eyes. There are bags underneath them, and he walks with a cane.

He's a tired version of the former man.

"I didn't cheat on Jenna." That's not how I wanted to start, but it flies out of my mouth, so I go with it. "Ever." He stares in silence, so I go for broke. "It's true, I fell in love with her when she was only sixteen. I was enamored with her, but I never pursued her until she was eighteen." I pause to think, and with a raspy voice, he speaks.

"You better come inside."

I'm surprised by his willingness to hear me out, let alone invite me in. He swings the door open for me, I step inside and look around. Not much has changed on the inside either.

"Go ahead, sit down." He points to the black leather couch, as he sits in his recliner chair across from me. Jenna had tried to get her parents to move to California for the longest time, but they wanted to stay put, and during our divorce, I had offered them the beach house

I bought for Jenna just before the first miscarriage. They turned me down.

I sit and rub my palms over my thighs.

"You sound like you're on trial, you coming clean about something?" He asks, a smirk on his face.

"Setting the record straight. I know you always thought I was the bad guy. I'm sure Jenna's book will paint the picture for you, but I want you to hear my version since I don't plan on writing a book."

"I see." He rubs his chin.

I lose my train of thought, my mind is all over the place. "I told Jenna to invite you and Maureen to our wedding, at the time she didn't think it was the right thing to do.

I knew it would be the catalyst for a lot of damage, but I always gave in to every one of her demands, right down to her asking me for a divorce that I didn't want.

I always did what I thought was for her protection. Maybe, it was me she needed protecting from after all. I was so focused on being unconditionally committed to us, to our marriage, that I couldn't see us spiraling, and, in the end, we couldn't climb out with so much shit on top of us."

He listens to my speech without interrupting. "Sounds like not much has changed." He rests his cane against the side table, and I wonder if Jenna has been confiding in her Father about us.

"Yeah, I guess not. I just thought you should know." I lose my nerve to ask him what I came here to ask. I stand to thank him so I can just go and let him get back to whatever it is that keeps him busy.

"Sit." He uses his forceful tone, the former man's demeanor that I'm used to. I sit back down. "When Jenna's mom got sick, I tried to help her. I knew she was mentally ill, but I tried to cover it up, make excuses for her because I didn't want to live without her. I knew she needed more help than I could give her." He shifts slightly in his chair. I see pain flash across his face. "I still go visit her, you know. She doesn't want me to, she hates that I put her in a psych home. But still, I go, because selfishly it's hard to let go.

I always knew you loved Jenna. In some ways, I might have been jealous, that you were showing me up in the husband department."

I wrinkle my brow in confusion. "Frank, I know I've never been a parent, but help me understand something. Doesn't every parent want their son or daughter to find someone who loves them, like I did Jenna."

"Of course."

"Then why the hell did you hate me so damn much then?"

He uses his cane to scoot forward on the chair. "You were an obstacle, a distraction to the plan. My plan. I didn't know till a few years ago that she didn't have the same dreams I did. She actually told me she would've given the Grammy's back, if I had just asked her once what she wanted."

I sit back, thinking about everything he's just said. *Did I ever ask her what she wanted?* "But she made it. Isn't that what you wanted?"

"Yes, but you got all the credit. You signed her, fell in love with her, married her, and no one looked twice at me, she didn't need me anymore once she had you.

I was the one who took her to voice lessons, made her join the choirs. I pushed her to perform the anthem at sporting events and come to find out, all the while she didn't even care. She wanted to be a vet.

That is until she got your gig. Then suddenly, she was determined, said someone told her she was awful. I think she used the word 'flat'. That lit a fire under her."

I shake my head and laugh. "A vet? Huh?"

"Can you imagine a diva like her as a Veterinarian?" He shakes his head as if he's picturing it. "She loved that damn dog though."

I nod. "Rocky." Jenna mentioned him from time to time until like all pets, he suffered from old age long before her.

"Jenna told me. About the baby." He clarifies.

I hang my head. "Did she?"

He nods. "She told me about running from you again. She thinks this whole thing is her fault, that she pushed you into that girl's arms and the universe is punishing her."

"She would think that."

"She's a lot like her mother in that respect."

I let his words hang in the air. I decide to go for broke. "There is something I came to ask you. I realize this may sound a little foolish being that another woman is pregnant with my child, but I should have asked the first time.

I have no intention of being with anyone else, there is no one else for me. I'm asking for your blessing to marry Jenna, again.

I love her. I've loved every version of her, and will continue to love the future versions of her."

He's quiet, his stern face is pinched into an expression and I'm not sure if he's considering my request or about to tell me to fuck off.

He clears his throat. "You can have my blessing, on one condition."

"Name it."

"I get to walk her down the aisle."

60

"I'm quitting the band." Jamie stands and paces the floor while Dave and Steve wait for me to go on. "It shouldn't really be a surprise." I've been delaying this for a long time. "I need a more stationary job. Jenna needs me more accessible. Growing the label is the perfect opportunity." I sell it to them.

Jamie shakes his head. "So that's it?"

I nod and take a seat. I called this meeting an hour ago, and even though they feel blindsided, they know deep down our fifteen minutes of fame has run out.

"You can replace me." I suggest.

Dave crosses one leg over the other. "You know that won't work. They only come to see you."

I hang my head and sigh. "I promised to take care of her. I'm breaking that promise and this is long overdue." The truth is, my priorities changed months ago after she separated from me. I had promised her a normal life, and she gave up waiting on me, and decided to throw herself into her work.

"So, you give up your dreams and she does what? Don't get me wrong, you know we all love Jenna, but would she do the same thing for you?" Jamie voices his concern.

"She wants fame, I want her. End of story." Besides the fact, I know she can't handle a third world tour on her own, but I don't say that. They look at each other, worried and concerned.

"Ok, well it sucks, but we support your decision." Jamie finally says.

"Thanks guys. I really am sorry." I stand and Jamie pats me on the back.

I slip my hands in my pocket, knowing my best friends would support me even if they are not in agreement with my decision.

"Give Jenna our best." Steve says on his way out.

I nod and head for the door.

I drive over to the new offices that are being renovated as the new home of Heartbeat Records.

We've long outgrown our small office and I know our potential reach by moving to these offices will propel us forward.

The guys know Jenna is our most successful artist, but we need to expand, we can't survive off her forever.

With me out of the band, I can move forward with my plans to expand the label into other markets, as well as international *and* be around to take care of Jenna.

I take the elevator up to my office. Jenna is already here sitting on my desk when I arrive.

"You wanted to see me?" She says in that serious voice she gets whenever she thinks we're talking business. "Do I need my lawyer?"

I laugh but the humor is not lost on me.

We're in an extremely fragile state since the separation. I want her to know we're on the same side.

I walk toward my desk, stopping in front of her. I rest my hands on her thighs. She's looking especially beautiful in a pale-yellow sundress, her makeup done natural and her blonde highlighted hair glows in the sunlight behind her. She looks angelic.

"I quit the band this morning."

She leers at me, like I just told her I bombed Kuwait. "Why on earth would you do that?" She pushes my hands off her and hops off of the round desk.

"I have my reasons. There are so many things I want to accomplish here, and I think given our current situation it's best if I were here, with you."

She folds her arms across her chest. "I don't need you to babysit me."

"Not everything is about you Jenna. I'm tired. I've been with the band since I was seventeen. I'm thirty-one, I just need something else."

"I don't need you to suffocate me. It's hard enough to hold myself accountable, I don't need that pressure from you too." I lean against the desk, staring at the woman who makes me crazy, yet, I'd gladly give everything up for.

"You don't make any sense. When I'm gone, you want me here. When I'm here, you act like I'm bothering you. Which one is it J? Are we in this for the long haul? Or do you want to make this separation permanent?"

She's quiet, I can read her like a book, and I've struck a nerve. She knows everything I said is true.

"Do *you* want it to be permanent?" She turns it around on me.

It wasn't my idea to separate in the first place, of course I don't want it to be permanent, but I keep that to myself.

"I'll give you whatever you want."

She shakes her head. "You didn't answer the question."

"No. Of course not. But I need you all in, no more living with Max. I want you to come home."

"Fine. There's something I want to talk to you about too, as my 'label,' Wes is no longer my manager, I'm replacing him." She stands her ground, prepared to fight. Just like that we're negotiating terms of getting back together.

"Any reason why?" He's been good to Jenna. I don't understand.

She chooses her words carefully. "We weren't seeing eye to eye. His contract was up and I asked him to resign."

"Ok, I'll find you someone else."

"No." She grabs her purse and throws it over her shoulder. "I've taken care of it already."

"Jenna, you have to vet a manager, you can't just work with anyone." *For God sakes, she's Jenna!*

She laughs. "I've vetted him, it was quite the process."

I roll my eyes at her nonchalance. "Well? Who is it?"

"Me."

I turn to find Max, standing in my doorway. He has zero experience as a manager. He's been a music producer for the last few years and I don't understand how he's supposed to seamlessly jump into this role.

Needless to say, I'm less than thrilled.

"You?" I scoff.

"Is there a problem?" Jenna asks standing next to him, her arm on his shoulder. They've always had a strong alliance, this will make that alliance impenetrable. Case in point, if I'm not on board, I'll lose Jenna.

They're not going to walk all over me though.

I walk forward, stopping in front of both of them but I look directly at Max. "I want to be really clear. One, you're under my label, my brand. I run the show here. I get final say on everything regarding Jenna, that's my right as her label.

Two, Jenna is my wife, until she decides that's not what she wants, you stay out of our marriage. Are we clear?"

Jenna glares at me but I keep my eyes focused on Max.

"We're clear." He responds.

"Good." I walk back to my unconventional round desk and watch as they turn to leave. "Jenna, I'll see you at home."

61

"Are you sure? I was really looking forward to spending Christmas with you." My Dad has suddenly flipped a switch on spending Christmas with me, and I don't understand why when it's only a week away.

"You stay with Mark. I'm just gonna do my own thing here."

I roll my eyes, he must think I'm choosing Mark over him again. "What does that even mean?"

"Jenna, I'm gonna be fine. I have Aunt Roe."

"Why don't you just come stay with us in Nashville then? Bring Aunt Roe." I was really looking forward to this.

"Nah, you know she doesn't like to travel."

"Ok, I guess. I'll see you soon. Ok?"

He agrees, then we say our goodbyes, and I hang up.

Mark wraps his arms around me from behind as I lay my phone on the counter. "Everything ok?" He asks.

"I'm not sure. I was supposed to go there for Christmas, but he just canceled on me."

"I'm sure he's fine."

I spin around to face him and narrow my eyes at him, he averts my glare, and I think he knows something that I don't. "Ok, I guess we'll stay here then."

He shrugs. "Whatever you want." He turns to load the dishes into the dishwasher.

"By the way, I'm flying to L.A. tomorrow." I say reminding him.

He leans against the counter and dries his hands with a dish-towel. "I know." He drops the towel and wraps his arms around me. "You don't have to go alone, but I don't want to intrude."

An errant tear escapes. I can't help it, I've been dreading this for a year. "I'd like it if you came with me."

He pulls me into him. "Then, I'll be there."

I rest my head on his shoulder, breathing in his scent, which is doing wild things to my senses right now. I sniffle and dry my eyes. "I have meetings pretty much all day." I kiss him on the cheek, but he pulls me into a tight embrace and kisses my lips, I know he wants more, but I need to go. "Stop that, or I'll never leave the house."

"I'm ok with that."

I back away, blowing him a kiss.

Forty minutes later I arrive at the cafe. I'm late for my meeting with Lily, and she's occupying a booth in the back reading when I come in.

"Good book?" I smirk.

"Can't put it down."

I take a seat across from her.

"I'm so grateful you let me read this first."

I nod, wondering which part has piqued her interest. She looks at me with tears in her eyes.

"I remember reading about the intruder. I don't remember hearing anywhere that you were pregnant."

I blow out a deep breath. "No, somehow I was lucky, that part never got out," I order a tall coffee with a double shot of espresso.

I was able to keep that secret. No one knew except for the intruder, and the small group of friends we had told during Christmas.

"Jenna..." She looks at me serious now. "How did you get over something like that?"

I knew opening this part of my life would be difficult. The truth is, I moved past it long ago, but I never really got over it. "I didn't do it gracefully, that's for sure. Those three years after the intruder are a blur. We moved, tried grief counseling, but I just couldn't get past it. I became a different person, my anxiety went through the roof, and it took me a long time before I could even be alone."

"Awful. What happened to him?"

"He did four years for breaking and entering, he passed away a few years after that."

She leans against the back of the booth. "You were recording before it happened, how did you finish?"

After I released that second album, something in me broke.

The songs on that album were written during a happy time, and nothing was happy after the intruder and the album took on a depressed tone. Many people thought it was intended to sound that way. I hated it. "It took a long time. In hindsight, I shouldn't have released that album. How do you win awards for something and be so miserable about it? Things went straight downhill from there."

She opens to a page and reads the words I've written.

'I worked endless hours for two years on a worldwide tour, so I didn't have to face reality. I was drunk for days at a time.

When I wasn't on stage or partying, severe exhaustion kept me in bed. Between the alcohol and the cocktail of anxiety medications, I was so far gone.

When I finally came home. Mark sent me to rehab, but I came out worse and took my aggression out on him. We fought a lot. Mostly, because Max was an enabler, while Mark was trying to curb my destructive behavior.'

I nod my head. "I went to rehab twice. Then in 2005 I got myself together enough to put out a third album. I won another Grammy, but by that point, I think people just felt bad for me because my life was such a disaster."

She looks from the book to me. "Jenna... I don't know what to say." I smile and repeat something Dr. Wild tells me all the time.

"Those years made me who I am today. I'm not proud of them, but I am who I am."

"And that fool stuck it out with you. What's wrong with him?"

I laugh. I used to wonder the same thing. "That you'll have to ask him."

She flips to another page and reads.

'After the release of my third album, Max became my manager, the album went platinum.

Mark quit Tainted Innocence to tag along with me on tour, and though I avoided it for years, my biological clock got the best of me, and we got pregnant again.

But three more times, it just didn't work out. I was so numb by then that I learned not to get attached to anything.

A specialist explained that my body treated the pregnancies as a foreign object and that it was a waste to keep trying. I had my tubes tied after that.'

She looks down at the book, resting her hand on top. "I'm so sorry." I smile, and clear my throat, fighting back the tears.

"What happened after that?"

I wag my finger at her. "Oh, no. You're gonna have to keep reading."

"Ugh, where are the perks of knowing you."

I throw a napkin at her.

My phone buzzes in my bag. I peek at it. "It's Mark."

"Go ahead. I need a bathroom break." She slides out of the booth, and I answer.

"Miss me already?" I joke with him, but I know he does, and I miss him too.

"More than you know. I just got a call from Tom Royce, the President of Halycon. He's under the impression I'm cockblocking them making a deal with you, by opening a Nashville office."

"I don't know why he would think that. I'm not making a deal with anyone, that's why I released the single on SoundCloud." I rub circles around my temples because I don't need this right now.

"Talk to Lily, maybe it's worth seeing what they offer you. You know what you're worth, Jenna."

"Exactly, and I don't need to be locked into a contract. I want to change the industry and how artists are treated. Who in their right mind signs away the rights to their music for seventy years?"

"You know who you're talking to, right?"

I close my eyes because this is going to be a divide between us, he represents the same thing I'm going up against.

"You know you will meet a lot of resistance along the way, releasing on your own. I'm just being honest."

I appreciate his honesty and form a very vague idea. "Then, change it with me."

"Change it how?"

"Make recording fun again, without burying the artist under years of obligations and making little to no money."

He's quiet, considering my idea.

"Honestly, J, I have to mull it over."

My heart deflates a little, he's always trusted my instincts.

"I do not disagree. The system is antiquated, but Heartbreak is already treading thin ice."

I stare at Lily, who slides back into the booth. "Well, while you're thinking about it, I'll be doing it, with or without you."

62

JENNA - AUGUST 2005

"When the cat's away, the mouse will play."

I look up at Max after I snort a line of coke off the table. Mark is back in L.A. for a few days and I'm bored and tired and alcohol just isn't cutting it tonight.

"Shut up." Considering its Max's damn fault that I'm on this shit.

"Ready?" He watches me as I clean up and check my face for residue.

As long as I'm dressed and able to perform somewhat on time who cares if I party a little. *No one.* "As I'll ever be."

Max fell into the manager role seamlessly, minus getting me hooked on coke, which I can't totally blame on him, because he was using, and curiosity got the best of me.

"Jenna..." Max says while he holds up a little baggie of white powder. "Last bag, you promised."

I nod as he tucks it into his pocket and leads me out of the door and toward the stage.

I don't need him to get it for me, Wes always sheltered me from the drugs, but backstage is a free-for-all, if I want it, I'll get it myself. That's the thing about having money, no one cares what you do.

We're supposed to be getting off this shit, but it's giving me the energy I need, and I literally don't think I can perform without it anymore. Caffeine pills will never replace the coke.

I trip over myself and laugh hysterically. I'm drunk and high, and right now I think I could fall off the roof and laugh my ass off.

Max grabs my arm and tells me to wait as the crew resets the stage for me, but my body is humming with restless energy and I fidget next to him.

I barely acknowledge that he's walked away to answer his cell. I sway and grab onto the arm of one of the stage guys, who holds me up by cupping my ass.

Obviously in my current state I think it's hilarious, which doesn't deter his hand and he's emboldened to reach under my twelve-hundred-dollar skirt, while all I can do is hold onto this guy's arm, so I don't fall on my face.

"Hey! Fuck off asshole." Max grabs me by the arm and pushes the guy off of me. "Touch her again and I'll personally cut your dick off."

I'm still in the giggle phase of the high. Max grabs my face, so I focus on him. "That was your husband, on the phone."

I shrug because I'm no longer in control of my emotions and I'm not sure what he wants me to say.

"Jenna?"

"Hmm?" I stare at him, trying to focus.

"You were only supposed to do one bump, you did two, didn't you?"

I don't acknowledge him. I turn and grab my glittered pink microphone dramatically and saunter away. I don't need a lecture.

"You ok to go on?" Max asks as he meets me at the edge of the stage.

"I'm holding a microphone, aren't I?" I wave it in front of him for good measure.

"Mark is on his way. He told me not to tell you, wanted it to be a surprise." He confesses.

"Fuck."

"Yeah, fuck is right, look at you." He waves his hand over me, from head to toe.

I do the math. It's almost seven now, a five-hour flight, by the time he gets from L.A. to Miami, I'll be ok. "I'll be fine by the time he gets here."

"Oh, yeah? That's like fifteen minutes."

I spin around to him, I may be high off my ass, but I process what he said just fine.

He takes a good look at me. "We're fucked."

"I'm going on. Now." I turn too fast in my heels, twisting my ankle and falling on my ass.

He crouches down and shakes his head. "I can't put you out there, not like this."

Again, I have no emotional control, so I go from crying to angry in a matter of seconds. "No. He can't see me like this." I panic and somehow, I manage to climb to my feet, and he helps me stagger over to the stage entrance. A medic comes over to ice my ankle, but I shoo him away.

"Go get a stool." Max yells to a stagehand and they run around as I hear the band start. The music cues my synapses and the adrenaline takes over and I'm able to put weight on my foot.

"Break a leg." Max calls out and I give him the finger as I walk— hobble out onto the stage to cheers and whistles. The lights are bright, and I squint to find the microphone stand, and once I do I hold onto it for support and lean against the stool, casually leaning my foot on the rung to get the weight off it.

I'm loud and boisterous as I perform, but I'm pretty much chained to the stool and very paranoid as I look to the side of the stage for signs of Mark.

I perform for two and a half hours, high as a kite on a twisted ankle, with no break. I'm beaming as I stand to walk off the stage, one more song, just the encore then I can stop and sit down.

I walk carefully, calculating each step because the pain in my ankle is unbearable and I know Mark is watching me, I feel him and I smile as I lock eyes with him but I can feel his stare analyzing me, he knows I'm off. I never sit during a show and with that, I lose focus and my ankle gives out.

I hit the stage with a thud, bracing my fall with my hands and a sharp searing pain shoots through my wrist.

I'm far enough off the stage that I'm mostly covered, but I don't give a shit if anyone can see me or if they take a picture because my ankle is screaming and so damn swollen along with my wrist.

Mark runs out to me, with a swarm of personnel right behind him but all I want is to get off my ass and away from the audience.

Everyone is yelling at me to stay still but I manage to get up on my feet and limp back stage. Mark and Max grab me under the arms, supporting my weight.

"What happened?" Mark looks from me to Max.

I hold my wrist against my stomach, which is now in excruciating pain, dulling the throbbing in my ankle.

"I tripped before I went on, twisted my ankle." I say truthfully.

"Why didn't you get medical attention?"

"The show must go on, right?"

He shakes his head, I've disappointed him. "I leave you for one day—"

"I tripped!" I yell and steal a glance at Max.

The medic is back and leans me back into a chair while he looks over my wrist and ankle.

Mark stands, pushing Max against the wall. "What is she on?"

I try to diffuse. "Jim Beam." I say but he's not buying it and gives me a look of fury for treating him like he's stupid.

"I know the difference, Jenna." Unfortunately, he does know quite well, what his alcoholic wife looks like day in and day out.

"Can we talk about this later. Please." I wince as the medic braces me up.

"Fine."

Three hours in the ER being poked and prodded by medical personnel and all I can think about is getting more coke. Getting high to relieve the pain.

Mark says nothing more to me until we're back at the hotel. I watch as he paces the length of the room, stopping suddenly in front of the window, staring out into space. Crossing his arms over one another. "Hairline wrist fracture, and a sprained ankle. Even drunk, you're not usually clumsy." He says exasperated.

"I'm tired and I want to go to bed. I don't need a lecture." I'm crashing and it's going to be bad.

"This is not a lecture. This is me telling you that you're done."

I sit upright, wide awake and ready to fight. "I've seen you and the band on something at one time or another. This is not a big deal."

"What is it?" He asks, his hands now on his hips.

Street names swirl in my head, but I don't beat around the bush, there's no reason to sugar coat it. "Coke."

He closes his eyes, but he doesn't seem too shocked. "Who gave it to you?"

I shrug. "I don't know. It was just there." I lie hoping to protect myself and Max. Mark always knows when I'm lying.

"I don't believe you. It's always been there. It's Max, isn't it?" He shouts.

I don't answer.

He flips the table near the window. His temper is beyond anything I've ever seen and he rushes to the night table, picking up the phone and starts to dial angrily. I panic and lean over to stop him, pressing the button on the receiver to hang it up.

"I'll stop. I'm done."

"Yes, you will. Or we're done."

63

"I'll give you a minute." He kisses my forehead and waits by the car. My heels crunch over the grass as I walk toward the cemetery plot. I don't walk with purpose, I walk with obligation, because I don't want to be here now, as much as I didn't want to be here the first time.

Being here means this is reality. Reality is a hard pill to swallow, and being sober doesn't make it easier.

I stand and read his name, artfully engraved onto the stone.

Maxwell J. Holden
June 4, 1980 - December 18, 2014
Best friend

I place my hand on the stone, overwhelmed with guilt that I haven't been here since the day he was buried.

My knees buckle, and I drop down, skinning them.

I don't feel it though, I'm numb, and the only thing I feel is my body shaking as I sob. An unwilling participant of my emotions as they spill out.

My grief feels a million miles away, yet on top of me at the same time.

"I wish you had let me be there for you," I say honestly. "I was never a good friend. Not really. I should've known you needed... something." I say the words to no one.

Had I known he needed something? Or was it an oversight of epic proportions.

I don't know how long I'm on the ground as my knees bleed, and my tears flow freely.

I'm stuck inside myself until Mark bends down next to me.

Carefully, he takes my hand in his, and I'm so grateful he's here with me. So grateful that we have another chance. I know Max would be happy for us.

I look over at him, it's clear how much his heart aches for me. How he feels my grief in the way, he grips my hand.

He dries my tears with his other hand and lifts me gently from the ground, wrapping me in his safe embrace, until Mother Nature interrupts and opens the sky on us.

Before we make it to the car, I stop him tugging on his arm. He needs to finally hear this. *No more secrets.* I drop his hand and back up a few steps, needing the distance to say what I have to. Out of all the secrets, all the trouble Max and I shared, this was the biggest one of all.

"The man... the intruder..." I say in a shaky voice.

Mark shakes his head. "J... Don't do this to yourself, on today of all days." He steps forward to grab my hand again, but I pull away from him.

"No. You don't understand." We stand in front of each other as the raindrops fall around us, and I try to find the right words. "Max was with him."

"In the house?" He looks at me, confused.

I shake my head. Obviously, those weren't the right words. "He was Max's boyfriend. He used Max to get to me." My voice is thick with emotion as he stares blankly at me as the rain soaks us. The minutes tick by before he grabs my hand and roughly pulls me the rest of the distance to the car.

We get in and drive off in deafening silence except for the squealing tires as he peels out of the cemetery.

The gravel sounds like bullets against the car, and my heartbeat matches the rev of the engine. Finally, he glances over at me. "Why didn't you tell me?" He growls.

I push wet hair off my forehead and wipe my face, my hands are stained from my mascara. "I didn't recognize him by the car, at the doctor's office. It wasn't until we were at the top of the stairs, before we fell, that I recognized him. When I snapped out of the shock, I wasn't sure. I wasn't sure of anything that happened before or after."

I stare out the window lost in my own thoughts, remembering Max confirming my fear and him blaming himself for bragging that he was my best friend.

Together, we went through hundreds of regrets and what-ifs. It was a huge burden to bear. I thought I was saving Mark from that.

I'm so lost in the fog of memories that I jump when Mark throws the car in park in front of my house in the Hills.

He jumps out and slams the driver's side door. The gentleman in him helps me out of the car, and up to the door, the animal inside him vibrates quietly, waiting to explode as I unlock the door.

He leads me by the elbow to the bathroom, not saying a word.

I shiver as I sit on the edge of the tub, Mark kneels in front of me to clean the scrapes on my knees.

That's Mark, always taking care of me, no matter how bad I hurt him, no matter what a disaster I am.

I watch in awe as he deftly unbuckles the strap on my high heel and slips it off my foot, massaging his fingers around the ball of my foot then dropping it to grab my other foot.

I pull it back as he reaches for it. "Don't. Don't take care of me like this. Like I didn't just tell you something awful, like I'm not a monster."

He stares at me in his crouched position, his eyes look wild, and he truly looks half-animal, half-man.

He screams and throws my heel across the room, hitting the

mirror that hangs on the door, shattering it and sending shards of glass across the floor.

"You protected him, over and over. You chose him over me every day that you didn't tell me. He could've—"

His words strike a nerve. I'm a coward for not telling him. "Max wanted to tell you, he said he tried. I asked him not to."

He shakes his head. "You're right, I forgot. Everyone does whatever Jenna wants. It's the Jenna show." He stands with his hands on his hips and loosens his tie and damn him, seeing that tiny bit of exposed skin makes me want him despite him being seethingly mad at me.

"It wasn't his fault, he didn't know the guy was a lunatic! What was I supposed to do? Lose him too? It was bad enough he lived with the guilt the rest of his life until he couldn't anymore." *Till he killed himself.*

"But this didn't just affect you and him. I lived with it too! Where was your compassion for me?"

I stand and reach for him, but he pulls away. He looks around at the glass-covered floor. "I'm sorry, I can't do this right now."

The sound of the glass crunching under his shoes and the door closing, fills the room with a sickening echo.

The emptiness fills me instantly, and with one shoe, I hop over the glass and run after him. "Shit," I yell, cutting my foot on a piece of glass, leaving a trail of blood all over the floor.

He's already backing down the driveway by the time I get to the door.

I slam the door shut and hobble into the kitchen, quickly sitting down to remove my other shoe. I grab a towel that's on the counter and apply pressure to my cut toe.

A wave of nausea hits me. I put my head down on the island. I sit there for what feels like an eternity with insurmountable guilt piling up.

Was I wrong back then? Should I have told Mark everything from the beginning? Did my pain and suffering give me a pass to call the shots? I'm an asshole.

I feel a hand on my shoulder and gasp. "What did you do?" I look up to find all six feet of him and icy blue eyes staring intently at me. He grabs the towel and examines my foot.

He came back.

Relief floods me, and I let myself cry the tears I was holding back. Tears from the past, and the present release like a tidal surge as the dam breaks.

"I think you need stitches." He says after examining my cut.

I grab his lapels and pull him to me. "I need you."

"When I saw the blood..." He trails off.

"I'm so sorry I never told you, but I swear that's it, I never kept anything else from you."

He nods. "Shh, let me take care of you." He leaves, returning a few minutes later with bandages, and I watch as he carefully butterflies and wraps my foot expertly.

"I was going to run after you, but..." I hold up my bandaged foot.

He smiles. "I didn't make it far."

"I'm so glad." I sigh a breath of relief.

The doorbell rings, and we both stare in that direction. "I'll get it." He says, leaving me to get the door.

At the same time my stomach decides to revolt, and I make it over to the garbage just in time.

"J?" He rushes back, hearing me as I retch and gasp, and my shoulders heave.

Finally, I stand and rinse my mouth with cold water. He looks at me, concerned.

"I'm ok. It's just been a horrible day." I assure him. He nods, understanding the emotional toll of today.

"Did you order something?" He points to a box.

I shake my head and examine who it's from, but I don't recognize the name.

He grabs a knife from the butcher block and cuts the tape, opening the flaps, he pulls out a mahogany box with a Manila envelope taped to the top.

The outside is addressed to me, and in bright red letters, it says that it's to be opened by only me.

I tear it open as Mark watches and stands next to me. "It's from a lawyer," I explain as I skim the letter, handing it off to him as I take the box and hobble into the living room.

I fall back onto the couch, resting the box on my lap as Mark follows me with the letter.

I lift the lid, and I simultaneously laugh and cry as I pull out mixtapes, notes from school, concert tickets, and I unfold a piece of paper and cover my mouth as I read it silently.

My dearest friend Jenna,

If you're reading this, my plan worked, I'm gone. I want you to know I spent a lot of time thinking and planning and protecting you from seeing me at my worst. This is what I wanted, and I hope you can forgive me for what I've done.

After all, you forgave me for much worse.

By the time you read this, I'll have been gone for one year. God, I hope you are ok.

If I could've just woken up one day, just one day, without remembering, maybe things could've been different, but no amount of pills, drugs, or alcohol ever made me forget, and I was so tired of carrying it around. You were always so much stronger than I was.

Anyway, enough about me. There's something I felt you should know, I never told you because, well, I owed it to him to keep a secret from you.

I just hope that I'm not too late telling you this.

I kept in touch with Mark every week since your divorce. He was a fool to sign those papers. I told him so many times, but he insisted that he couldn't tell you no.

He's still hopelessly in love with you. I hope he found a way to keep tabs on you without me around, and I hope that you're no worse off than you were.

Jenna, if I had found in someone even one ounce of what Mark feels for you, I would never let them go.

I know you can find it in your heart to forgive him because you forgave me.

Please, please, don't waste any more time. I know you're still in love with him too.

Oh! and please don't ever, I mean ever, wear anything with feathers, or I will haunt you.

Thank you for everything, and for accepting me for me.

I love you, my dear friend.

Max

64

MARK - DECEMBER 2015

J enna reads the letter from the box and hands it to me, before looking inside the rest of the box. I skim the letter quickly and watch her reaction as she sifts through dozens of emails and texts between Max and I. *He kept all of it.*

"Whose idea was it? To keep in touch." She asks slightly irritated.

"He caught me outside your lawyer's office. He wanted the truth, whether I cheated on you or not. He said he blamed the divorce on himself for being in the way, and for your addiction. Now in hindsight, I see how I might have made him feel responsible." I watch as her face contorts.

"I'm gonna be sick." She hobbles past me and makes it to the kitchen garbage just in time. I stand behind, holding her hair as she empties her stomach. When she has nothing left, she's pale and weak and I carry her to the bedroom, gently laying her under the covers.

Almost immediately she falls asleep, the depth of her emotion exhausting her into a deep sleep. I crawl behind her, pull her close and watch as her chest rises and falls, but I'm restless and can't sleep.

So, I carefully slide out of bed and down the hallway to the bathroom, to clean up the mess of glass that I caused earlier.

My head is spinning with the information Jenna told me earlier about her attacker and I'm angry at her and Max for not telling me, but, really, I'm angry because I feel left out.

Regardless, the outcome is the same.

Jenna and I lost the baby, but maybe Max lost more than we did.

The guilt that must have consumed him as he watched his best friend suffer a psychotic break and battle alcoholism and drugs for years after.

She was never the same.

I bag up the rest of the glass and throw it in the kitchen garbage.

The box on the couch catches my eye. I sit down next to it, flipping the lid open and looking through the contents.

I laugh. They sure were a dynamic duo from the pictures I find. A time before I knew either of them. There are concert stubs, there's even one from a Tainted Innocence show back in 1995 at one of the stops we did in New Jersey. Dozens of football shaped folded notes between them from high school.

But what draws me to tears, at the bottom of the box is a scrap book. I flip through the pages to find Jenna's accolades starting with her choir days back home, newspaper articles, interviews, mentions and - list appearances all the way through 2014.

He saved everything. Her whole career is documented between the laminated pages.

"Anything good?" Jenna walks sleepily toward me, taking a seat on the oversized chair across from me.

"I couldn't sleep. I hope you don't mind." I point to the box on my lap and she shakes her head. "Leave it to Max to meddle with us from the grave."

She laughs. "Yeah."

"Actually, that doesn't really surprise me." Max was a character.

She pulls her knees up and looks intensely at me. "I'm sorry."

"It's—"

"No. Let me finish. I was wrong to keep information from you. I protected Max because he was fragile, instead of confiding in you and when I wanted to tell you, too much time had passed.

But I swear I loved you, Mark. I really did, I know that it seemed like I chose Max over you, and in some ways maybe I did, but... he only had me, and in the end I wasn't even there for him.

The night he died, I was passed out drunk. He had called me a few hours before and I didn't answer, because I'm an addict and getting drunk was more important.

He had been nagging me for six months to get sober and God, I was tired of hearing it, but I couldn't commit to doing it, so I avoided him. Maybe if I had answered..."

I kneel in front of her as she stares into space, wishing she had made a different choice. "Don't think like that."

She focuses her eyes on me, tears fill her eyes, but she holds them at bay. "I'm not the same person." She admits. "I don't want to be that girl again."

I nod but her admission has me second guessing all the intentions I had for our future. "Come on, let's get some sleep."

"Holy fuck! It's like seeing a ghost." Dave says as he spins Jenna around while she squeals with joy. When she's on her feet again, Steve hugs her warmly and Jamie kisses her cheek.

"Glad you're here Jenna, I need a date." Jamie says to her with a wink and I give him an if-looks-could-kill stare.

The guys always cared for Jenna, she became one of us when we were on tour and they protected her, as if she were their little sister.

When we divorced, she cut everyone off that had anything to do with me, it wasn't fair, but they understood.

I clear my throat. "Ok, if we're done with the family reunion. Jenna, tell them your idea."

She casually flips her hair over her shoulder, like an innocent school girl, but she commands the conference room better than anyone I've ever seen, while she prepares to pitch her idea. "As you know I recently released my single on SoundCloud. It's doing very well, but it was quite the process, and even having released four studio albums I found it a little intimidating. My hope was to release the album on my own, but then I started thinking about indie artists, how they release their tracks. It got me thinking can we streamline the process for them? While allowing them to maintain their rights. I came up with a few different ways for Heartbeat to corner the market." She hands out her proposal to each of us and we confer amongst each other.

She twirls a piece of her hair between her fingers as she follows the conversation between us.

"I think it's a good idea, but I think the only way it would work is if you were the face of this, Jenna." Jamie says as he leans against the table.

Jenna considers his suggestion quietly with her arms over her chest. "I'm not opposed. I'll have my lawyer and Lily reach out to you."

"Wow, so formal." Steve jokes.

Everyone laughs but I sit quietly as they iron out a tentative plan. My phone vibrates and I slide it out of my pocket. *Marissa.*

I don't answer and it goes to voicemail, only to ring again a few minutes later. "Excuse me. I have to get this." Jenna looks to me for confirmation that nothing is wrong, but I avoid her stare and once I'm out in the hallway, I slide the green button to answer.

"Your lawyer is being a real dick, you need to put an end to this now." Marissa shouts.

"Hello to you too." I roll my eyes.

"I'm serious Mark, and you can tell whoever you have following me they need to stop. It's an invasion of privacy."

"I don't know what you're talking about." *I plead the fifth.*

"You have shown zero percent interest in me or this baby. How do you think the media would respond to that story? You fathered this child, whether you like it or not, so call off your henchman."

I'm about to burst her bubble. "You know what's interesting, the power of the internet, it's scary what you can find if you put a little effort into looking. And you know what I found out? Before me, you were seeing Brody Thompson, linebacker for the bears and oddly enough, it looks like we overlapped."

"You don't know what you're talking about." But I hear the surprise in her voice.

"You're not the first person to fabricate a pregnancy with a celebrity. I want the paternity test." I hang up and shove my phone back into my pocket as I walk back into the conference room.

I look at Jenna whose smiling and seemingly carefree despite the emotional roller coaster she's been on the last few days with the Anniversary of Max's death.

Tonight though, I'm going to take her mind off everything.

"Are we finished here?" All eyes turn to me. "Jenna and I have plans."

"We do?" She eyes me skeptically.

I stand behind her and wrap my arms around her waist. "Baby, you have no idea."

65

"Where are we going?" After a short flight from LAX, we flew to God knows where and I was immediately blindfolded and put into the passenger seat of a car.

"Shh, It's a surprise," Mark says as he gets behind the wheel.

My heart is pounding with anticipation, and it doesn't help that his fingers are drawing tiny circles on my knee, driving me crazy.

"I hate surprises." I pout, and he laughs.

"No, you don't." His fingers stop circling, and his hand slides up my thigh, making me shiver as they climb higher and higher, and I practically growl when his fingers slide my panties to the side, growing increasing wanton as he rubs his fingers over my sex.

"Ok, maybe not. Oh, God, that feels good."

"Be patient, my love."

I lean my head back against the seat as he continues stroking me, teasing me until suddenly the car slows to a stop. He removes his fingers, and I hear his door open and then close. He's talking to someone outside the car, but I can't make out the words.

Seconds later, my car door opens, and Mark grabs my hand and pulls me out of the car. There's a slight chill in the air, and I shiver despite my jean jacket.

I walk blindly with him leading me. One hand on my lower back and the other holds my hand, keeping me from falling on my face.

Finally, we stop, and I hear water flowing. It must be almost dusk by now, and I can't imagine where he has brought me.

He slides the blindfold off, and I open my eyes to find a creek situated beneath us, and I look around for clues as to where we could be.

"Sedona." He answers before the question rolls off my lips. "I know you were upset about your Dad canceling on you for Christmas, but honestly, I think he got the short end of the stick."

I smile despite the disappointment I feel about not seeing my Dad. "I love you."

He puts his arms around me. "I'm glad, because for the next seventy-two hours we may not leave our room."

I grip the back of his shirt and pull him tightly against me. "I'm more than ok with that."

"Come on, our room should be ready." We walk back up the hill toward the resort, and a bell boy leads us to our private vista cottage.

"Oh my god." I gasp when we step inside the romantic cottage. The sun is setting, and there is the most spectacular view of the Grand Canyon, reds, and oranges litter the sky in front of me. It's serene and breathtaking. I tour the rest of the cottage and find a luxurious jetted tub for two, a deck with an outdoor shower, a king-size bed, and a gas fireplace. This place is truly a lover's paradise.

"Please let us know if you need anything." The bell boy leaves, shutting the doors behind him.

I leap into Mark's arms. "This is beautiful, thank you."

He kisses me, a slow-burning kiss that quickly evolves into the promise of more and God do I want more. So, when he pulls away and removes a piece of hair from my forehead, I feel robbed of the moment.

"Don't stop." I plead and grab hold of his hips, pulling him back to me.

"It's getting late."

"As in bedtime?"

He laughs, which makes me laugh. "Come on, I'm not that old. No, as in, we have dinner plans."

"Oh." Somehow, I forget simple necessities, like eating, when I'm with Mark.

"Don't sound so disappointed. I fully intend to make it up to you later." He kisses my forehead and pulls his shirt over his head before disappearing into the bathroom to change.

I sit on the bed reflecting. Part of me still can't believe that I'm with my ex-husband on a romantic Christmas getaway, while the other more prominent part of me feels at home.

My suitcase is on the bed behind me. I turn to unzip it and pray that there is something nice to wear inside. I wasn't allowed to pack for myself, and I'm not sure what I'll find inside. I hope that Mark had the good sense to let Lily pack for me. *What does Mark know about dressing a woman?*

I find several dresses, a short red—Christmas dress with rhinestones covering the top, a seductive little black dress, and then a gold one that's low cut in the front but longer than the rest. There are also comfortable clothes and some lingerie.

I change into the sexy black dress, and an hour later when I emerge from the bathroom, Mark's heated stare is so appreciative, that I think for a second he might change his mind about going to dinner and just undress me. Unfortunately, he does not, and we walk arm in arm until we reach the restaurant.

The room is decorated for Christmas in an understated yet upscale theme, in whites and golds, and it's gorgeous. We order, and I spin in my chair to take in the room, which has spectacular views of landscape before us.

"J?" Mark calls my attention back to the table. "I have to talk to you."

"Ok..." I spin back to him, giving him my full attention.

"I don't want to lose you again." He grabs hold of my hands, and I'm about to make a joke, but his deadpan face tells me he's trying to tell me something important.

"You won't lose me, I feel like things are different this time. I'm different."

He nods and wraps his fingers around his wedding band, hanging from the chain around his neck.

I'm nervous about where this conversation is going, my stomach is twisting in knots.

"I went and saw your Dad." He confesses.

Ok, I was not expecting that. I shift nervously in my chair."You did? When?" *This is news to me.*

"A few weeks ago. I wanted to clear the air between us."

Funny, my Dad didn't mention anything about Mark visiting. "Oh. I'm sure that went over like fire and ice."

He smirks and sits back. Folding his arms across his chest with a cocky grin on his face. "Actually, it went well."

What the hell is going on here? "It did?" I say in disbelief.

"It did." He affirms.

"Well, did he tell you why he canceled on me for Christmas?" My voice is agitated.

He nods, and I start to take it personally that neither of them told me about this meeting. "I asked him to."

I feel anger rising up, and I know my face is heated and flushed. "Why would you do that?" I remove my linen napkin from my lap and throw it on the table.

"Because I wanted to bring you here."

I take deep breaths and count like Dr. Wild told me to when I feel irrational. "I know you think I needed all of this," I wave my hands around the luxury restaurant inside the resort. "But I really just wanted a quiet Christmas with my Dad. I missed out on a lot of Holidays with family, and I was fine with this trip when I thought he canceled on me, but..." I rise from the table. "I—I need a minute." I don't want to say anything else in the heat of the moment, so I excuse myself.

It's Christmas Eve, I'm not sure what my Dad is doing now that Mark made him cancel on me. So, I grab my phone and call, praying he will answer because it's late on the east coast, but I want him to know this trip was not my idea and that Mark shouldn't have asked him to cancel.

He doesn't answer. I leave a message and head back into the restaurant, disappointed.

I pause only feet from the table, my steps falter, and I must be hallucinating. There's no other explanation. He starts walking to me, but I can't move.

"Jenna. Baby." He greets me.

"Dad," I whisper as my Dad crashes into me, giving me the biggest bear hug. "What are you doing here?"

Mark stays sitting at the table, his leg crossed over his knee, and a huge smile spreads across his face.

"I hope you're not upset that I'm here."

I'm very emotional, and I can't stop the tears from falling. "Upset? God, no."

"Well, don't be upset with Mark either, he just wanted us to have a special Christmas together."

I cry and laugh through the tears.

"Come on, I'm starving. Despite my first-class meal." He winks at me, and I laugh.

Mark stands and pulls out my chair as we return to the table. I grab hold of his arms and lean forward to kiss him. "Thank you," I whisper.

He bends forward to whisper in my ear, his words are smooth like honey. "You can thank me later."

We eat our meal, and it's surreal that my Dad and Mark are sharing a meal so cordially. It's a first.

"So, Dad, Mark told me he came to visit you." They exchange a look, and that's when I know for sure they're both up to something.

"He did." My Dad doesn't look me in the eye.

"Good. I'm glad we are all finally putting the past behind us."

Mark grabs my hand and gently squeezes. We finish our meal, dinner is fantastic, and it's one of the best evenings I've ever had. We walk my Dad back to his cottage, and Mark and my Dad tell me that their plans for tomorrow include a golf day for them and a spa day for me.

"I still can't believe you and my Dad made amends."

Mark and I are walking hand in hand down by the creek, he caresses the top of my hand with his thumb.

"I thought he was going to slam the door in my face." He wraps a shawl around my shoulders as he leads me to a gazebo covered in thousands of tiny lights. He helps me up the few steps, and I walk to the other side of the gazebo, staring out at the beautiful vista in front of me.

"He's soft in his old age. He just wants me to be happy." I don't know why we couldn't get to a place of forgiveness sooner.

I breathe in deeply. The smell of firewood burning from the cottages leaves a romantic essence in the air.

"I know, and I want the same thing. I think we finally realized we're on the same side, where you're concerned at least." He stands behind me while his hands hold onto my hips, and his warm breath tickles my ear. "Which is why he said yes when I asked if I could marry you again."

I turn surprised in his arms. "You did what?"

He takes a step back, then bends down onto one knee.

I press my hands against my lips when he pulls out a ring box.

"My last proposal sucked, but I meant what I said then, and I mean it now. I love you, Jenna. I want the world to know you are mine and nothing, and no one will ever change how I feel about you. The universe is giving us a second chance. Marry me this time because you want to, not because I want you to. I'd rather hear you say no, then tie you down for all the wrong reasons. I want us to be in it for the long haul, as a team. So, J, will you marry me?" The lights from the gazebo dance in his eyes. I can't help but think about so many things in the matter of a millisecond, but the only thing that sticks out in my mind is one word. *Yes.*

"I don't need a piece of paper or a ring, because all I ever needed was you. I thought you gave up on me when I was at my worst and that killed me, that's why I walked away. But I can't imagine anyone else making me feel the way you do. The way you always have. So yes. I'll marry you. I want to marry you, I love you."

He claps his hands together and stands to kiss me before sliding the biggest rock I've ever seen onto my ring finger.

I'm elated and he spins me around, making me laugh.

"I'm really glad you said yes."

"Oh? Why is that?"

"Lily said you would say no."

I roll my eyes and laugh. "I can't believe you told her."

He cups the back of my neck and kisses me deeply. "It was pretty hard to convince her to clear your schedule otherwise. She is impossible."

"You can say that again."

He leads me back out of the gazebo. "You know, I hear there is a hot tub waiting with our names on it."

"I can't wait." We start back toward our cottage, but I have a burning question, and I pull him to stop. "Hey, how did you get my Dad to say yes? It couldn't have been as easy as you're making it sound."

He winks at me. "We made a deal, you'll just have to wait and see."

66

JENNA - MARCH 2006

"I'm so glad you're out. I missed you." Max is sitting at our kitchen table and I'm sitting next to him, trying to readjust to normal life outside of a posh rehab center.

"What can I say, I'm stubborn." Max and I entered rehab together, but what he completed in three months took me six.

I didn't think I needed treatment. I thought I had everything under control. I didn't think I had a coke habit, I admit to being a drinker, but I didn't have a choice. I was losing Mark, I was losing everything. After the first two weeks of withdrawing I realized I needed a new addiction. Something else to fixate on.

Anorexia was what I fixated on. It was a high seeing how long I could go without eating, a new kind of adrenaline rush. Which did nothing but set me back months inside rehab and got me put into another six months of outpatient therapy.

It's only been two weeks.

Mark didn't want me to see Max this soon, but after Max convinced him he was 'rehabilitated' he agreed to let him come over for a short visit.

"Beyond stubborn." Mark calls from the couch.

I roll my eyes and lift my knees to my chest. "You look great." I say to Max while Mark continues eavesdropping.

"Got me a handsome guy too. Wait till you meet him. Don't worry Mark, he's clean cut, real straight edge." Max turns to where Mark thinks we don't notice him.

I slap Max playfully on the hand. "Oh my god. When did that happen?"

"A couple months ago."

I nod, feeling cheated, like I've missed so much. "Well, we should do dinner ASAP."

Mark lifts off the couch and comes into the kitchen. "J, I think we should take things slow. It's gonna be hard going out." He kisses my forehead, grabs a bottle of water and heads out to the patio to sit in the sun.

"I've been a prisoner in rehab and now I'm going to be locked away in my own house." I slap the counter for good measure.

"He's just trying to protect you. It was really hard on him." Max sticks up for Mark.

"Wow, way to be on my side." I slide off the chair and head to the fridge. There are bottles of cranberry and grape juice. Substitutions for alcohol since this is a dry house now.

"I didn't mean it like that, Jenna. I'm just playing devil's advocate, it's hard to be away from the person you love."

I look at Max like he is a completely different person. "Well, *he* put me in there."

"Ew, don't be a brat to me, you could've said no."

I slam the refrigerator door empty handed. "No, I couldn't. His ultimatum was 'get better or we're done'. That left a lot of options."

"We were out of control." Max admits.

"Ok, fine. I'm wrong." I drop back down on the chair and fold my arms over my chest.

"Let me talk to him, maybe you guys could just come to my place."

I squint my eyes at Max. "Since when are you and Mark best

buddies?" He stands and puts on his fedora, the one I bought him in Italy after a night of clubbing.

"Alright, I'm out. I don't want to argue." He leaves slamming the front door. I glance out at Mark who turns to look when he hears the door.

"What happened?" He stands in the doorway eying me carefully before walking over to me.

"Apparently, I'm picking fights." I roll my eyes.

He pushes my arm playfully. "You are a little moody."

"That's because I *am* moody. I'm so damn angry."

He puts his hands on his hips. "At me?"

"Yes, at you, at Max, at myself."

He hangs his head, but I'm not going to make it easy for him. I'm ready for a fight. A fight that he's not ready for.

"Tell me what I should have done?" *Ok, maybe he is ready for a fight.*

"I could've done it on my own. You didn't have to drag me there while the media took every shot at me that they could."

He shakes his head. "Why are you really upset? Is this because of what I said? About dinner with Max?"

"No, this is about you treating me like a child. I have to ask you permission for everything, you're officially my keeper."

He grabs me by my biceps and pulls me to him. I try and break free, but he keeps his hold on me, shocking me to the core. He's never put his hands on me like this. "You're not a child, so stop acting like one. Open your eyes Jenna, you needed help. I forgave you for a lot of things, but I won't forgive you for saying that I don't love you or that I put you in rehab out of spite."

"Forgave *me*! Forgave me for what?" I interrogate him.

He drops his hands and walks into the living room, opening and slamming a drawer closed, returning with an envelope. He throws it on the counter and folds his arms over his chest.

I scoff even though I have no idea what the contents inside are. I flip it over and let the contents drop onto the counter. I hold my composure when I see the pictures, but I'm sure the shock still registers on my face. "Where did you get these?" I slide my hand over them to fan them out, it makes me sick. At least a hundred candid shots of me. Some of me clubbing, severely intoxicated or high, backstage with a crew member, his hand up my skirt, me topless at a strip club. Totally distasteful and humiliating shots.

"A photographer sent them to me, he was going to do a documentary on you. I had to pay him off. He was going to sell these."

I scream and push them off the counter until they are scattered all over the floor. "I didn't cheat on you." *I know I didn't, I'm sure of it.* Despite all my fuck ups I love Mark, I would never hurt him like that. We stare so intensely at each other until he finally speaks.

"Are you sure you would even remember if you did." He leaves me standing there while he goes back out to the patio.

I know I need to change, he deserves better than this. I vow in that instant to change. I should follow him and tell him this, but I don't. I slide down on the floor and pick up the pieces that are my life.

67

"I'll meet you there around three." We've been back in Nashville for a week now. The press has been relentless about a Mark and Jenna reunion and insinuating a love triangle with Marissa, and despite me resting the last week, I'm still exhausted and not feeling well.

I was supposed to meet with Lily, but instead, I'm sitting in my doctor's office. I hang up with Lily just as the Doctor walks in.

"Jenna, how are you?" That's a loaded question.

"I feel awful, like I have the flu."

He takes my temperature and makes a face before lifting his iPad and making a note. He leans against the counter, crossing one leg over the other.

"Jenna, you don't have the flu."

"Ok. What is it?" I prepare myself for the worst and know that whatever it is, I'm a fighter and I'll deal with it.

He puts the iPad down on the desk and takes seat on a round stool on wheels, leaning against the wall with his arms folded over his chest. "You're pregnant." He smiles like he's just told me I've won the lottery.

"That's not even funny." I hop off the exam table and start to grab my things.

"I was never very funny." I glare at the Doctor and wrap my fingers around the doorknob. "But I'm not trying to be funny."

I turn back to him. I've had enough of his antics. "That's ridiculous and quite impossible. My tubes are tied."

He nods, he knows this, and he knows my history of miscarriages. "Well, the universe must have aligned just right, because you *are* pregnant."

I drop everything. My bag hits the floor with a thud. *What do I even have in my bag that makes it sound like that?* "How could this happen?" He laughs, and before he can make any more jokes, I correct myself. "How could this happen medically?"

"It is rare, but sometimes the tubes just... reattach and poof! Pregnant."

I sit down in the chair instead of on the exam table, shock setting in.

"The high-risk obstetrician will see you shortly. Congratulations."

I swallow over the lump in my throat because not only is this unexpected, but also because it's extremely dangerous for me to try to conceive.

My body doesn't work like every other woman's, which is why I had my tubes tied after the last miscarriage.

I sit anxiously waiting until the nurse comes in and brings me down to the OB's office. I say a quick prayer and look up at the ceiling as if I'm talking directly to God, then I lock any remnant of a feeling inside a black box within myself. I don't let myself feel or contemplate anything. I just go through the motions.

After several vials of blood are taken, I'm sent for a sonogram where I close my eyes and put my arm over them, so I'm not tempted to look. I'm literally so locked up inside myself that when the OB doctor comes in, it takes me a minute to snap out of it as he does the internal exam.

"This is nothing short of a miracle." He says as he pulls off his glove and studies the sonogram on the computer, which I still refuse to look at. "It's almost as if the surgery fixed you." He says as if he's just discovered a cure.

I look at him, puzzled. "Come again?"

He spins away from the computer to face me. "All of your levels are perfect. The placenta is right where it should be, and the baby is measuring a little over fourteen weeks. For a normal pregnancy, you've made it past any point of concern, and even at your age—with all due respect, I have no doubt at this point that this is a normal, healthy pregnancy."

I shake my head. "What do I do now?"

He laughs and points to the rock on my finger. "Well, you might want to tell the father and then succumb to some awful pregnancy craving. We'll see you back here in two weeks." He hands me the sonogram pictures and leaves. Once the door shuts, every emotion that I locked up in that little box comes pouring out.

"You're what!" Lily says with a deafening 'what!' I'm pacing the kitchen floor nervously, stopping to hand her the sonogram pictures, which I still haven't looked at.

"Preggers, you heard it here first." I say jokingly like a tabloid headline.

She shakes her head. "Is this some cruel joke? You told me you couldn't have babies."

I stop pacing and face her. "The doctor proclaimed me a medical miracle."

"Praise the Lord, Jesus Christ." She makes the sign of the cross and stares at me in disbelief.

"When are you going to tell Mark?"

I shake my head. I haven't had much time to think about that. "Do I have to tell him?" I whine.

"Do you think he won't notice? Now that I look, you do have a bump. I thought you were just packing on a few pounds."

I look down at my stomach, self-consciously. "Thanks," I roll my eyes and continue pacing the floor. "I guess I'll tell him tonight."

"Sure is interesting, though."

"What's that?" I pull a bag of chips from the pantry.

"That Marissa lied about having his baby, and now here you are, actually having his baby. It is his right?" She smirks.

"Oh my god, of course, it is." I jump at the sound of the front door slamming. Mark has been in a foul mood since finding out the results of the paternity test. *Not that I blame him.*

"The media is going to be all over this three-ring circus." She says, her voice low.

I know she is right, and I imagine all the headlines and what they will say. I shove the sonogram pictures into my purse just as Mark walks into the kitchen.

"What's going on, ladies?" He kisses me on the cheek.

"Jenna was just telling me the most interesting thing I've ever heard."

I glare at her.

"Oh? What's that?" He turns to me, and I spin to the fridge for a bottle of water, nervous he will notice my stomach.

"Just something I heard on the news, it's not that interesting, she's exaggerating."

He nods. "What time do we have to be at the Ryman?" *Shit, I forgot all about the fundraiser event.*

"Eight." Lily answers for me.

He nods and leaves the kitchen.

"Jenna, you have to tell him. He's walking around moping for no reason."

"I will, as soon as I find the right moment."

"The moment is now." She waves me off.

I throw my hands in the air. "Ok. Ok. I'm going."

"Good. I'm leaving." I walk behind her to the front door, past where Mark is sitting in the TV Room. "Bye Mark." She calls in a sing-song voice. "Call me later, Jenna."

"I will."

She winks and opens the door, and I close it behind her taking a deep breath as I head in to talk to Mark. His eyes are glazed over as he watches the TV.

"Hey," I say, sitting on the ottoman in front of him.

"I'm not pouting." He says, and I rub my hands nervously over my thighs.

"I mean, you have every right to be. What she did was awful." He nods but doesn't say anything. "We don't have to go to the event tonight." I offer because he doesn't look like he's in the mood to go anywhere to socialize, and I don't really feel up to it anyway. He doesn't respond. He just sits, staring into the idiot box hanging on the wall until he finally sits up and says.

"I'm leaving Heartbeat."

68

MARK - JANUARY 2016

"I don't understand, why?" Jenna's fury is directed at me as she paces from the living room to the kitchen, slamming things as she goes.

Some things never change. I channel surf from the couch, there is no point in fighting about this. I made up my mind.

"I told you, it would've swayed your decision." I say, knowing she would've changed her plans to release her new album independently.

"You don't know that for sure."

"Look at you. If I gave you a contract right now you would sign it in blood."

"I don't understand how you're so calm about this, the label is your baby. Why would you leave now? What was the whole expanding into Nashville campaign?" She comes back into the living room with her hands on her hips. "Mark," She pauses. "Are you having a mid-life-crisis?"

"Maybe." I admit. I never thought I'd leave the label, but maybe it's time to do something else.

"And the guys? How do they feel about you leaving?"

I put the remote down and go to her, resting my hands on her shoulders. "I have a plan Jenna. Just trust me ok?"

She rolls her eyes. "How about this. I sign with Heartbeat, you don't have to quit, and we can all make a lot of money."

I sit back down on the couch and start channel surfing again, ignoring her offer to fix everything. We both know I would stay if she were to sign under the label. I would feel responsible to make sure she did well, just like she feels responsible to keep me there. We would all come out on top. She's a phenomenal artist.

The truth is I've been in a mood since I found out Marissa lied about the baby. There is no baby.

Only God knows why I feel like this. Maybe it's because deep down I wanted it. I wanted to be a father.

I should be thrilled to be off the hook, but I can't help feeling melancholy. I don't tell Jenna any of this though.

"I set up the Nashville office just as I said I would. I promised the guys I'd fix the business and I did. Now I need to move on."

She stands in front of the TV. "Move onto what? The 'clothing line'?"

"For the record, there is an actual clothing line."

"Ok, fine." She puts her hands in the air and storms out.

I grab my phone off the table and respond to Jamie about meeting on Thursday, to remove me legally from the label. Then I head into the bedroom to change for the event.

"J?" She's on the bed, on top of the covers sound asleep. I sit next her and run my fingers over her cheek. I know having her back in my life should be enough, and God it is, she's more than enough, but I need to tell her how I feel, what I really want.

And what I want is for us to adopt. I want to be a father. I want us to raise a child together, and though it may take a while for a child to come to us, I hope Jenna will be open to the idea of adoption this time around.

I strip off my shirt and climb behind her, resolving to talk to her about it first thing in the morning.

I SLEEP LATER than planned and Jenna is already gone by the time I wake. I'm frustrated because I need to talk to her about adopting, and sooner rather than later.

I call her cell hoping we can talk over lunch, but she doesn't answer. So, I send her a text instead, which also goes unanswered.

By the time five rolls around, I'm borderline losing my mind, so I break down and call Lily.

"Lily, are you with Jenna?" I ask, hoping I'm not crossing any lines.

"She's in L.A., didn't she mention that? She said she had something to take care of, I assumed you were going with her."

Fear slices through me. "No, I don't know anything about it, and she hasn't answered me all day. Can you call and see if she answers for you?" *Maybe she's just pissed at me.*

We hang up and two minutes later she calls back.

"Sorry Mark, she didn't answer for me either." I can hear the worry in her voice, it matches my own because we both know Jenna wouldn't leave without telling me.

"I'll call you back." I hang up, my head is spinning and I'm not sure what my next move is. I'm about to call Jamie and ask him to call Jenna when her purse catches my eye. It's just sitting there on the kitchen counter. *Why didn't she take it with her?*

I rifle through its contents, normal chick stuff, lip gloss, a compact, a bottle of ibuprofen, but I notice her wallet is gone. Then I see something strange, I pull out a long strip of paper that has been folded loosely in half. I know I shouldn't snoop but curiosity gets the best of me and I unfold the sheet to find six black and white, square sonogram photos.

I see Jenna's name in the top left corner of each picture, and I lean against the kitchen counter trying to figure out why she's carrying these around with her.

I look at the pictures again, and notice the date. "Yesterday?" I hold the pictures in my hand and my heart puts it together before my brain. "Oh God. Yesterday!" I call Jenna again and get no answer.

Now I'm sure that something isn't right. She's either really upset with me or something has happened to her and for the first time in my life I pray she isn't pregnant, because I don't think either of us will survive that again.

I grab my wallet and my keys and in minutes I'm out the door and on the way to the airport. I'm boarding the plane when my phone rings. *Finally.*

"Jenna, what the—"

"Hi Mark." Ice cold fear grips me.

"Marissa? Where's Jenna?" I stammer, trying to sound calm.

"She's here, with me. We're having a lovely girl chat, comparing stories." A flight attendant taps me on the shoulder to sit down.

"Let me talk to her."

"We're getting along so well, I don't think that's a good idea. Besides, don't you want to talk to me?"

"Marissa..." I have no idea what condition Jenna is in, and it's going to be hours before I can get to her. "I want to talk to you. I'm actually on my way there. Just don't do anything else until I get there. We can work this all out."

"I loved you, Mark." The plane is pushing back from the terminal and I only have a minute until the flight attendant tells me to shut my phone off.

"Riss, I love you. Don't do anything stupid. I'm coming." I end the call and send a text to Jamie telling him the short version and to pick me up at the airport.

69

JENNA - JANUARY 2016

I took the bait.

She knew I would. She knew I would be a martyr for Mark, and her pleas for me to talk to her wouldn't go unanswered.

Now, I am the bait.

I planned on giving her hell, and at some point, I realized this could end badly, but I thought I had it under control until she must've slipped something in my drink, and I woke up in her house.

My arms are tied behind my back. They ache from being in this position for so long, and no matter how hard I try to keep my eyes open, they want to close.

The sound of the front door opening and closing jars me awake. I listen for sounds but only hear silence. *Did she leave? Is Mark here?* He has to have figured out by now something is wrong.

I do my best to undo the ties on my wrists, but so far, it's been a futile effort.

Vigorously, I move my wrist back and forth. The tie cuts into my skin, but I can feel it slipping down onto my hand, and I wiggle and twist until finally, I slip my hand out.

Very quietly, I work on the other side using my free hand until the door opens and closes again. I hear voices, but they are too far to make out who it is.

I get the knot loose enough to slide my wrist out, and I jump out of the chair like it's on fire.

I look around in the dark for my phone, but I don't see it, and I'm pretty sure Marissa took it with her. I look around the room for anything else, a landline, or an escape or anything that can be used as a weapon.

After a quick look out the window, I realize there's no escape. We're up too high. I hear footsteps, and I look around the room for a hiding place, but there isn't much in the room. So quietly, I sit back down in the chair and slip my wrists back into the loosened ties.

The steps get closer, but they don't stop, they keep going then I hear another door open and shut.

I tiptoe over to the door and put my ear against it. I don't hear anything, so I slowly turn the knob, opening the door a fraction of an inch, just enough so I that can see out. The hallway is empty, so I slowly push the door open until I can squeeze out without opening it all the way.

The floor beneath me squeaks, making me pause. The stairs are too far for me to get to without making noise.

I look up, there are crisscrossed wood beams above me that overlook a living room, and I look for a way to get up there. If I can slide across the beams to the other side of the room, I can reach the front door.

I climb on top of the railing and use the height of it to grab onto the beam above me, carefully hoisting myself up and onto the beam. My legs hang on either side of it.

I'm not afraid of heights, but I'm dizzy from not eating and from whatever she drugged me with. I close my eyes to refocus, taking a deep breath and prepare to crawl across.

Behind me, a door opens, I'm totally visible up here, and I curse myself because I didn't calculate how long it would take me to cross the beams and now, I'm nothing more than a sitting duck.

Marissa is standing at the railing, figuring out no doubt how I got up here.

"What an interesting way to escape." She calls to me.

I ignore her and crawl further along the beam, and I'm almost halfway across when she takes the same route, climbing up onto the railing and lifting up onto the beam behind me. "You're making this way too easy, everyone will assume you were high when you climbed up here and accidentally fell, what a shame."

"When I get down, everyone will know *you're* insane and that you brought me here against my will."

We both freeze when the front door is kicked in. Mark and Jamie stand in the open foyer, gaping at the two of us on the beam above. The look of pure terror on his face speaks volumes, and he has no idea what to do as he looks from me to Marissa.

"You were supposed to come alone, Mark." Her agitated voice snaps him out of it, and he slowly makes his way to the stairs.

"Riss, don't move. Let me get you down."

I can't see her, but him calling her that makes the hair on my neck stand on end, and I look at Jamie, who doesn't say anything but puts a finger casually to his lips telling me to be quiet and wait. *I hope they have a plan.*

"No, don't come up here. I'm not stupid, Mark. You have no interest in saving me."

"That's not true. I don't want anyone to get hurt." He says truthfully.

I crawl a few more inches before stopping so I can sit and straddle the beam and look behind me. I see Marissa standing on the beam, facing Mark, who has made it to the railing. "Come here." He calls to her, but she shakes her head.

"I just wanted Jenna to know the truth." She starts to cry.

"Riss, it's ok. Just come here, walk back to me."

"There was a baby, but I lost it." She shakes her head and walks a few steps toward him. "Ironic, isn't it? That I lost it, just like Jenna, just like that."

He shakes his head. "It doesn't matter, I'm not upset with you.

Please, come down from there." She shakes her head, and he climbs up onto the railing, holding his hand out to her. I look back to Jamie, but he's gone, and I'm sliding infinitesimally across the beam to the other side. I make eye contact with Mark, who nods his chin up slightly, for me to keep going.

"I just wanted you to see me so I could explain."

He looks at her sympathetically. "I'm here. I'm listening." His voice is so even and calm.

"You didn't even recognize me. I made no impression on you at all." I look to Mark, who looks just as confused as I am. "That's what I thought." She says when it's clear he doesn't know what she's talking about.

"Recognize you when?"

"2010."

He squints as he thinks. I see the moment he remembers, the moment it clicks for him, and I pause my journey on the beam. I count back the years trying to put it into perspective for myself.

"The surrogate." He says, connecting the dots before my brain can.

"You would think between that and working at your label you would've remembered me a lot sooner. Especially after how great our meeting went that day."

I remember her now. She was the girl in the tabloids. The one that sparked the affair rumors. The girl who didn't deny she was sleeping with Mark.

"You, bitch," I say without regard for being suspended up in the air, on a beam with a crazy woman only feet away. Both of them look at me as I move to stand.

"Jenna." Mark looks at me, shooting me a warning glance. Blame it on the hormones, blame it on adrenaline, but something primal comes over me, and I see red as I move away from the end of the beam back toward Marissa.

She has a cocky grin on her face. "You're the tabloid girl. You fabricated the whole thing. You made it look like he was having an affair."

Her smile is sadistic. "Did I? Did I make the whole thing up?"

"He didn't sleep with you, not then, anyway." I'm sure of it.

"Didn't matter. Everyone believed it."

I'm inches away from her now. "I divorced him because of that, you fucked with our lives."

She shrugs, her face is cold and uncaring. "I know, and then he pined over you for so long. I didn't think he would ever get over it. I was sure after the first six months at the label, I could make him forget you, but he walked around like a heartsick puppy. It drove me crazy. It took me longer than I expected to wind up in his bed, but I had him. I had him, and then you came back. Why did you do that? Everything was perfect." She walks forward as I take a step toward her.

Mark climbs out onto the beam.

I hear crackling and smell smoke coming from the other side of the house. "You are crazy. He never wanted you. You were a... a tool to make me jealous. He loves me, he's always loved me. You will never be anything to him." I say, distracting her as Mark wraps his arms around her, pulling her back toward the railing. They fall to the floor, and he wrestles with her as I turn back the other way on the beam. I hear sirens off in the distance, and I freeze, being pregnant and captive is treading way too close to bad memories.

Smoke is filling the room faster, making it harder to see, and I'm losing valuable time. "No, Jenna, come back this way!" Mark yells as Jamie runs back inside, screaming something about a wildfire as he rushes around, frantically moving the furniture about and pushing the couch toward the beam.

I see flashing lights outside and hear people rushing inside, but the smoke is so thick that now, I can't see either side, or the beam under my feet.

Pieces of ash fly all around me, and the crackling sounds as the fire engulfs the house, and I fear there is no way out. I cough and carefully lower to a sitting position on the beam.

"J! You have to crawl to the other side." I can hear that Mark is below me now, and the firefighters are yelling for him to get out.

"I can't see," I yell to him.

"Then hang off the beam. I will catch you." I shake my head even though he can't see it.

"I can't." I put my hand over my stomach, I can't imagine willingly falling from this beam, but Mark doesn't know why, and I can't bring myself to tell him right now. "I can't," I repeat and cough, the smoke filling my lungs.

"I found the sonogram pictures." He yells and I cry out when I realize he knows. "J, jump. I promise, I will catch you." I shriek as I look around. I don't have any other options.

I say a prayer, making the sign of the cross as I do, and lower myself down, and for all that is Holy, I don't know why, but I take that leap of faith and let go of the beam.

EPILOGUE
JENNA

"Can you tell me *now* where we're going?" I must admit spontaneity is not my strong suit, but here I am on a plane letting Mark whisk me away to who knows where, doing God knows what.

"Where is the fun in that?" He winks at me.

It's useless, he's a steel trap. I lean my head back against the seat, resting my hand over my stomach and hoping that wherever we are going has a great buffet.

In addition to not knowing where we're going, my cell phone and tablet have been confiscated, and I feel completely cut off. "What if Lily needs me for something?" I ask, but he smiles patronizingly.

"She knows how to reach me."

"Wait, does she know where we're going?"

His lip twitches, and I know I'm right. Well, he's not the only one with a surprise up his sleeve. I smile knowingly to myself.

I take a nap, and a few hours later, I sit up to look out the window as we fly over a paradise of blue water and palm trees, and I instantly recognize where we are.

"Aruba," I say it slow, almost seductively as memories of the time spent here rush back as if it were only a week ago and not more than a decade ago.

Mark rubs his middle finger over his bottom lip, no doubt, reminiscing himself about our time here. "You loved it here." He says, and I laugh, remembering how I thought moving here would solve all our problems.

"If I remember correctly, you loved it here too." I wink at him.

"It had its perks." He lifts his brow and smiles coyly.

"So, what exactly is on the agenda?"

"It's about time I make an honest woman out of you."

"Oh?" How fitting for us to come back here and tie the knot, full circle, I love the idea.

"Unless, of course, you just want to keep things the way they are. Either way, you're mine. I'm not letting you go."

I slide my hand into his. "I love the idea."

He wraps his arms around me as he kisses my forehead, and we wait for the ok to disembark.

From the airport, it's only a short drive to the resort. It has been updated, but it's not much different than I remember.

Mark entwines his fingers through mine, and I'm so damn giddy I actually skip, which makes him laugh, and he twirls me around. We must look like two lovesick kids.

We check-in and go to our suite. The view is breathtaking, and I run out onto the private Veranda where the warm breeze wraps me in familiar memories and immediately relaxes me. Mark stands behind me, running his hands up and down my arms, leaving a trail of goosebumps.

"Did I do good?" He whispers in my ear.

"You did *very* good." I turn in his arms, one kiss turns into two, two turns into four, and before I know it, we're naked on the veranda worshiping each other in a slow, unhurried rhythm until we're breathless and sated laying on the lounge chair.

After a little while, Mark turns to me. "I'd rather do nothing else, but I did make reservations. It would be rude not to show."

"I'll put some clothes on then."

His eyes are heated as I lift off the chair and head back inside.

We eat an amazing gourmet dinner and take a walk down the beach, but I'm exhausted, and sleep is calling to me.

I sleep so soundly that I don't hear Mark leave for his run the next morning. I call for room service and help myself to a large breakfast and just like last time we were here a rack of designer wedding dresses show up as well as a wedding day coordinator, who hands me a wedding day itinerary and lets me know the hair and makeup team are on their way.

I mostly stick to the itinerary timeline that Mark has obviously put so much time into, and I get to the outdoor patio area only fifteen minutes behind schedule.

The wedding planner is waiting for me, and the doors are closed so that I can't see the beach area beyond them.

"Mommy!" A small voice screams behind me.

I turn around just in time as my handsome little boy throws himself into my arms. I squeal in surprise. "Max!" I kiss a million kisses all over his little face stopping only to look up to see where he came from. I swing Max onto my hip and watch as my Dad walks a few paces behind.

"Dad," I say with tears in my eyes.

"Jenna, you look gorgeous." We both shed a few tears, and I hug him tightly, while Max squirms in my arms. "I can't believe you're here."

"I wouldn't miss it for the world."

I smile, and he puts his arm out for me to hold onto.

It's been two years since the night I took a leap of faith to jump off the beam into Mark's arms. Mark kept his promise to catch me, and the worst thing that happened was an overnight stay in the hospital for minor smoke inhalation. Marissa's family checked her into a mental health facility, and I visit her from time to time. Life is too short to stay angry.

Our son, Max John McGinley, was born a healthy eight pounds, four ounces, and a week late. My country album topped the Billboard chart for twelve consecutive weeks, and Mark went back to Heartbeat, where he and I developed a platform for indie artists to release music under a label, without the pressure of a Contract. The guys all gave up some of their shares to make me part owner, and business has never been better.

Mark and I have never been better.

"Ready?" Dad asks as the piano starts.

"I've never been more ready." The doors open, and to my surprise, our friends occupy the many rows of chairs along the patio.

Lily and Jamie are on either side of Mark, who is quite dashing in his tux. I blow him a kiss before I walk down the aisle with my Dad and Max, and I know I'm beaming.

Dad and Mark shake hands before he leans down to kiss me on the cheek then he takes Max from me, as Mark and I join hands.

The ceremony is short and sweet, and our guests throw tropical flowers as the three of us walk back down the aisle and head into the reception.

Lily dances with Max while Mark spins me around for our first dance.

"This was an amazing day," I say, linking my hands behind his back.

"Perfect." He says and pulls me closer, but Max has other plans, tugging on my dress until I scoop him up in my arms. He gives me a kiss, and I hug him tightly.

"What about Daddy, bud?" Mark puckers his lips for a kiss.

"No. Mommy." He shakes his head at Mark, and we both laugh. I kiss my little boy and bask in the joy of being a Mom.

I made peace with all the evil in my life, forgiving myself, continuing therapy, and my biggest accomplishment of all, staying sober.

I thank God for giving me a second chance, for letting me experience this beautiful life, and I'm grateful for all the miracles.

Life may not have always been perfect, but those times were lessons learned, and I wouldn't change a thing.

Ok, well, maybe a few things, but those things did make me who I am today.

Mark hands me a glass of sparkling cider, before taking one for himself—sharing a life of sobriety with me. We listen as Lily and Jamie each make a toast, and then I *finally* get to dance with my Dad at my wedding. Which leaves us both blubbering like babies.

When all the women line up, it's Lily who catches the bouquet, and I wink at her when I see her and Jamie dancing a little while later.

I'm ready to call it a night. So gracefully, I interrupt Mark talking to a friend and pull him out onto the beach.

"You can't wait to get me alone again, huh?" He says playfully.

I shrug. "You know me so well."

"We can go back to the room now, no one will miss us."

"A very enticing offer, yet, I have to decline." I pull him to a stop.

"Oh? Why is that?"

"I'm starving."

He looks at me, puzzled. "We just ate." He grabs my hand and continues our walk.

"We did, but... I'm eating for two these days." He stops abruptly and turns to me, staring and speechless.

I smile satisfied that I've been able to keep a secret for this long. "You're not the only one capable of surprises."

"You're..."

I nod. "Nineteen weeks."

He squeals and spins me around before he sets me on my feet and pulls me into his arms. His forehead resting on mine.

"Oh, and Mark, it's a girl, and if she's anything like me... You're gonna have your hands full."

He smirks. "I think I can handle it."

I shrug and say a prayer for him as he puts his arm around me. I rest my head on his shoulder and look out into the vast ocean, dreaming of what our forever looks like.

ACKNOWLEDGMENTS

I just want to start by saying I may not have been a writer my whole life, and if it weren't for the encouragement of my best friend (she knows who she is), I might never have had the guts to try this thing called writing. I am, first and foremost a reader, a fan, my love for books is soul deep. I love to get lost in a good book, and although I've mostly been hanging out in the romance genre, I find all of you authors out there truly inspiring and amazing.

Thank you to J.C.R for always letting me bounce ideas off of you and never telling me to 'Shut up about the book already!' You truly are an amazing person, and I hope the rest of the world gets to know you one day. Without you, this book would be sitting on my laptop for eternity.

Thank you to my family for understanding that this is what I want to do and letting me have a little time to do it.

Thank you to my beta readers for your kind words, honest feedback, and encouragement. Thank you from the bottom of my heart for giving my work a chance to be in your to be read pile. Without you readers, books wouldn't come to life.

Thank you for buying & reading my book, I am eternally grateful. Please consider leaving a review, I read each and every word.

ALSO BY R.J. ROME

Twelve Naughty Nights

Becca Sullivan doesn't do commitment. Until a one night stand turns into everything she ever wanted. There's just one problem, he's her new boss.

Cupid's Sacrifice

Aiden Blackwood has been in love with his best friend's little sister since they were kids, but there's one problem, he made a pact that she's off-limits. Now she's about to get engaged to the wrong guy. Will he risk losing his best friend and the girl of his dreams with the truth? Or will he sacrifice himself for her happily ever after?

Heart Overboard

(Coming Soon - join my mailing list for updates)

A summer cruise brings them together. She's not looking for love, but their connection is hard to ignore. They say everyone has a soulmate, will she walk away from hers?

ABOUT THE AUTHOR

R.J. Rome is an author of contemporary romance. Born in New Jersey, she currently resides near the Jersey Shore with her husband, two children, and her German Shepherd, Penny.

She is a self-proclaimed hopeless romantic, a sucker for a tear-jerker, and when she isn't writing, she likes to read steamy NSFW novels, and Hallmark movies are her jam.

R.J. is a co-founder of The Phantasm Effect, a support network for writers, and also a co-host on the Married to My Writing Podcast.

Follow Me

You can find me online @ www.rjrome.com (please sign up to receive my newsletter, I promise I won't spam you) or feel free to contact me in an email rjromebooks@gmail.com